BEWARE

OF THE

ELEPHANT

A MIDCOAST MAINE MYSTERY

Also by Lawrence Rotch

Gravely Dead: A Midcoast Maine Mystery
Bulletproof: A Midcoast Maine Mystery
Standing Dead: A Midcoast Maine Mystery
Mistletoe and Murder A Midcoast Maine Mystery

BEWARE

OF THE

ELEPHANT

A MIDCOAST MAINE MYSTERY

LAWRENCE ROTCH

Shoal Waters Press

Printed in the United States of America

ISBN: 978-0-9839079-2-3

First Edition: May, 2015

Published by
Shoal Waters Press
Liberty, Maine
Shoalwaterspress.com

10 9 8 7 6 5 4 3 2 1

"Change is the law of life, and those who look only to the past or present are certain to miss the future."

John F. Kennedy

Chapter 1

With her delicate features and long black hair tied in a ponytail, Phoebe McTavish looked ten years younger than her real age of twenty-seven. Adding to the youthful effect was the fact that she stood just five-feet tall. Not that Phoebe was standing up at the moment, it being a bit after midnight. Nor was she lying down, as one might suppose at that hour. She was, in fact, sitting behind the wheel of a Peterbuilt 379, maneuvering her eighteen-wheel rig down the back roads of Northern Pennsylvania on a warm Friday night in May.

"The turn is just ahead on the left," her companion said, his voice sounding tense.

Phoebe nodded and proceeded up a short driveway to a pair of ten-foot wrought-iron gates. This must be a high-class place, she thought, where even the back entrance sported such an elaborate set of ironwork.

"I've got the key," the man beside her said, getting out and approaching the gate.

Phoebe watched Asim as he stood, skewered by the headlights. She figured that he must be at least six-and-a-half feet tall, and about her age. She waited as he struggled impatiently with the stubborn lock, while the tractor's engine idled with its typical diesel clatter. "Hurry it up," she said half-aloud, checking the side mirrors. She scolded herself for getting caught up in the man's unexplained nervousness. She was just the driver, after all.

The road behind her was dark and still.

The gates swung open at last with a metallic groan of surrender, and Asim waved her through, closing the gates behind the semi.

"The service road branches off to the right," he said, sliding back into his seat. "Go slowly; I don't want to make too much noise."

"Is there a night watchman?"

"He's all taken care of."

Phoebe wondered what that meant, but didn't have a chance to ask before Asim directed her to a loading dock.

"Stay here," he said, once she had the rig in position. "I'll do this alone. The fewer people around, the better." He started to get out and added, "You'd better turn off the engine."

Phoebe sighed as she shut down and Asim disappeared into the darkness. She didn't like it that the man seemed so on edge, and so worried about making too much noise.

She sat, listening to the night sounds and the cooling pings of the engine. Clouds hid any chance of moonlight, so it was pitch dark except for an anemic security light, barely visible in the distance through the spring foliage.

Phoebe sat for almost half an hour, and was beginning to get antsy, when the trailer gave a lurch that made her jump in her seat.

It was just Asim, loading up.

After what seemed like an eternity, he slid into his seat.

"Did you padlock the back?" Phoebe said.

"Of course."

Phoebe held out her hand. "Gimme the key."

"That's okay. I'll keep it in case there's an emergency."

"Key," Phoebe repeated, jiggling her hand in front of his face. "I'd rather—"

"We're not going anywhere until I have the goddamn key in my hand."

Asim reluctantly dropped it in her palm.

She wondered what kind of emergency was he thinking of as she slipped the key into her jeans pocket.

*　*　*

For about the hundredth time in the last ten minutes, Phoebe checked the side mirror, and for about the hundredth time she didn't see a prowl car bearing down on them with its lights flashing. In fact, there was nothing to be seen behind her but the black stillness of a blossom-scented May night.

Her companion had noticed Phoebe's repeated, furtive glances at the mirror. "She won't be missed before dawn," he commented. Asim Okiro towered above Phoebe, even though she was perched on a cushion in order to see over the Peterbuilt's hood. She glanced at him. Asim's skin, almost as dark as her raven hair, made his face unreadable in the dimness.

"Why all the secrecy, and the sneaking around in the middle of the night?" she asked. "I didn't sign up for some kind of crazy, midnight kidnapping."

"We have discussed this before." His voice betrayed a faint accent, a precision of speech that Phoebe couldn't place. "This isn't a kidnaping. We are just getting her out of harm's way. We're saving her life. She will be killed if we don't do anything."

Phoebe turned back to the road just as a hard right turn swept into the headlights. The rig lurched and swayed as she struggled for control. She scolded herself for her inattention on these winding, back roads. That sort of mistake was an amateur's blunder, and she was no amateur. "Sorry," she said, slowing.

"It would be unfortunate to run off the road at this point," Asim observed dryly.

She nodded her head to indicate the trailer box. "Are you sure she's tied up securely? I don't want her getting loose and making a racket while we're stopped at a light somewhere."

"She won't get loose. Besides, I gave her a tranquilizer."

"A tranquilizer? You gave her a tranquilizer? It'll take us a good eight hours to get up to Maine. Are you going to keep her doped up for all that time?"

"Of course not. But you're the one who was worried about her making a racket while we're driving through town."

"Are you planning to keep her tied up with the freight all the way to Maine? Aren't you going to let her out somewhere along the way?"

"Certainly not. Where would we find a place to let her loose that's safe, with nobody around to see?" There was a flash of irritation in his voice.

"This isn't what Kermit and I were told to expect, that's all."

"We talked about this yesterday, and you were fine with it then," Asim pointed out.

"Talking about something is one thing, but actually doing it is different. You never said anything about having to sneak around in the middle of the night."

"You worry too much."

Phoebe braked abruptly as another turn came into view, too fast.

Asim looked at her sharply. "Would you like me to drive for a while?"

"Do you have a commercial license?" Phoebe snapped.

"No."

"Then you're not driving."

Asim sighed.

"Look, this isn't like driving the family Toyota," she said. "This is my father's rig, and he didn't loan it to me for some amateur to wreck it."

"Eight hours is a long time behind the wheel, on top of everything else."

"I've done longer." She bit her tongue, fearing for a second that he might start quoting time-behind-the-wheel regulations. Of course he couldn't afford to do that, not really. The man obviously didn't care much about regulations—not if they got in the way of his mission. Whatever that was.

Suddenly, she wanted to be alone. She wished the cab had a bunk so she could send Asim off for a nap and be in peace, without the man looming beside her. The truck's speed was creeping up again, and she made a conscious effort to ease off on the accelerator.

"You could ride in the box with Mabel for a while, if you want," she suggested.

"Maybe later, when we're on the turnpike."

"Suit yourself." It had been incredibly naive to let Asim talk them into this crazy escapade.

"Tell me more about this Ziggy Breener," she said. "How is he going to help when we get there? Does he have a place to keep her out of sight?"

"I haven't actually met the man, but a friend recommended him," Asim said vaguely. "He assured me that Breener is very reliable."

Phoebe was a person who liked certainty, and Asim's vagueness made her uneasy. What was he hiding? Had he really thought out what he was doing? She knew very little about the man, having just met him two days ago when he walked into the office of McTavish Transport. Her father had been out at the time, leaving her in charge of the family-owned trucking company. She had doubts at the time, and never would have taken the job if they weren't desperate for the money.

"Exactly what is this guy going to do when you get her there?" she asked.

"Keep her out of sight, of course," Asim said with a hint of irritation. "Maine is a big state, you know."

"Keep her out of sight? How?" Their speed was creeping up again. "You're sure this is legal? I've never broken the law before, except for some speeding tickets, and I don't want to get caught now, just because you didn't plan this out right."

"You picked an awkward time to get squeamish about the law," Asim said coolly. "We both know that McTavish Transport isn't exactly licensed for this kind of job. Why didn't you think about that before?" Asim paused, reining in his temper. "Stop worrying. You've been well paid for this trip. What happens when we get there is my concern, not yours."

"You have no idea what you're going to do with Mabel when we get to Maine, do you? All you have is a name and that's it." Phoebe shook her head in frustration. "Have you even talked to this Breener?"

"Not directly, but I've been assured that he'll help us," Asim said doggedly.

"And suppose this man, who you've never met, or even talked to, decides not to help you? Then what?"

Asim looked at her with surprise. "Why wouldn't he help? After all, we're bringing him a gift."

A gift? The man was creeping her out. "Look, Maine isn't like your country, whatever your country is. Things don't work the same way here. It's not that easy to go off and disappear. Maybe up in the County you could, but not in coastal Maine."

"I thought we'd been over this several times. Your job ends when you get the cargo to Maine, and that's all."

The rig lurched as she went into another corner too fast. She swore to herself. "But part of the cargo is alive—"

"Get us to Maine in one piece, and your worries are over," Asim assured her.

Chapter 2

The midcoast area of Maine is riddled with countless inlets, coves, peninsulas, and islands. In the early 1700's, when the village of Burnt Cove was first settled by a German immigrant named Gerhard Burndt, the waters teemed with codfish, lobsters were deemed suitable only for feeding the indigent or fertilizing vegetable beds, and people thought it was inconceivable that the state's 3,500 miles of rocky, desolate coastline would ever be fully settled.

How times have changed.

No longer an isolated fishing village, Burnt Cove was now a haven for tourists, gift shops, lobster connoisseurs, and lavish summer homes.

Ziggy Breener happened to be a resident of picturesque Burnt Cove, though he could never live long enough to become a true native by Maine's strict standards.

Ziggy was somewhere in his fifties and well weathered, as befit a man in his profession as Burnt Cove's "Can Man." To be precise, it was his self-appointed job to bicycle over the town roads, picking up bottles and cans in order to collect the deposit.

Few people knew it, but Ziggy had once been an Emergency Room doctor in a prestigious Boston hospital. Unfortunate circumstances, and a vengeful Massachusetts politician, caused him to abruptly move to Maine and start his present career in the can collection business.

Ziggy wasn't cruising for recyclables on this fine, sunny Saturday morning. Instead, he was gazing into the cellar hole of what had once been Myra Huggard's home before it burned down some eighteen months ago—with the old woman inside. The unkempt beard covering most of his face, combined with the grimy watch cap pulled low on top, made it impossible to guess what he was thinking beyond the fact that he wasn't smiling.

The freshly cleared land sloped gently down beyond the ruins to a scruffy line of trees, which stood along the rocky shoreline.

The flame-blackened foundation stones, along with the three acres of prime waterfront land around it, belonged to Ziggy now, since the eccentric old woman had chosen to leave the property to him instead of her own sister.

Ziggy Breener was a man of very modest means, recyclables notwithstanding, and the inheritance was a mixed blessing as it placed him solidly in the land-rich, but cash-poor, category.

Pastor Leonard Briskin, spiritual leader of the Golden Arms of Faith Full Gospel Church, stood beside the pensive Can Man. Misinterpreting the cause of his companion's gloom, Pastor Briskin said, "Myra Huggard is in a better place, Brother Ziggy. We can take comfort from that."

"She's certainly in a hotter place," Ziggy replied grimly.

Pastor Briskin's bushy eyebrows twitched with irritation at these words. Like Ziggy, he was in his fifties, and also like Ziggy, much of his weathered face was bearded. The fact was that Leonard Briskin led a double life. When he wasn't leading his church flock towards salvation, he drove a pulp truck carrying logs to the area paper mills.

"I'm saddened that you should talk that way," the bi-vocational cleric said. "Remember what the Good Book tells us, 'Judge not, lest ye be judged.'"

Ziggy wrinkled his brow.

Undeterred by the furrowed face, Pastor Briskin expanded on the biblical words of wisdom. "It's unworthy of you to speak ill of the dead, especially someone who has shown such affection and generosity to you." He faced the shore, which was just visible through the trees, and spread his arms wide to encompass Ziggy's new domain. With his lush beard, Pastor Briskin looked for all the world like Moses about to part the waters.

The waters of Kwiguigam Sound remained unmoved.

Ziggy remained unmoved as well. He turned to his left and glanced at a newly-built sixteen-foot-high privacy wall, locally referred to as "the Great Wall of Borofsky," or simply, "the Great Wall," which could be seen through the strip of woods that separated his property from the Borofsky's mega-mansion, next door.

"Her affection and generosity come at a cost," Ziggy said balefully, "like the embrace of a rabid porcupine."

"I will pray that you come to appreciate Myra Huggard's generosity, Brother Breener." He spread his arms once again. "This is a magnificent gift. There's plenty of room for the youth camp, as well as a modest house for yourself." He paused and turned to the right. "Even if you do insist on giving that strip of land with Gerhard Burndt's old grave site to the town for a park." Pastor Briskin nodded to himself. "Yes, this is a magnificent gift."

"Beware of friends bringing gifts," Ziggy murmured, unaware that an eighteen-wheeler was even now approaching with a troublesome gift for the Can Man of Burnt Cove.

* * *

Bernie Knowles clambered into the cab of his elderly excavator, which was parked next to the bearded duo, and began to the grind the starter noisily. Dressed in a frayed white dress shirt, his pants held up by fire-engine red suspenders, and his head topped with a battered fedora, Bernie was an unusually well dressed machinery operator.

The engine finally came to life with a smokey roar that sent the bystanders scurrying to safety.

"It's time to fill in that old cellar hole," Pastor Briskin said briskly, as Dudley "Dud" Tibbs joined them.

"It's an eyesore, and dangerous, too," Dudley said. "Somebody's likely to fall in there one night."

"Who would want to do that?" Ziggy inquired.

Dudley, in his mid-sixties, was of medium height, muscular build, with his balding head covered by a John Deere cap. "Who the heck knows? Anybody could fall in there and hurt themselves what with all the old boards, pipes and whatnot lying around in the bottom."

Pastor Briskin put a beefy and consoling hand on Ziggy's shoulder. "It's time to put the old lady to rest and move on. We've almost finished clearing the trees and brush, except for that strip along the shore that Harvey is working on, so we're almost ready to start clearing the tree stumps and digging the foundations for the camp's new bunkhouse and the main building." He peered worriedly into Ziggy's eyes. "You still haven't told us where you want your new cottage. There's that little stand of trees down by the water. It would have a nice view, and some privacy..."

Ziggy stood in silence and stared into space, apparently lost in thought.

"How about building up next to the road, then? It would mean less plowing in the winter."

"I must ponder many things," Ziggy said, staring up at the sky.

"You've got to stop pondering, and start deciding," Pastor Briskin said impatiently. "You have to make up your mind before we can do much more. There are building permits and the town planning board to consider, after all."

"The top foundation stones are nice and square," Dudley commented. "You could sell them to one of those landscape places and get good money."

The excavator belched more smoke as the machine began to trundle slowly up to the foundation hole, its treads scarring the soft ground.

"Good suggestion, Brother Dudley. I can load them onto my pulp truck and take them into Rockland tomorrow."

"I want to keep them," Ziggy announced.

"May I ask why?"

"Because Myra would want it."

Pastor Briskin pursed his lips.

The men watched in silence as the excavator's jaw flipped the first foundation stone away from its resting place.

It was a warm Saturday morning for mid-May, and half-a-dozen members of Pastor Briskin's flock were taking advantage of the good weekend weather to clean up brush and trash from the overgrown area around Myra's former yard.

Contrary to popular belief, Maine's state bird is the black-capped chickadee, not the black fly. Unfortunately, the lack of wind was giving the pesky insects free rein to swarm the brush-clearing crew down by the water. As a result, they moved to higher ground where there was a breeze, and watched the excavator as it began to root out the old foundation stones from where they had lain for nearly three centuries.

"I bet it took a lot longer to lay those stones than it'll take to dig them out," Harvey Cassell observed. Harvey was in his early sixties, and like a number of Pastor Briskin's flock, had grown up in Burnt Cove.

Ziggy turned away just as the excavator made a loud clanking noise and stopped with a jolt that sent a spasm through the machine. Bernie leaned out of the cab, muttered an oath, spotted the clerical frown, and caught himself. "Hydraulics let go. May take a while to fix the old bird," he explained.

A gust of cold air blew in from the icy waters of Kwiguigum Sound, ruffling the tender new leaves. "Myra isn't pleased," Ziggy murmured.

"Foolish superstition," Pastor Briskin scolded. "You know this is what she wanted, and she chose you to fulfill her wishes. It's in her will."

Ziggy gazed solemnly up into the treetops. "But is this *how* she wanted it?" His stare returned to ground level, where he noticed a diminutive young woman approaching.

"I'm looking for Ziggy Breener," she said.

"Why would anyone look for him?" Ziggy replied cautiously.

Pastor Briskin came to the stranger's rescue. "You must be Phoebe McTavish, and the tall gentleman with you must be Asim Okiro," he said. "I'm Leonard Briskin and this is Ziggy Breener. We've been expecting you."

"We have?" Ziggy said.

"Of course. They've brought lumber for the camp buildings, and for your new house." The cleric seemed uncharacteristically flustered, adding, "and a few odds-and-ends."

"Odds-and-ends?" Ziggy said.

Phoebe's eyes crossed for a moment before she recovered. "We want to unload the truck as soon as we can. Mabel has been tied up in there since last night."

"Mabel has been tied up in the truck since last night?"

Asim looked around dubiously. "Somewhere private where we won't be seen from the road."

"Private?" Ziggy said.

"Does this guy know what's going on at all?" Phoebe asked Pastor Briskin.

"We haven't had a chance to discuss all the details," Pastor

Briskin replied evasively.

"What details?" Ziggy said, his eyes sharpening on his clerical companion.

"Why don't you back in and unload over there," Pastor Briskin said hastily, indicating the brushy, half-cleared area which was destined to become the town park. "It's well away from the road. Just make sure to stay away from the old grave site; it's an historic monument."

"Where's the zoo?" Asim inquired, looking around with confusion.

"Zoo?" Ziggy said.

"Ziggy's Zoo is just a figure of speech," Pastor Briskin replied glibly.

"Yes, my zoo is over on Meadow road, where my former house used to be," Ziggy said, relieved to be on firmer ground. "It's only about half-an-acre, but I have two piglets, a flock of chickens, and a goat named Annabelle. I had a pig, but she moved into my freezer last fall." He paused before adding, "and I hope to add a pair of geese later this spring. There's nothing better than a good pair of guard-geese to keep foxes away."

"You don't know anything at all about Mabel, do you?" Phoebe said to Ziggy.

"I had an aunt named Mabel," The Can Man replied. "I hope you don't have her tied up in there, because she died twenty years ago."

"Mabel is an elephant, for crying out loud!" Phoebe screeched. She turned to Asim. "I thought somebody had arranged all this! I thought you said there was a zoo here!"

"You may not be aware of it, but I've had a long week."

"It's going to be a lot longer if you don't get your act together," Phoebe retorted.

"If you back the truck over there, our work crew can help you unload," Pastor Briskin repeated. "Meanwhile, Mister Breener and

I will go to one side and discuss matters in private."

He turned to Ziggy as soon as they were alone. "Those building supplies were donated by our sister churches in Pennsylvania, and our friends had everything trucked up here for free," he said urgently. "How could I not let them bring their elephant for a day or two? Or maybe a week, at the most."

"Beware of friends bringing elephants. Remember Hannibal crossing the Alps."

"Hannibal? Why do you insist on seeing the worst in life? We are doing God's work here. It's not for us to question how He chooses to lead us forward." Pastor Briskin shot a glance towards the eighteen-wheeler. "Besides, they're paying us very handsomely to board their elephant, and we need the money badly to build the camp."

The petite trucker had grumbled to herself as she tramped over the area, checking for soft places before backing her semi over the spot where Myra's vegetable garden had once produced its bounty. Ziggy watched the wheels dig deep ruts in the soft ground.

"This is a lot harder than I had expected," he said, half to himself.

* * *

It was noon by the time Mabel, her temporary enclosure, one-hundred bales of hay, and a small mountain of lumber had been unloaded from Phoebe's semi.

"She'll need water, lots of water," Asim said as the tired group stood and watched Mabel working on a small mountain of hay.

"You must have a water pump back home, don't you, Harv?" Dudley said. "I know you've got most everything under the sun piled up over there."

Harvey nodded. "I got a portable pump with a gas engine on it. We can run a hose right out of Myra's old well. It's just a dug well, so it's not too deep, and she's got plenty of water in her."

"Bless you for your generosity, Brother Harvey," Pastor Briskin replied.

"Don't get too close to the elephant," Asim warned as the group pressed up to the fence. Mabel was standing up against the heavy wire, waving her trunk at them in what looked like a greeting. "She loves to shmooze people, but don't forget that an elephant is a very large wild animal, and like most wild animals, elephants aren't always predictable."

"I thought elephants were pretty easygoing," Harvey said.

"They usually they are, but Mabel is a little stressed after being shut up all day."

"I bet you'd be stressed too, if somebody locked you up in a semi all day, Harv," Dudley commented, to a titter of laughter and an angry glare from Harvey.

Asim smiled dryly. "It's important to remember that people seem pretty small to an elephant, and Mabel's eyesight isn't very good, so she could easily step on you or knock you down by mistake, without even noticing you're there."

"Ouch," somebody said.

"On the other hand, elephants have an excellent sense of smell."

"That's a pretty long nose she's got, for sure," Dudley said.

"Better watch out for Dudley," Bernie said. "He's a hunter. An elephant would look wicked nice over your fireplace, Dud."

"You'd need to build a bigger house for it, Dud," Harvey Cassell said.

"Old Dud couldn't hit an elephant if he was standing next to it," somebody else added.

"That ain't funny," Dudley grumbled.

"Tomorrow's sermon will be on loving thy neighbor," Pastor Briskin announced.

"Elephants can get stressed out in new situations, just like people," Asim lectured the group, ignoring the byplay, and clearly comfortable to be talking about his favorite subject. "Fortunately, I've worked with Mabel for several years, so she trusts me. But she's not a performing circus elephant, and she's not used to having a lot of people being too close to her."

"How much does she eat?" Harvey said, eying the pile of hay.

"Mabel will eat over six hundred pounds of food a day. In fact, she spends almost all her time eating."

"How much does she weigh?" somebody asked.

"About five tons," Asim replied. "Mabel is an African elephant, and they tend to be bigger than Indian elephants. They can also be a little more aggressive and harder to train, which is why most circuses use Indian elephants."

"I bet she could walk right through that wire fence," Dudley commented.

"She could probably walk through most anything she wanted to," Phoebe said.

"Mabel has been trained to respect fences," Asim said, frowning at Phoebe.

"Let's hope so," Phoebe murmured.

"Elephants are gentle, sociable animals," Asim said, still frowning at Phoebe, "but they're like any other wild animal, or a person, for that matter; they will react, sometimes violently, if they feel threatened. That's why it's important for you all to give her space until she's acclimated to her new quarters."

"Are elephants afraid of mice?" somebody asked, "because there are a lot of them in that rough grass."

Asim looked irritated. "Elephants are *not* afraid of mice, any more than horses or people are. Of course a mouse or, any other any small animal, can startle an elephant, or a horse or a person, for that matter," Asim paused. "And before you ask, a mouse won't run up an elephant's trunk and suffocate it."

"I thought only male elephants had tusks," Bernie said, admiring Mabel's ivory.

"That's mostly true for Indian elephants, but female African elephants almost always have tusks."

"So don't get fresh with a lady African elephant," Phoebe advised.

"What about an elephant's memory?" Bernie said.

"That bit of folklore is true. Elephants have excellent memories, like most other social animals. They can remember another elephant, or even a person they haven't seen for years."

"So don't cross an elephant, 'cause they never forget," Dudley said.

"Elephants have the largest hippocampus of any animal, on a percentage basis," Asim went on, "even bigger than a human, percentage-wise."

"What's a hippocampus?" Bernie inquired.

"I'm glad you asked," Asim said with a smile. "It's the region of the brain that's associated with the processing of memory and emotion, which means that an elephant has both memory and feelings. They suffer real grief at the loss of a family member. Elephants have even been observed to suffer from post-traumatic stress disorder if members of their family are killed. They have large and complex family structures, sophisticated language, and are adept at using tools to forage for food."

"Sounds like my grandson," Dudley said. "He sure knows how to forage for food."

"And it shows," came an anonymous voice from the back of the group.

Dudley opened his mouth to issue a retort, but Pastor Pastor Briskin stepped in. "I think it's time to quit for the day, my friends. Don't forget, there will be a picnic lunch at the church tomorrow at noon! Afterwards, we'll come back here again."

"I hope you can be with us tomorrow," Pastor Briskin said to Phoebe and Asim as the rest of the work crew wandered away. "We have plenty of room to put you up for the night."

"I'll sleep in the truck tonight, to be near Mabel," Asim replied. "I want to make sure she's settling in all right."

"I have to go back home tomorrow," Phoebe said, "but I'd be glad to stay with you tonight, if you're sure it's not too much trouble."

"It's the least we can do, and you're both welcome to our eight o'clock service tomorrow morning," the ever-hopeful divine said enthusiastically.

Mabel was not invited to the church service, nor was she mentioned at all. For all intents and purposes, she appeared content to shamble around her new home, pulling down branches from the numerous saplings, pulling up brush, and working her way through the bales of hay in front of her.

Chapter 3

Oliver Wendell's weathered Colonial sat on the side of Hound Hill some ten miles away from Ziggy Breener and his new four-legged guest. The large barn attached to the house had been converted to a boatbuilding shop, and Oliver and Sarah Cassidy were conferring with their own two-legged guest, for whom they were building *Daisy,* a thirty-foot sloop.

Oliver, in his mid-fifties, was tall and thin, with curly blond hair, showing white at the temples. Sarah Cassidy, about the same age, with shoulder-length dark hair and an open Irish face to match her name, stood beside him.

Many people come to the relative quiet and isolation of Maine in order to escape their past. Sarah and Oliver were two such individuals.

Oliver had given up his career as an engineer and moved to Maine some ten years ago, shortly after his wife and daughter were killed in an auto accident. Settling in Midcoast Maine, he had begun a new life designing and building boats in an area that was famous for its boatbuilding tradition.

Sarah had come to Maine a year ago with the intention of

spending a quiet summer regrouping after her divorce. It had not been the quiet summer she planned, nor had she intended to become involved with Oliver Wendell, or any other man, for that matter.

Sarah's father had been a carpenter who specialized in cabinet work, and she had learned basic woodworking skills from him at a young age. Whether by fate or accident, Sarah had found herself using those skills to help Oliver build *Daisy* the previous fall. The vessel was nearly complete now, except for the usual myriad of last-minute odds and ends.

Abner Haskins, the eager owner, was in his mid-forties. His five-foot- three-inch height, curly brown hair, and youthful face hid the fact that he was a human dynamo—and an immensely rich person. He was, in fact, a "quant," a mathematical genius who made vast riches for his employers by creating dizzyingly complex computer programs designed to coax huge profits from arcane derivatives, swaps, and variuos other financial devices.

Oliver would normally have intensely disapproved of Abner Haskin's profession for a variety reasons, both ethical and philosophical. Indeed, one would hardly expect them to even be on speaking terms. One would be wrong, however, because both men shared a passion for boats.

Like everything else he did, Abner Haskins had done his homework before having Oliver build *Daisy,* now so tantalizingly close to completion. Part of Abner's homework had involved persuading Oliver's father, a well known and long-retired yacht designer, to come out of his retirement long enough to design the boat.

Though he hadn't expected to, Oliver came to enjoy Abner's hyperactive involvement in *Daisy's* creation. The multi-millionaire had put his stamp on every aspect, dimension, and detail of the boat's construction. Wouldn't it be better, he'd suggest, if the compass was mounted over there? Should the berths be an inch wider? Wouldn't it be better if the winches were a little closer? How about using varnish on that little piece of trim?

Oliver had grumbled at first, but the man's unflagging enthusiasm and good-natured humor had won him over. By now, Abner knew every inch of the boat as well as Oliver and Sarah did.

Abner's enthusiasm was reaching a frenzied pitch now that *Daisy's* launch date was approaching, and he turned up for a few hours nearly every weekend.

He was here this morning, having landed his plane at the Owl's Head Airport an hour ago. Abner wandered around *Daisy* like a hyperactive child on Christmas Eve, fairly fit to explode with anticipation.

Wes, Oliver's ebullient black-and-white springer spaniel, sensed Abner's excitement and followed him around, his tail wagging busily. Their guest had been a Favorite Person in Wes' book ever since the day when Abner first stopped to scratch behind his ears.

Sarah and Oliver watched with amusement.

"It's perfect," he said at last, "but there is one little thing..."

"You want us to make the boat a foot longer?" Sarah inquired impishly.

Abner considered her question. "No," he replied gravely, after a moment's deliberation. "That might be a bit much to ask at this stage of the game. It's her name..."

"I thought you told us that her name was *Daisy*. Is it spelled wrong?"

"That's not her whole name."

"*Daisy* isn't her whole name?" Oliver asked. "What is it, then? *Daisy Mahitabelle Mahooligan?* Are we going to have to nail a billboard on the transom to fit the name on?"

Uncharacteristically, Abner blushed "No, it's just that I have a nickname, you see."

"A nickname?" Sarah prompted.

Abner's blush deepened. "Li'l Abner," he murmured.

"So her full name should be *Daisy Mae?*" Oliver said solemnly.
Sarah turned aside and convulsed silently.

"I've brooded over this for months. It's not an easy decision,
but I've concluded that it should be—"

"Consider it done," Oliver said. "Daisy Mae was a beauty, as I
remember the comic strip."

"So is the boat," Abner said, beaming like a proud father.

Oliver's father had often said that the best way to get to know
a person was to design a boat for him. Oliver figured it was much
the same thing to build a boat for someone. He was going to miss
working with "Li'l" Abner.

Perhaps his client was thinking along the same lines. "Do you
two have another project coming along?"

Sarah wondered about the phrase, "you two."

"Sasha and Anton Borofsky are looking for a boat," Oliver said.
"They have a summer place in Burnt Cove, and I'm going over to
talk with them in a day or two."

Abner looked surprised. "Anton Borofsky, the rotten fish czar?"

"The very same."

"I didn't know they were sailors."

"They aren't. As near as I can tell, it's mostly an ornament so
they can keep up with the neighbors, though Sasha claims that she
wants to learn how to sail."

Abner frowned at the thought. "Make sure you get paid in
advance."

"What do you mean?" Oliver said. "I thought they were rolling
in money. Have you seen their summer cottage?"

"Summer castle," Sarah said.

"I can believe the castle part, knowing the man," Abner said,
"but the place is almost certainly mortgaged to the hilt. I probably
shouldn't tell you this, but he's skating on the edge. He may be a
brilliant chemist, and a genius when it comes to fish preservation,
but he's not much of a businessman.

"I thought he pretty much had a monopoly on deodorizing dead fish," Sarah said.

"No monopoly lasts forever, and Borofsky is starting to get some real competition. From what I hear, it's beginning to hurt his bottom line."

"He certainly acts as though he's got money to burn," Oliver said.

Abner nodded in agreement. "He and his wife both have expensive tastes. It can be very hard for people like that to rein in their spending."

"That's not reassuring," Sarah commented.

"It's not as though he's going broke or anything, but I wouldn't extend him a lot of credit. If I were you, I'd work on a cash-and-carry basis. I'm told it can be hard to get money out of him otherwise."

Chapter 4

Phoebe pleaded exhaustion as an excuse to sleep in and avoid Pastor Briskin's Sunday church service. The evangelical soul had grumbled unhappily until his wife, Hazel, came to Phoebe's rescue. The truth was that she was more tired than she realized, and she slept much later than usual. As a result, the house was quiet and still while she ate breakfast.

Her father called as she was finishing off her second cup of coffee.

"When are you planning to bring the rig back?" Kermit said.

"I'm hoping to leave in an hour or two," Phoebe replied, made wary his tone of voice.

"There's an interesting story in the local paper about the Hart's Ridge Zoo," Kermit commented. "Apparently their elephant disappeared last night."

"Their elephant is gone? Really?" she replied innocently, playing along with Kermit's game, whatever it might be. Her father knew perfectly well where the zoo's elephant was, and how it got there. Phoebe figured he was just toying with her. Or warning her.

"The zoo says they sent the elephant away because they're

remodeling its enclosure—"

"That makes sense," Phoebe cut in, trying to hide the relief in her voice. It sounded as though Asim and the zoo were working together after all, in spite of her doubts yesterday.

"It would seem so," Kermit said blandly. "The interesting thing is, the article mentioned that the elephant has a history."

The morning sun had found its way through the kitchen window and onto the table, where it was stealthily creeping up to Phoebe's coffee mug. She took a swallow before saying, "What kind of a history?"

"The article referred to her as a 'Killer Elephant.' I don't know where they dug that phrase up, but you know how the papers are. Anyhow, it seems that the elephant has killed two people."

"*Two* people?"

"One last week and another a couple of years ago. She trampled them to death."

"Oh," Phoebe said, her mind churning.

"A private eye came by yesterday, asking me about it. Apparently he's checking with all the local trucking companies. I don't suppose there's been anything in the papers up there?" Kermit asked in a tone of voice that made her nervous again.

"Not a word." Phoebe wondered if the story was big enough to reach Maine, and how long it might take. "You'd need to have a special truck to transport an elephant, wouldn't you?"

"Yes, you would—to do it legally, anyhow," Kermit said. "There must be a ton of regulations."

Which meant that McTavish Transport could be in big trouble if people started asking questions. Phoebe vowed to have a serious talk with Asim.

"Anyway, the reason I called was to find out when you were planning to be back, and to tell you that there's no rush to get here."

"Okay," Phoebe said, reading between the lines.

"I don't know where you are right now, but if some work turns up locally and you need the rig for a couple more days, that would be fine with me."

"As a matter of fact, I probably could come up with a couple of day's work here."

"Just don't haul anything that'll stink up the trailer," Kermit warned.

"Don't I always bring it back clean?"

She was rewarded with a snort. "Take care of yourself, lass; that's all I care about."

* * *

Meanwhile, on the flank of Burnt Cove's Hound Hill, Sarah was looking at Oliver incredulously as they stood beside *Daisy Mae*. "I can't believe you still want to go ahead with building a boat for the Borofskys after what Abner said yesterday."

"Why not? Progress payments. It's simple: we just have to make sure to get the money in advance at each step of the way, no payments, no progress. The worst that could happen is that we end up having to sell the boat ourselves. It's the best way to deal with tightwad millionaires."

"You sound like an expert on tightwad millionaires."

"One deals with all kinds in this business."

"I guess we're lucky that Abner isn't a tightwad."

"He's spoiled us," Oliver said. "The thing is that we've almost finished building *Daisy Mae*, and it's time to move on to the next boat."

He was right, of course. *Daisy Mae* was nearly complete in spite of the last minute odds and ends. Even so... "We've talked about this before," she said, "and you know perfectly well that Sasha Borofsky doesn't give a hoot about having a boat, except as some kind of status symbol to one-up the Vincent's boat next door, and if they can't pay for it then why put up with the aggravation of trying to pry the money out of them?"

"All I'm going to do this morning is drop off some drawings and a few pictures for them to look at, so they can decide what they want."

"I know what she wants," Sarah said. "Sasha Borofsky is a man-hungry vampire, and you're a potential victim."

"But I'm a good ten years older than she is," Oliver protested.

"At least—"

"Thanks."

"—and that just means that she likes older men."

"Which shows that she has good taste," Oliver replied smugly.

They finished putting the breakfast dishes in the dishwasher. "Maybe I should go with you to fend her off and save your good name."

Oliver suppressed a smile. "Are you going to bring some garlic? That's a very thoughtful offer, and you're welcome to come along, but Anton will be there to protect me."

"You know how jealous he is. He had Sasha's last fling beaten and shot, remember?"

"That was a special case. After all, that particular boy-toy happened to be a hired killer. Anyway, how do you know that she'll even let you into the house? As far as she's concerned, the place catches fire every time you go through the door."

"That's not true. I've been there three times—"

"—and there were two fires in your three visits. Two-for-three is a pretty good batting average. And she did try to punch your lights out the last time you were there."

Sarah scowled. "She was hysterical, and that fire wasn't my fault."

Oliver paused and took her hand. "I'm not your ex, and Sasha is definitely not my type. And I'd be glad to have you come with me."

Sarah gave Oliver a kiss on the cheek. Claude, her ex, had been and still was, as far as she knew, a philanderer who thought any woman was fair game. The experience had destroyed their marriage. Were the scars poisoning her trust in Oliver and their relationship?

"I'll drop you off at the vampire-lady's castle," she said, "and go next door to see how Ziggy is doing while you talk about boats."

"I'll scream if things get dicey."

"And I'll come to the rescue with my garlic and my sharpened stake."

* * *

Sarah dropped Oliver off at the Borofskys and parked on the road opposite Myra Huggard's driveway, which by Maine tradition, would remain Myra Huggard's driveway for at least two generations to come.

The drive itself was perhaps thirty feet long with a screen of scraggly trees and brush between the road and the clearing where the old woman's house had stood. It was almost a year since Sarah had last seen the burned out ruins of the house, and she walked slowly and a bit reluctantly up the drive, bracing herself for the changes that she knew had occurred in the last few weeks.

Those changes made it hard to be sure of its location, but Sarah paused at the place where she guessed Myra's chicken coop had been located in Sarah's youth. It was here that she had first met Myra. Sarah had been thirteen and was spending her first summer at the Migawoc Camp for Girls, which abutted the Huggard's unkempt property. The camp was long-gone now, the land sold off for house lots, one of which now held the Borofsky's mega-mansion.

She and her new friend, Marlee Sue Ruggles, were both city girls, Sarah from a middle-class Boston Irish family and Marlee Sue from a wealthy New Orleans background. They had wandered into a nearly impenetrable thicket of fir and spruce one morning and managed to get themselves lost. Eventually, they emerged behind Myra's chicken coop, inspiring its residents to create a racket which brought Myra out to investigate. She was in her fifties then, a tall, boney, hard-faced woman, her gray hair in an unkempt bun. Myra unceremoniously shooed her visitors away, calling the young campers spoiled brats, among other epithets.

Sarah felt strangely drawn to the cantankerous woman, and braved Myra's scorn to visit many times during her years as a camper, and later a counselor, at Migawoc.

It wasn't until after Myra's death last year that Sarah learned that *Owl*, the camp's sailboat, had been on loan from Myra, and the old woman had inexplicably left the boat to Sarah in her will.

An excavator sat near the old cellar hole. Its arm drooped tiredly over the foundation, looking a bit like the neck of a dead giraffe.

She walked around the excavator and saw several members of Pastor Briskin's flock hard at work clearing trees, brush, and saplings between the old house site and the water's edge. There were three of them: one with a chainsaw, one carrying brush over to a pile, and the third digging up sapling roots with a pickaxe. Sarah could just catch a glimpse of the ocean through the remaining wall of trees.

Myra, who had encouraged the stand of thick, brushy growth on the theory that it held back the fog, would have been appalled. As if to prove the crotchety old lady's point, a light east wind was already wafting cool wisps of fog in from the sound.

To her left as she faced the water, Sarah could see the so-called Great Wall, which the Borofskys had erected earlier this spring to protect themselves from their new, unwelcome neighbors. To the right, an eighteen-wheeler and a large pile of lumber blocked her view. Curious, she strolled over, stopping short when she saw an elephant scraping bark off a sapling with its tusk and stuffing the fibers into it's mouth.

There were also voices coming from the other side of the semi.

"You never told me that Mabel was a serial killer," a woman said.

Sarah didn't usually eavesdrop, but the woman's words froze her in place.

"Mabel is *not* a serial killer," a man replied impatiently.

"What else would you call it? She killed two men! So far! That's not like Fido biting the mailman's leg! People are looking for her!"

Sarah glanced at the elephant, who was now contentedly working her way through a bale of hay. Was that Mabel-the-serial-killer? She looked pretty placid for an animal who was prone to killing people, not that Sarah considered herself to be an expert on homicidal pachyderms.

"You can't keep her hidden forever, Asim," the woman said, "Kermit told me there's a private eye checking the trucking companies back home. Somebody is serious about finding her. They're bound to be looking for you, too, considering that you're her handler."

The man mumbled something that Sarah couldn't hear.

"That's the whole point! It's not going to blow over in a few days! For all you know, the cops have gotten involved and have issued an APB or whatever they do for elephants, and they're looking for you, too."

Sarah struggled with the temptation to move closer so she could hear the man's mumbled reply.

"How long do you think she can stay here before the word gets out?" the woman went on. "Do you really think Briskin can keep his people from talking about Mabel? And how long do you think it'll be before somebody comes around to make trouble for McTavish Transport?"

The man mumbled inaudibly some more, much to Sarah's growing frustration.

"It *is* my business dammit! Thanks to you, I'm involved it the transport of a serial killer!" Sarah could hear the woman's sigh. "I don't know how I let you sweet-talk me into this mess."

There was more conciliatory mumbling.

"You damn well better figure out something, because I'm taking the rig out of here as soon as I can find a place to hide it." The woman's voice sounded closer, and Sarah scuttled back to the dead giraffe just in time to avoid being spotted. As it was, the woman glared suspiciously at Sarah as she stalked by.

The man she'd been talking to, as tall as the woman was short, and as dark skinned as she was light, went over to the brush pile, took an armful of greenery, and dropped it into Mabel's enclosure. The "killer elephant" ambled over and began eating contentedly.

* * *

Sasha had opened the door at Oliver's knock, and she looked over his shoulder with satisfaction as Sarah's Ford Explorer pulled away. With a smile, she focused on her guest.

Sasha Borofsky was tall and slender, almost to the point of emaciation, with long, ash-blonde hair, bright blue eyes, and pale skin.

Oliver was not an expert on women's leisure attire, but Sasha's skin-tight leotard showed off her slender figure to good advantage. He suspected the woman would make a good fashion model. She ushered him into the vast three-storey front hall and trapped him in a skin-tight hug.

Oliver contemplated the idea of Sarah bursting through the door with her sharpened stake. What kind of wood was it supposed to be made of?

Prying himself free of Sasha's octopus grasp, he held out a manila envelope. "I brought some pictures and sketches of different boats for you and Anton to look at."

"Later," she said urgently, grabbing his hand. "There's something you have to see upstairs."

"Where's Anton?" Oliver asked uneasily.

"He's upstairs in the dressing room." She tugged impatiently at Oliver's hand.

"The dressing room? This sounds like a bad time for a visit. Why don't I just leave the envelope for you and Anton to look at later."

Sasha was stronger than she looked, and she hustled him across the entrance hall and up the Grand Staircase. "You know what we want: a boat like the one you made for the Vincents, only bigger."

"But they have a rowing boat."

She urged him further up the stairs. "We certainly don't want to row our boat, silly."

"But there are all kinds of power boats—"

"All we want is a power boat that's bigger than the Vincent's," Sasha said as she maneuvered Oliver into the bedroom. "And it has to be designed and built by the son of a famous yacht designer, like you."

Oliver was relieved to find that Anton Borofsky, a great bear of a man, was seated in an easy chair in front of the dressing room window. "You have to see this," he said, relinquishing his seat and handing Oliver a pair of binoculars.

The window looked over the Great Wall and into Ziggy's new estate. From here, Oliver could see the foundation of Myra Huggard's old house through a thin screen of trees. An excavator drooped tiredly across it. To the left, he caught a glimpse of Pastor Briskin and some of his congregation turning the woodsy growth into piles of brush.

"Look just beyond that big truck," Anton urged.

"Oh," Oliver said.

"Do you see it?" Sasha said excitedly.

"It's an elephant."

"Of course it's an elephant," Anton said impatiently. "What I want to know is why that man has an elephant in his backyard."

Oliver spotted Sarah hurrying away from the semi and up to Myra's cellar hole. "I wouldn't dare to guess why Ziggy might have an elephant, or any other animal, for that matter."

"Is he planning to open a zoo or a circus over there?" Anton said.

"Ziggy already has what his neighbors call a zoo—a few farm animals: a goat, some chickens, and a pig," Oliver said. "Maybe he's branching out."

A woman appeared from behind the semi and stalked off. "Anything is possible with Ziggy," Oliver murmured, his eyes still glued to the binoculars.

"I won't have it!" Anton boomed. "I'll call the Animal Control Officer, and have the beast removed!"

"But darling, it's such a nice looking elephant, and you do enjoy watching the goings-on over there."

Anton scowled at his wife.

Oliver knew the Animal Control Officer in town—an elderly gentleman who was notorious for refusing to deal with any animal that happened to have claws, or a bad temper, or was too heavy for him to pick up by himself. He also had a particular dislike of skunks. "I don't think the Animal Control Officer will be much help with an elephant."

"Then I'll call the state. It has to be illegal to keep an elephant without some kind of permit." He turned to Oliver. "You're my witness that there's an illegal animal on private property."

"Yes, well, that *is* an elephant," Oliver admitted. "But I have no idea whether it's illegal to have it there."

Sasha massaged Anton's knotted shoulders. "But I *like* the elephant," she wheedled.

"I'm not buying you an elephant, and I won't have one living next door. Who knows what that man will bring in next, if we let him have an elephant. A lion? A hippopotamus? He'll be opening a real zoo over there, and charging admission if he isn't stopped."

Oliver thought that a real zoo was unlikely, but not impossible for Ziggy Breener.

"I loved the *Dumbo* movies when I was growing up," Sasha said dreamily. She picked up the binoculars and gazed out the window. "And this elephant has great big ears, just like Dumbo, and it seems to be very peaceful. I don't see why we can't let it stay for a while."

"It would give you a chance to find out what Ziggy is up to," Oliver suggested. He didn't say it, but in his experience, it wasn't possible for anybody to figure out what Ziggy Breener was up to at any time, or in any place.

Sasha beamed at Oliver.

Anton Borofsky heaved a great, rumbling sigh.

Chapter 5

Unaware that she was being observed from the battlements of Borofsky Castle, Sarah watched as the mysterious woman walked down to where Pastor Briskin was working beside his crew. Sarah gave an involuntary yelp when a pounding noise came from the old cellar hole beside her. She peered into the gloom and saw a man working underneath the excavator's arm.

"Sorry to give you a bad turn," the man said. "I didn't know anybody was up there." He eased out from under the excavator and clambered up a stepladder to the ground. "I'm Bernie Knowles." he said, holding out a grimy hand.

"Sarah Cassidy. I'm a friend of Ziggy. I thought everybody would still be in church." She guessed that Bernie must be in his early sixties, a small, lightly-built man wearing a battered fedora.

"Pastor Briskin is a fast worker when the weather is good," Bernie commented. "Ziggy doesn't go to church, but he should be along most any minute. He's been out cruising for cans. Weekends are suppose to be good for hunting them; he might even make a couple of bucks this morning." He gave an indulgent shrug at Ziggy's eccentricities. "How do you like our new elephant? I saw you down there a few minutes ago."

"Where did it come from?"

Bernie wiped his hands on greasy rag, which did little to improve their condition. His white dress shirt was already showing grease stains, and Sarah suspected that he owned a drawer full of worn-out white shirts, dating back to the Kennedy administration. A mane of curly grey hair crept out from under his partially crushed fedora, which looked like it dated back to the Eisenhower presidency. He glanced over at the elephant. "I think it's something Pastor Briskin cooked up, but I don't know why. Anyhow, he said to keep it a secret and not tell anybody."

"Good luck with that."

Bernie nodded with a laugh. "Just because you can't see Mabel from the road doesn't mean people won't find out she's here."

"Mabel?"

"Apparently her real name is some African word that nobody can pronounce." He shrugged. "Lucky for me, I'm not in charge of the elephants at this particular circus. I've got enough problems trying to get that old bird up and running again," he said, indicating the excavator.

Sarah noticed two men working on one of the enclosure's fence posts, trying to straighten it. "Is Mabel pushing over the fence?"

"She could push those fence posts into next week like they were nothing if she wanted to, even with those big steel posts, but she doesn't bother the fence at all. It's just that the topsoil is pretty thin down at that end, and it's all blue clay underneath—harder than hell to drive anything into the stuff. They couldn't sledge that post in worth a darn yesterday, and it started to lean, so Harvey and Dudley are digging a hole to set it in solid."

One of the men was swinging a pickaxe, which made a dull, wet thud in the damp clay with each blow. "It looks like heavy going," Sarah observed.

Bernie nodded. "The beefy guy with the pickaxe is Dudley

Tibbs; most people call him Dud. The taller one who's keeping the shovel from falling over, is Harvey Cassell. The three of us grew up in town."

Sarah guessed that they were probably all old enough to be retired. Mabel ambled over to the men, and Harvey put down his shovel long enough to give her a handful of brush from a nearby pile.

"Harvey spoils that elephant something wicked. Asim, he's her handler, isn't too happy about it—says Harvey'll make her fat, though I don't know how you can tell if an elephant's fat. Anyhow, Harv does what he does, and Mabel sure likes it."

"You've certainly done a lot of work on the place," Sarah said, looking around.

"Old Dud is sure doing a lot of work right now," Bernie observed. "He's swinging that pick like he was a hard-rock miner digging for gold."

Sarah noticed another man digging with a small spade not far from Gerhard Burndt's grave site. "Who's that down by the grave?"

Her question was greeted with a scowl. "Some damnfool archeologist."

"Archeologist?"

"Pastor Briskin says he's looking for Indian artifacts down there. Some kind of state thing. He turned up a couple of days ago."

"Was there a Native American settlement here?"

"I doubt it. Pastor Briskin thinks that Borofsky told the state there are artifacts buried down there just to stir up trouble—a midden, I think he called it."

"Trash heap," Sarah said.

"Right. Anyway, it seems there's an antiquities act that requires somebody to poke around and make sure we don't dig up some archeological treasure. Long story short, there he is, Bert Farley, rooting around with his shovel."

"How long will it take for him to finish looking?"

"Not long, if Pastor Briskin has anything to say about it. He doesn't want anybody holding up the new camp from opening." Bernie glared in Bert's direction. "Me, I don't trust the guy."

"Why not?"

"How do we know he isn't looking around for the Huggard family's stash?"

Sarah nodded. When she was young, the girls at camp had traded ghost stories which were sometimes embellished with tales of pirates and buried treasure on the Huggard's land. She was surprised that Bernie actually gave credence to them. "I thought that buried treasure business was just a legend."

He gave her a pitying look. "Just because something's a legend doesn't mean it isn't true. Who knows what the Huggard family might have squirreled away back in the old days? Or pirates, even? There were stories going around when we were kids."

"Did many people take them seriously?"

"All I can say is that so-called archeologist brought a metal detector with him." He lowered his voice. "How many prehistoric stone tools is he going to find with a metal detector?"

"I suppose it would depend on how old the tools were," Sarah said.

Bernie ignored her implied skepticism. "I'd throw the guy out, if I were Ziggy. Archeologist, my foot. He's just trying to steal what isn't his."

Their conversation was interrupted by the familiar rattle of Ziggy's bicycle as he rolled in the driveway and pulled up beside Sarah. The five-gallon buckets tied on each side of the rear wheels were filled with cans.

"It looks like the can business is going well," she said.

Bernie gave a short laugh and retreated into the dimness beneath the excavator.

"It's the only thing that is going well, Ditch Lady Sarah," Ziggy replied gloomily. His laden bicycle gave a tinny rattle as he set it in its stand.

Sarah cringed at the Ditch Lady title. As it happened, she'd been climbing out of a roadside ditch just across the road, bruised and shaken after nearly being killed by a hit-and-run driver, when they first met last spring. In Ziggy's oddball mind, she had been Ditch Lady Sarah ever since, despite her best efforts to break him of the obnoxious habit. She supposed that Ziggy's weirdness was an essential and unavoidable part of his nature.

At the moment, Ziggy's worn, knitted watch cap and the unkempt beard seemed to radiate discouragement.

"Where are you planning to put your new house?" she said brightly, in an effort to cheer him up him.

Ziggy looked around dispiritedly. "It's impossible to decide with an elephant in my midst."

"But you do have to decide where to build a new place—here or Meadow road. You can't stay in Doctor Carnell's cabin much longer; he'll want it for the summer, and that's not far off."

"I can't decide until the elephant is gone," Ziggy repeated stubbornly. "My psychic living space is filled with pachydermia. It disrupts my serenity. The feng shui eludes me."

"Pachydermia? Is that a real word? You made that up, didn't you." Sarah frowned. "Okay, Breener, what's really the problem?"

Ziggy eyed her solemnly. "I am beset on all sides by well-meaning people. People who offer to help, but put us all in grave danger."

"What are you talking about? Pastor Briskin's people are here to help set up the camp that you and Myra wanted. I really don't think he's trying to run your life, and I'm sure he'd be glad to do things differently if you asked."

"Did I ask for an elephant?" Ziggy grumbled. "I have been cursed, oh Ditch Lady." He lowered his voice. "Myra Huggard's ghost is not pleased, and I fear the worst."

"Get a grip, for heaven's sake. Myra is long gone. Besides, she wanted a camp here, and you're doing what she wanted."

"But is it what she *really* wanted?" Ziggy said earnestly. "It's so easy to think you want something to happen until it does, and then you don't. Did she really want her hen house flattened, or trucks driving over her vegetable garden, or all those trees cut down? Did she really want a camp here, for that matter?" Ziggy sighed. "Words are such powerful weapons. It's like asking some devious Aladdin to grant you a wish—the devil is in the wording." He looked around sadly. "There's so much change, so quickly."

"But you can't build a camp here without making changes."

"Perhaps not, but she is showing her displeasure," he insisted, indicating the defunct excavator.

"Are you trying to tell me that Myra's ghost sabotaged the excavator because she didn't want her old house foundation filled in?"

"She died a violent death in that house."

"You can't really believe that kind of superstitious foolishness. The idea of her wrecking a piece of heavy equipment from beyond the grave is ridiculous. You know better than that."

"You and Pastor Briskin make the same mistake of underestimating Myra Huggard," he warned with a meaningful look into the cellar hole.

"Yes, but—"

"She died in that very spot." Ziggy pointed an apocalyptic finger at the excavator's bucket. "And she is very angry with us."

"Be sensible, Ziggy," Sarah pleaded. "You can't just leave the cellar hole there, like some kind of junk-filled mausoleum. It's dangerous to let it sit open like that; somebody will fall in."

"You know perfectly well that she's right, Brother Ziggy," Pastor Briskin said. He and Dudley had come over, and they looked into the semi-darkness where Bernie was pounding with a hammer underneath the excavator's prostrate arm.

"I didn't know the old lady died down there," Dudley said,

looking nervous.

"She died down here?" Bernie echoed, peering around the shadowy space uneasily.

"Myra is very angry," Ziggy repeated.

"I'm shocked that you, a man of science, a doctor, would believe such heathenish things," Pastor Briskin said sternly.

"I might have been a doctor on another astral plane, but now I'm a simple Can Man with a wider view of life. And death."

Chapter 6

"This morbid talk doesn't suit you, Brother Can Man," Pastor Briskin said. "The Lord has taken Myra Huggard home, where she lives in Glory, and has no interest in mere earthly things like excavators and cellars."

"So you say," Ziggy replied, "but I can feel her restlessness in the air. She is not at peace."

Pastor Briskin's beard twitched. "I hope you're not working yourself up to suggest some sort of religious frippery, like having an exorcism."

Ziggy gave his companion a look of pure horror. "That would be extraordinarily dangerous. Myra would be furious. I shudder to think how she might react."

Pastor Briskin shook his head sadly. "You are fantasizing. After all, we are doing God's work here, and not even Myra Huggard can withstand the will of God. I shall pray that you may find peace in this matter."

Ziggy's eyes narrowed beneath lowered brows. "You don't understand Myra at all. She doesn't *want* to be exorcized. She doesn't *want* to find peace. She wants to supervise us. She wants things done *her* way. She doesn't care about God's work; she wants us to do *her* work."

Ziggy leaned forward until his nose came within inches of the cleric's weathered proboscis. "Besides, how do you *know* we're doing God's work?"

As if in answer, the excavator gave a convulsive twitch, and a spurt of hydraulic fluid rained down on them.

"Godalmighty!" Bernie said, shooting out from under his unruly machine.

"What happened?" Dudley said as he peered into the darkness.

"Bad karma," Ziggy murmured.

"More like a bad hydraulic line let go," Bernie said. "I'm not going under there again 'til can get something to prop up that arm."

"That machine is mighty old," Dudley observed uncertainly.

"She may be old, but she's a good runner," Bernie retorted.

"She isn't running so good right now, and if one hydraulic line let go, others will probably let go, too," Harvey said.

"Bad hydraulic karma," Ziggy commented.

"You try my patience, Brother Breener. Myra Huggard may have been a cantankerous old woman, but she's not some kind of satanic poltergeist."

"What's a poltergeist?" Bernie inquired, turning to Harvey.

"It's a kind of baby chicken," Harvey explained.

Pastor Briskin stared into space, his lips moving in what could have been a prayer. Or an imprecation.

The excavator groaned and settled further into the cellar.

"Maybe you should get a crane or something to pull the machine out of there, so you can work on it more safely," Pastor Briskin suggested.

"No need," Bernie said. "I'll just get a jack and put some blocking under it."

"Mark my words," Ziggy intoned in a voice of doom, "your elephant will bring disaster down upon our heads, Brother Briskin."

"Disaster and hydraulic fluid," Dudley amended as he wiped at the oil stains on his cap.

"What in heaven's name does Mabel have to do with anything?" the irritated churchman demanded. "And you know perfectly well that is not my elephant. Besides, Mabel will only be here for a few more days—certainly not more than a week or so."

Sarah wondered about the mysterious woman and the conversation she'd overheard. What did Pastor Briskin know about Mabel's homicidal past?

Just then, Bert Farley the archeologist walked by as he headed to his pickup. Sarah guessed that he was in his mid-thirties, with straight, dark hair and Harry Potter glasses to go with an earnest, Harry Potter face. Pastor Briskin waved him over. "Sister Sarah, this is Brother Bert Farley. He has arrived, like the proverbial hoard of locusts, to torment us. We can give thanks that locusts are short-lived." He gave the embarrassed young man a predatory grin. "How long do you expect to stay?"

"It's difficult to say exactly," Bert stammered. "This is really just a survey to see what other artifacts there might be. A day or two, maybe a week."

Ziggy looked at Bert as though he'd heard similar words in reference to Mabel. "And you're going to look at all my waterfront, not just what's going to the town?"

"To be thorough, yes."

Pastor Briskin frowned. "We have a very tight schedule. The buildings need to be finished by late June. I thought you were just looking at the area where the town park is going to be."

"That's true, but where an artifact has been found—"

Harvey gave a derisive snort.

"An artifact has been found?" Ziggy said, his eyes boring into Bert's face.

"Yes. A gentleman found it while doing some beach-combing along here last week. A handsome spearhead, very well made for this area. Quite sophisticated."

"The gentleman was Anton Borofsky, perhaps?" Ziggy asked.

"Why yes. A very public spirited person; he was conscientious enough to turn it over to the town so they could report it."

"Of course he did," Pastor Briskin said. "He's a fine person all around."

"Yes indeed," Bert replied enthusiastically. "He's even agreed to pay for my services to come and look over this area."

"We'll have to remember to thank him next time he comes by," Harvey said.

"Sarcasm doesn't become you," Pastor Briskin commented.

Bert went on, seemingly oblivious to the byplay. "A lot of people would pick up an artifact like that, take it home, and leave it on the mantle without realizing the possible significance. Maine has quite strict laws to protect archeological sites."

"Why do you have a metal detector if you're looking for stone tools?" Bernie wanted to know.

"This area has probably been in use for many years. Later Native American groups may have had contact with English settlers and traded with them—knives or other metal goods. We know Gerhard Burndt built here, but what about earlier Euroamericans?"

"What about pirates burying treasure?" Dudley asked.

"That's not my area of expertise, but I suppose anything is possible." Bert shrugged. "The point is that even though the park only covers an acre or so, it would be more desirable for the town if it had some archeological significance in addition to the grave site."

"I suppose the town might even want a bigger piece of Brother Breener's land if a major find was discovered," Pastor Briskin said coldly.

"That would be between Mr. Breener and the town, or possibly even the state." Bert looked at the group uncomfortably. "Anyway, my lunch is in the pickup." With that, he hurried off.

"My neighbor is a true patron of the sciences," Ziggy murmured.

"Your neighbor has planted a Judas in our midst," Pastor Briskin replied.

"He's looking for the Huggard treasure," Bernie grumbled. "Borofsky was over here asking about it a few of days ago, so he knows about the legend."

"There isn't any treasure," Ziggy retorted. "He's planting weed seeds."

"Weed seeds?" Bernie said, looking confused.

"I think Ziggy's suggesting that Anton Borofsky is spreading rumors to stir up trouble," Sarah replied.

Ziggy bowed to Sarah. "Discord is a powerful weapon."

Pastor Briskin looked thoughtful. "A buried treasure?" he mused.

"There isn't any treasure," Ziggy repeated.

"Yes, but suppose there really is?" Pastor Briskin said, a hint of greed in his voice. "Just think what a boon it would be for you. And perhaps for the camp as well."

"Nobody is going to see any buried treasure if that phony archeologist gets to it first," Bernie growled. "He's already digging holes all over the place down there."

"Why do all of you suddenly have this buried treasure fantasy, when nobody took it seriously before?" Ziggy said.

"You're telling us that *we* have fantasies?" Dudley retorted.

Ziggy scowled. "I'm saying that you're all getting a case of gold fever and it's clouding your minds."

"Ziggy's right," Harvey said, "that buried treasure business is just a fairy tale."

"Let's keep an open mind on the matter," Pastor Briskin said. He clapped his hands to get everybody's attention, and announced, "It's time for lunch, and the ladies have put together a magnificent Sunday potluck meal for us back at the church, so let's not keep them waiting!"

Sarah begged off the potluck invitation, planning to wait for Oliver to return from Borofsky Castle.

To her surprise, even Ziggy caught a ride with Pastor Briskin, glum mood notwithstanding. The bewhiskered duo made a contentious pair, Sarah thought. She wondered if they could work together long enough to complete the camp before coming to blows.

Of course she didn't put any stock in Ziggy's idea that Myra was controlling things from the spirit world—some other "astral plane" as he put it. Even so, now that she was standing alone in the quiet stillness with nobody to talk to, there was something about the place, a certain, dare she say it, aura.

Sarah scolded herself. She needed to think about something else.

How much longer it would be until Oliver turned up from his meeting with the Borofskys? What would it be like for him, or even her, to build a boat for them? Certainly nowhere near as satisfying as their relationship with Abner Haskins; she was sure of that.

More to the point, how would she feel about helping to build a boat for Sasha, considering her strained relationship with the woman?

A cool breeze coming in off the sound swept through the trees, and Sarah zipped her windbreaker. Her mind wandered as her gaze swept over the landscape again, looking for familiar landmarks from her youth.

Except for a strip of woods running around the four sides of the property, and a dozen trees scattered around elsewhere, much of the land had been laid bare, stripped of the familiar landmarks, wiped clean like a blank slate awaiting the writing of a new story. She supposed that some of the trees which remained along the water's edge were still awaiting Harvey's chainsaw—assuming some long-lost Native American settlement didn't turn up to get in the way.

The property, which had seemed cramped and closed-in by woods when Myra and her house were there, looked bigger and somehow sterile now, as though the last bits of Myra's life had been disinfected.

The hardest part wasn't the size of the change, she decided, it was that the change had happened so quickly.

Sarah felt a sudden sympathy with Ziggy's feelings of grief at seeing the place leveled. He'd known Myra during the last years of her life better than anybody else, and had managed to see a measure of goodness in her where most people in town saw only evil.

She saw Oliver walking in the driveway, and hurried up to join him.

"That didn't take long," she said.

"What's with the elephant?"

"How do you know about that?"

"See the left-hand window on the second floor?" Oliver replied, nodding at the Borofsky's castle.

"The bedroom window?"

"The dressing room window."

"So, you discussed the Borofsky's new boat in Sasha's dressing room?"

"Actually, neither of them has much interest in a boat right now. They're too absorbed with elephant-watching to think about anything else. They have binoculars and an easy chair up there by the window."

"I've already told you Sasha wasn't interested in boats," Sarah said coolly. "Her mind is elsewhere."

"Don't even think about thinking what you're thinking," he said primly. "Anton was there—"

"In the dressing room? With you and Sasha?"

Oliver sighed. "Could we stay on track? That window gives them a good view of the area where the elephant is penned, and as near as I can tell, Anton is spending a lot of time up there with his binoculars, watching what goes on over here. Partly, I think he's watching for building code violations, as well as illegal animals. What's the elephant doing here, anyway?"

"The elephant is named Mabel, and apparently Pastor Briskin has something to do with her being here," Sarah replied. "Are the Borofskys planning to file a complaint or something?"

"Anton is inclined to call the Animal Control Officer in town, or maybe the state, if he can figure out who regulates elephants. He's pretty sure there must be something illegal about having an elephant in one's backyard, but he doesn't know what. In any case, he'll have to wait until the state offices are open Monday. Sasha, on the other hand, likes elephants. She's a bit of an animal lover, and it gives her something to watch, and she used to like *Dumbo* cartoons when she was a kid."

"Mabel will only be here for a few more days, according to Pastor Briskin," Sarah said. She glanced up at the dressing room window. "Perhaps he should visit them and explain the situation before they do anything to stir up trouble."

"Sasha is his best bet to talk to," Oliver said innocently. "She'd certainly be the most sympathetic."

Sarah suppressed a wicked look and nodded agreement. "I'm sure she'd pay attention to him." Pastor Briskin was actually a fairly good looking man, in a beefy, rough-hewn, hirsute way, Sarah thought. And she suspected that his being married and a few years older would only make him a more appealing target for Sasha's predatory nature.

Yes indeed, Sarah concluded, he might be able to exert some influence over Sasha. Or the other way around.

"I hope your matchmaking doesn't get poor Pastor Briskin into trouble," Oliver said.

"I'm not matchmaking, and he doesn't have to take my suggestion. Besides, I'm sure the man is adult enough to be immune to her blandishments. He is a man of the cloth, after all."

Oliver rolled his eyes.

Chapter 7

"I'm sorry I yelled at you about Mabel this morning," Phoebe said around a slice of pizza. "But did she really kill two people?"

"They were accidents. It's one of the dangers of working with animals that size."

Phoebe wiped a dab of tomato sauce off her chin. "One accident is okay, but two accidents start to look bad. I can see why she's lying low."

They were sitting in the comfort of Phoebe's Peterbuilt, sharing a pizza as the Sunday afternoon sun crept down into the trees.

Asim finished the last slice of pizza, taking his time. "It's not really like that. There are public relations issues. The zoo just wants her out of the public eye until things get sorted out."

"Things get sorted out? How does that happen, and how long will it take?"

"It shouldn't take long. A week, maybe two."

"Does the zoo know where Mabel is?"

"They don't care that much where she is, exactly. As far as

they're concerned, Mabel is on sort of a road tour, at least that's the official line."

"It sounds as though you've been left holding the bag." Phoebe stared into the growing shadows for a while before adding, "For what it's worth, Kermit didn't tell the private eye anything, but that doesn't mean they won't track you down one way or another. Kermit and me just don't want to get into trouble ourselves, and we won't so long as nobody connects me to you and Mabel."

"Mmm," Asim said.

"One of the people in Briskin's church has a farm where I can keep the rig out of sight for a day or two." She tidied up the remains of their meal. "I'll take it away tonight."

"Good," Asim said.

"Do you really need to stay here? Mabel seems perfectly happy in her corral, and Pastor Briskin said he could put you up, no problem."

"I've got a tent set up, and I should stay here with Mabel. She's still a little upset from all the travel."

"She was all right last night, wasn't she?"

Asim paused, thinking. "Yes, as a matter of fact, she seemed very comfortable."

"You didn't get any sleep driving up Friday night, and it can't have been very comfortable sleeping in the cab last night, especially where it got so cold after the sun went down," Phoebe went on.

"It's a lot warmer tonight."

He was right, Phoebe thought with frustration. As a matter of fact it was unseasonably warm. "That just means there'll be a lot of bugs out, especially where you're sleeping on the ground. Do you have a pad for that sleeping bag?" She paused. "A decent night's rest in a real bed would do you good."

Asim was quiet for a while, and Phoebe suddenly became aware of his presence in a way she hadn't before.

"I can come back and move Mabel in a day or two, if you want. You really can't keep her here much longer; word is bound to get out."

"Yes."

Seated, her eyes barely reached up to his shoulders, which made it hard to read his face in the fading light. "So, are you going to come with me to Briskin's place, or stay here and sleep on the ground tonight?"

"Mabel isn't a killer."

"You need to give yourself a break, Asim."

"Most people don't understand elephants. All they see is a trunk, and a pair of tusks."

"Don't forget the ears. Mabel has really big ears," Phoebe said.

Asim gave her a disapproving look. "The point is that elephants are much more than that. They're smart, communal animals who form strong bonds, not just between themselves and other elephants, but with people, too." He paused before going on.

Chastened, Phoebe held her tongue.

"When I look into an elephant's eyes I see an intelligent, compassionate, even altruistic creature looking back at me. An elephant will sacrifice its well-being to help a friend, even a human." Asim fell silent.

"I've heard that a trainer can develop a strong bond with an elephant," Phoebe said softly. "I'm beginning to understand why."

"I think I'll go with you tonight after all, but I need to check on Mabel first."

Phoebe followed him out of the cab.

The place looked deserted at first, and Asim was startled to see that Bernie was still working underneath the excavator. He'd spent most of the afternoon placing timbers under the machine's arm to keep it from shifting again, and he was now working by the light of a lantern. Shadows danced and flitted out of the hole, while faint scraping and occasional hammering noises disturbed the evening stillness.

Asim checked on Mabel's water and tossed in an armful of the slash and brush that Harvey had piled up nearby. Harvey seemed to have taken a liking to Mabel, and had gotten into the habit of tossing greenery into her enclosure, much to her delight.

Asim watched Phoebe heave a bale of hay over the wire fencing. God, the woman is tiny, he thought. It was hard to believe she could handle an eighteen-wheeler like that, even with booster blocks on the pedals. She must be a lot stronger than she looked.

Phoebe clambered into the cab and waited while Asim stayed by the fence a little longer. Mabel shambled over and reached her trunk across to snuffle at him. Her breath felt hot on his face.

"How do you like your new digs?" Asim asked her. Mabel's pen covered half-an-acre and contained a dozen saplings and small trees. She'd managed to scrape the bark, an elephantine delicacy, off several small trees, before pushing them over to devour the leaves. Even one of the bigger trees was leaning dangerously. Asim hoped that Ziggy didn't mind Mabel's impromptu forestry efforts.

Mabel reached her trunk under the wire and worked at his jeans pocket.

Asim pushed her trunk away and fished out a peanut.

She devoured the gift, and started to reach for another.

"Just one," he said, pushing her trunk away again. "We don't want to ruin your girlish figure, and Harvey is already spoiling you rotten. Besides, you're going to reach into the wrong person's pocket someday, and they may take offense."

The Peterbuilt rumbled to life, but Asim stayed where he was, reluctant to leave.

As though sensing Asim's ambivalence, Mabel draped her trunk over his shoulder and pulled him against the fence.

"Oh, what a nice hug," he said, scratching her forehead. Her right tusk pressed hard against his chest.

The memory rose, unbidden and unwanted: Ray's crushed and twisted body lying in a corner of Mabel's enclosure, abandoned like a child's broken toy.

Asim scolded himself and moved away from Mabel's embrace. It was dangerous to assume too much when it came to animals, or people for that matter. Did Mabel's hug really mean the same thing to her as it did to him?

It was easy, at times like this, to forget that underneath the human-like veneer of sociability and affection, Mabel was, after all, a wild animal—a very large wild animal—whose urges and motivations were just as hard for a human to understand as it was for an elephant to understand a human's behavior.

He hadn't been present during either of the two accidents—hadn't even known Mabel the first time she killed—so he had no first-hand information as to what had caused them.

He had, however, arrived just after Ray's death and seen his body lying like a rag doll in her enclosure. Had Ray gotten careless and fallen under her feet? Had he unwittingly done something that Mabel saw as a threat? Had she simply tired of the human presence in her enclosure and eliminated that presence?

He'd thought at the time that Ray's corpse bothered Mabel, but it was hard to be sure what her reaction had really been. The sight of it was certainly burned in his mind.

Whatever her reaction to the accident, his relationship with Mabel, whatever it had been before, had changed and would never be quite the same again. The doubt would always haunt him.

Why was he thinking about these things tonight? Was it because of Phoebe's reaction to the killer-elephant thing? Was she right?

Had he had been idealizing elephants?

He stood for a while longer while the Peterbuilt idled patiently behind him.

Mabel ambled off to eat more hay, and she barely noticed when Asim climbed into the truck.

He was already looking forward to hot water, a shower, and a comfortable bed.

Chapter 8

Sarah and Oliver hadn't even finished breakfast on what promised to be a sunny Monday morning when she made her first mistake of the day. She answered her cell.

"Ditch Lady Sarah," Ziggy said, "we need to talk about ditches."

A feeling of dread tramped heavily across her mind. "Ditches? What kind of ditches?"

"The dark and murky kind that you are so good at exploring."

"I do not explore dark and murky ditches if I can help it. I don't explore any other kind of ditches, for that matter. Ditches are your bailiwick, Breener, not mine."

"I'm not asking for me, but for a poor, defenseless animal—" Ziggy caught himself. "Well, not completely defenseless, but one who can't speak for herself. Mabel needs your help."

"What are you talking about?"

"It's a gruesome tale of murder most foul, Ditch Lady Sarah."

Sarah held the cell so Oliver could hear. "Okay, talk. And speak in English."

"Bernie Knowles was killed last night."

"Mabel attacked him?"

"Possibly," Ziggy replied uncertainly. "The police are still talking to people about it, though they haven't questioned Mabel, yet."

"What happened?"

"A picture is worth a thousand words," Ziggy replied. In a lower voice, he added, "which is a lesson Pastor Briskin has yet to learn."

"Get on with it, Ziggy."

"Technology is a wondrous thing," Ziggy said, undeterred by Sarah's impatience. "Pastor Briskin took a picture of the prime suspect with his cell phone when we first got here last night, and I will send it to your phone, as soon as I find the right button—"

There was a muffled exchange, the sound of a brief struggle, and a photo of Mabel's head appeared on Sarah's cell, remarkably clear for a nighttime shot.

One of her tusks was smeared with blood.

"That's a pretty damning snapshot," Oliver said.

"Even an elephant is innocent until proven—" Ziggy began.

The sound of another brief struggle came through the phone.

"Mabel was framed." Pastor Briskin had obviously repossessed his cell. "Bernie's wife called me in the middle of the night when he hadn't come home, so I came over and found the body." He paused to collect himself. "I managed to take that picture before the police arrived. They're here like a plague of locusts now, of course. Apparently, Sasha Borofsky heard voices around ten o'clock last night, so it may have happened then."

"Bernie was still working on his excavator that late?"

"Yes. He told me that he wanted to have the machine up and running by this morning so he could fill in the cellar hole and start digging up tree stumps and leveling the ground before starting on the new foundations. He may not have been the most intelligent person in the world, but he was very conscientious."

"Did she break out of her pen?" Oliver said.

"It looks like Brother Bernie went into her enclosure, for some reason. I only got a brief glimpse, enough to see that he was dead. His head was bloody and his stomach had obviously been gored."

"Mabel has killed twice before," Sarah said.

There was a momentary silence on the line. "Where did you hear that, Sister Sarah?"

"I overheard a conversation between Phoebe and Asim."

"That's most unfortunate. Are you sure you heard correctly?"

"It seemed perfectly clear to me," Sarah replied stiffly. She wondered if Pastor Briskin thought it was unfortunate that Mabel had killed before, or that Sarah knew about the deaths.

"It appears that I have brought a great evil into our midst," Pastor Briskin said in a sad voice. "I have led us all down a slippery slope towards perdition. My own carelessness and lust for lucre has led my feet to stray from the straight and narrow path—"

"Where is Mabel now?" Oliver said, breaking into the gloomy monolog.

There was a pause, more muttering, another struggle, and Ziggy answered. "She's in her enclosure. Phoebe was tending to her while Asim was being questioned, and now Asim is taking care of her while Phoebe is being questioned. Oh, and a policeman is guarding Mabel as well. I fear, oh Ditch Lady, that Phoebe may be in trouble with the law for bringing the beast up here."

"Asim is the one who brought Mabel up here," Pastor Briskin said in the background.

"He's just her handler," Ziggy corrected. "Mabel is the zoo's elephant, and she's doomed unless you can prove her innocence."

"What zoo?" Sarah asked.

"That's a secret, according to Pastor Briskin."

"A secret? Why?" Sarah said.

"I'm sure the police can handle this perfectly well," Oliver said in an effort to derail the conversation.

"It can't hurt for us to see what Asim has to say," Sarah said to Oliver, "and we can go from there."

Oliver muttered.

"Tell Asim that we'll be down to see him in a little while, though I don't see how we can do anything to help."

"Speaking of perdition and slippery slopes, here we go again," Oliver grumbled.

* * *

Asim was standing next to Mabel's enclosure when Sarah and Oliver arrived. He eyed his visitors suspiciously. "I'm not supposed to talk about an ongoing police investigation," he informed them. "Besides, I don't know what happened after Phoebe and I left yesterday evening."

"Of course not," Sarah said. "But Ziggy and Pastor Briskin asked us to talk to you and see if there was anything we could do to help."

Sarah saw that the lower end of Mabel's enclosure had been marked off with yellow tape and rope. A big crime scene van was parked nearby, and two men were kneeling over the spot where Bernie had presumably been killed. Meanwhile, Harvey and Dudley were at work thinning more brush along the shoreline, and adding to the pile of elephant snacks in the process.

Sarah noticed that the pair were studiously ignoring Bert Farley, who was also working with his shovel down by the shore. She reminded herself that she needed to talk to Bert.

She turned to Asim "I understand that Mabel has attacked two other people in the past. I was wondering about them, and what happened."

"I didn't see either attack," Asim said coolly.

"When did they happen?" Sarah said.

Asim looked at them for a moment, trying to make up his mind. "I suppose can't won't hurt to talk about it," he said reluctantly. "Pastor Briskin told me you two might want to ask some questions, and that you were discreet. The first attack was about three years ago. Her handler was trampled to death. That's when I took over her care. I was told that the handler had been abusive and she finally snapped. Some elephant handlers can be brutal with their training, and African elephants tend to be stubborn."

"I gather the second attack was more recent?" Sarah prompted.

"About a week ago. A maintenance worker got careless and fell. He really shouldn't have been in her pen. It was a clear violation of the zoo's safety rules for a maintenance worker to be in there without a staff member being present."

"And both victims were trampled?" Oliver asked.

"Yes. As I've said before, people are small to an elephant, and they don't always see a person."

"And I suppose that's why the zoo had you bring Mabel here?" Sarah said.

"One attack could be passed off as a tragic accident, but twice and they start to think about putting the elephant down. It depends on the circumstances." Asim paused and glanced at Mabel, who was cowering nervously at the back side of her pen.

"She looks upset," Sarah commented.

"Can you blame her?" Asim frowned at them. "I don't understand why Pastor Briskin said there was a zoo here, or why nobody checked into this Ziggy Breener. The man looks more like a street person than the owner of a big piece of waterfront land, much less a zoo."

"Ziggy is a long story," Sarah replied. "He may talk strangely—"

"And think strangely," Oliver added.

"—but he's got more on the ball than most people realize."

"Could it be that the zoo was in a hurry to get rid of Mabel, and didn't check carefully?" Oliver suggested.

Asim nodded. "They talked about a clerical error, whatever that means, when I called them about it."

"A 'clerical error?'" Oliver said. "I wonder if Pastor Briskin oversold Ziggy's so-called zoo in order to get paid for boarding her."

Asim shrugged. "It probably would have worked out well, except for Bernie getting killed."

"Would Mabel be likely to attack Bernie if he went into her enclosure after dark?" Sarah said, returning to the world of dead bodies.

"Probably not." Asim sighed. "It least I don't think so, unless she felt threatened somehow." He gave Mabel a haunted look. "I don't know for sure what she might do at this point. I thought I knew her, but now..." He sighed again. "It may not have showed, but she was stressed by the long trip up here. On top of that, she's accustomed to living in a zoo, and this is obviously very different. She seemed to be perfectly happy here, but one can't always be sure."

"I wonder why she gored him, instead of trampling him, like the others," Oliver mused.

"Goring him makes no sense," Asim said numbly.

Sarah brought out her cell and showed Asim the photo of Mabel. "Pastor Briskin took that when he first got here."

"She looks so upset," Asim said sadly. He looked again, his brows furrowing. "Wait. There's something wrong..."

"What?" Sarah said.

Asim looked at Mabel, who was still standing unhappily at the farthest corner of her pen, and looked at the cell again. "I can't believe I didn't see this right away. All the police, with their constant questioning must have confused me—" He snatched the cell from

Sarah's hand and bent over the image, then looked at Mabel again. "How could I have missed it," he repeated. "Look at the blood on her tusk."

"What about it?"

"It's the wrong tusk, for God's sake!"

"The wrong tusk?" Sarah said.

Asim looked at the cell again, as though unsure the image and the elephant were the same. He turned to Sarah at last, saying, "Elephants are like people; there are left-handed elephants, and there are right-handed elephants."

"How can you tell with an elephant?" Sarah said, bemused.

"Don't you see? They use their tusks to dig in the dirt, scrape bark off trees, all kinds of things, just like we use our hands to do things. That's why an elephant often has one tusk more worn down than the other."

"The blood is on her left tusk," Oliver murmured.

"Mabel is right-handed," Asim said. "She would never attack with her left tusk, any more than a right-handed person would stab somebody with their left hand." He shook his head. "The fact is that she'd never attack a person with her tusk anyway. She's not a killer, and this picture proves it." He shook his head again, and turned back to Mabel, muttering, "How could I have missed seeing it?" He hurried off to share his discovery with the police.

* * *

"What do you make of this right-handed elephant business?" Sarah said as she and Oliver walked back towards the driveway. Oliver had promised the Borofskys that he'd stop by this morning after they'd had a chance to look at the drawings he dropped off yesterday.

He turned to look at Mabel. "Her right tusk does look a little duller, though it's hard to be sure without getting a closer look. Which I don't plan to do, by the way."

Sarah peered at the photo on her cell and nodded. "On the other hand, maybe that's why she used her left tusk to stab Bernie. After all, if you had a butter knife in your right hand and a dagger in your left, which hand would you use to stab somebody?"

"A pretty question," Oliver replied as he turned back towards the Borofsky's mansion. "I gather that you're not buying the right-handed elephant idea?"

"It's not that I don't believe in right-handed elephants. I'm just not convinced that it's a bulletproof alibi."

"Is it possible that Mabel is more ambidextrous then Asim realizes?"

"Maybe she is. And maybe he's using the right-handed business as a way to protect Mabel. He's obviously very fond of her."

"Which could make him less objective," Oliver said. "Plus, he's being paid to take care of her. No elephant, no job."

Sarah glanced back at Mabel, who was half-heartedly rooting up a small sapling. "Look, she's digging in the ground with her tusk. Her right tusk."

Sure enough, Mabel had deftly flipped a tasty bit of greenery out of the ground with her right tusk.

"Definitely a right-tusked elephant," Oliver said. "Score one for Asim. I'm not sure that proves she's innocent, though. We'll have to study her tusking habits more closely to see how ambidextrous she might be."

"Before she manages to dig up everything in her pen," Sarah added. "This does raise a question, though: why did she crush her first two victims, and gore her third? Why not be consistent with her modus operandi?"

"My thought, exactly." Oliver stopped as they reached the end of the driveway. "I can understand how an elephant might trample somebody by mistake. After all, as Asim said, we are pretty small to an elephant. But goring somebody is a personal, in-your-face, on purpose kind of thing."

"Maybe she is a killer elephant, after all."

Oliver looked at Sarah worriedly. "Promise you won't get involved in anything dangerous."

"Don't worry. I expect the state police will prove whether or not Mabel killed Bernie. What could possibly be dangerous about that? It's their investigation, not mine. I'm just a bystander."

Oliver grunted skeptically. "Just don't let Ziggy talk you into anything crazy. Remember the last time we got involved with one of his boondoggles."

"You know perfectly well that this boondoggle is about Mabel-the-elephant, not Ziggy-the-kook. Besides, he's been remarkably coherent lately."

"A fact which fills me with dread," Oliver said.

"You need to cut the poor man some slack. It's got to be a difficult time for him, with all the changes in his life right now. It must be a big readjustment to go from living in a shack on Meadow road to a waterfront estate on Squirrel Point road. Personally, I'm glad that he's talking a little more like a normal person. It's a sign that he's readjusting after all those years in hiding."

"Even so, there may be more to Mabel than meets the eye," Oliver said darkly.

Sarah frowned. "There probably isn't even a crime, for heaven's sake, except for Bernie being criminally stupid enough to go into Mabel's pen after dark. He probably scared her half to death, and that's why she skewered him."

They walked out to Squirrel Point road, where an assortment of official vehicle were parked along the pavement. Oliver paused to give Sarah a quick kiss before turning up the road towards the Borofsky's driveway.

"Promise you'll stay out of trouble," he said again over his shoulder.

"I'm safer here than you'll be over at the vampire's den," Sarah replied with a wave.

Chapter 9

Anton Borofsky was practically bouncing up and down with excitement when he greeted Oliver at the door. "Have you heard the news?" he said, his voice showing a mixture of outrage and delight. "Our crazy neighbor's elephant killed a man last night."

Oliver groaned to himself. "Yes, I have heard the news, and the elephant doesn't really belong to Ziggy. It belongs to a zoo down in Pennsylvania."

"It doesn't matter!" Anton proclaimed happily. "The man is keeping a dangerous animal on his property without a permit, and a person was killed. He'll be in big trouble over that. I've already filed a complaint with the state about keeping a circus animal in a residential area, and they're coming over later this morning to look into it. Maybe we can finally get him and that rowdy bunch out of there, so we don't have cars going in and out all day."

Oliver glanced over his host's shoulder and saw Sasha, wrapped in a beach towel, making her way down the Grand Staircase. Her long blond hair was wet and her bare feet left damp marks on the marble entry hall floor as she hurried over to welcome their guest.

"And to think that animal killed somebody, practically in our back yard!" Sasha exclaimed. "I'm not sure I dare to ride my bike by there any more."

"We can't have those roughnecks making it too dangerous for you to go riding, my dearest; it's an important part of your day."

"I'm sure you can fix it," Sasha said as she wrapped Oliver in a damp embrace, which resulted in the towel falling to the floor.

"Walking around in a bikini is not the proper way to greet our guest," Anton scolded mildly.

"I know, darling," Sasha said, retrieving her towel and draping it carelessly around herself, "but I just got out of the pool, Oliver is an old friend, and I'm so upset about what happened. What was that man doing in the elephant's pen in the middle of the night?"

Anton nodded. "That's exactly the kind of thing that can happen when you keep a dangerous animal without a proper enclosure. It should be obvious after this disaster that those people aren't fit to run a youth camp in the middle of a residential neighborhood." He frowned as Oliver opened his mouth to protest. "Yes, I know that Burnt Cove doesn't have zoning laws, but the man isn't competent to run a youth camp *anywhere*."

Oliver didn't think the Borofskys would get rid of their eccentric neighbor as easily as they hoped. "Pastor Briskin will actually be running the Spruce Cone Camp. Ziggy is just leasing them the land, except for the part he's planning to live on, and the piece he's donating to the town for a park."

The Borofskys knew all this from their confrontation with Ziggy last December, and they didn't appreciate being reminded of it now.

"Leasing the land doesn't get him off the hook," Anton growled. "And that fraud he's leasing it to is nothing more than a truck driver who parades around, pretending to be a minister."

"The 'Golden Arms of Faith Full Gospel Church?' Isn't that what he calls the place?" Sasha said scornfully.

"I wouldn't underestimate Leonard Briskin," Oliver replied. "He's managed to organize a group of churches, some as far away as Pennsylvania, to support the camp."

"That doesn't give him the right to let wild animals run loose on his property and kill people," Anton said. "We have rights, too."

"The poor elephant was probably terrified to have to have a stranger going into her pen in the middle of the night," Sasha said. "No wonder she killed him."

"Yes, of course," Anton replied distractedly. "In any case, you can rest assured that my attorneys will see to it that *Mister* Briskin is put in his proper place—behind the wheel of his pulp truck."

"I've had some experience with Pastor Briskin and his flock," Oliver commented mildly, "and that crew can be a handful when they decide to go on a crusade."

"A crusade?" Anton snorted. "We'll see about that. There are some powerful people in town who feel the same way we do. Breener and his phony friend, Briskin, are making a lot of enemies with this supposed 'camp for troubled teens,' as they call it."

"Powerful people? Like who?"

"Like Brian Curtis, for one."

"Brian Curtis?" Oliver said. Brian was the Realtor in town. About Oliver's age, he'd shown a romantic interest in Sarah last summer.

"He came over yesterday, very concerned about the elephant," Anton replied. "He's trying to sell the lot next door, and potential buyers are put off by having that animal living there."

"But the place where Mabel's enclosure is will be part of a town park, eventually," Oliver said, "and Mabel will be gone in a few days, or a week."

"That's not the same as the elephant being gone now," Anton countered. "People are funny about that sort of thing. On top of that, it smells like a stable over there. We can even smell it here, when there's a south wind. Anyway, Brian wants the elephant removed as soon as possible, and he's threatening legal action. It's money out of his pocket, and that piece of land is worth a lot more without Breener's eyesore. Anyway, I think Brian's planning to talk to him about it."

"I wish him luck," Oliver said. "Ziggy is mighty stubborn, as you know."

"That may be true," Anton said, "but I expect Brian can apply a good deal of pressure. He certainly can work with the authorities to make sure that having a town park there won't be disruptive."

"Brian was asking after Sarah," Sasha purred. "He seems quite interested in her. I didn't realize that they knew each other." She smiled sweetly at Oliver. "You may have some competition there."

"Oliver didn't come over to hear about Brian Curtis' love life," Anton said, pulling himself together and mentally shifting gears. "He wants to talk about our new boat. Sasha, dear, why don't you put on some clothes and we'll look at Oliver's drawings in the study?"

"I was thinking we could sit by the pool, and look at the drawings next to the water," she said. "For inspiration," she added, readjusting her towel in a way that revealed just how scanty a bikini could be.

Oliver had never seen the Borofsky's third-storey swimming pool. Nor, in fact, had he ever seen anywhere near as much of Sasha Borofsky. "The study, where we could spread the papers out, would be better," he said.

"Excellent!" Anton replied heartily, leading the way.

Sasha pouted.

* * *

Sarah was irritated to discover that she had to get permission from

Charlie and a state police officer before she could walk back in Ziggy's driveway, in spite of the fact that she'd just walked out a few minutes earlier. A light north wind wafted a strand of hair into Sarah's face. She swept it back behind her ear impatiently.

She found Pastor Briskin standing beside the excavator, and Dudley rummaging around inside the cab with a trash bag in his hand.

"A terrible thing, what happened last night," Pastor Briskin said, with unusual brevity.

"Damned elephant," Dudley said. He shot a hostile glance at Mabel, who was moping at the far side of her pen. Dudley muttered something under his breath as he clambered down to the ground.

Pastor Briskin opened his mouth to address Dudley's oath, but closed it again with nothing more than a sigh. He looked at the bulging trash bag. "What's in there?"

"Just some of Bernie's personal stuff: extra boots, jacket, lunch box, tools and junk. The cops are through looking around in there, so I figured I might as well take the stuff away for his wife in case she wants it. Not much in here, really." He opened the bag so they could see the contents.

"What's that thing that looks sort of like a hoe with a pie plate on the business end of it?" Pastor Briskin said, pointing to the oddly shaped object.

"It's a metal detector," Dudley replied. "Bert Farley has one just like it. You sweep that round plate over the ground, and it makes a noise when it passes over any buried metal. Bernie said he was going to use it to find where the water pipe came into the basement, so he wouldn't dig it up by mistake."

Sarah thought she knew what else Bernie had in mind for his metal detector. She glanced down towards Gerhard Burndt's final resting place and saw Bert digging with his spade. What did Bert *really* plan to use his metal detector for? She needed to talk to the young man soon.

"You're right," Pastor Briskin said, "we should take all that stuff over to his widow." He shook his head sadly. "I'm afraid the poor woman blames me for his death."

"She's not thinking straight," Harvey said. He'd abandoned his chainsaw to come over and hear any new gossip. "I can take it over, if you like. I know her pretty well, and maybe I can talk some sense into her. There's no reason why she should blame you. After all, it was his fault for going in there in the first place, especially in the dark—probably spooked Mabel into attacking him. That was just plain dumb."

"I wouldn't tell her that last part, even if it's true," Pastor Briskin advised, as his cell burst into song. He walked off to answer it.

Harvey glared angrily at Pastor Briskin's departing back. "I can think something without saying it, for crying out loud," he grumbled.

Dudley handed his burden to Harvey with relief, and went off to pick up some more brush. Meanwhile, Harvey put the trash bag in the back of his pickup and left to visit Bernie's grieving widow.

Pastor Briskin's face was flushed as he put his cell away. "We've been betrayed!" he proclaimed. "It's time to rally the faithful!" Without a word of explanation, he leaped into the church van and roared away.

With Harvey and Pastor Briskin gone, and Dudley puttering around the excavator, Sarah wandered down to Mabel's enclosure where Phoebe was tossing more hay over the fence. Mabel wandered over, snuffled in Phoebe's direction, and went to work on the hay.

"How is Asim holding up?" Sarah asked.

"The police spent a lot of time questioning him," Phoebe replied. "He seems fine, but he's convinced that Mabel was framed."

"I don't suppose they're buying the right-handed elephant theory."

Phoebe shook her head worriedly. "I doubt it. He's going to have big trouble with the zoo over this. They were paying him good money to keep Mabel out of sight."

"And paying Pastor Briskin good money too, from what I hear."

Phoebe, her mind somewhere else, said, "Asim's feeling guilty about not staying with Mabel last night."

"He had no way of knowing what would happen."

Phoebe gave Sarah a rueful look. "I'm the one who persuaded him to leave her so he could get a decent night's sleep, and I think he blames me for luring him away."

Sarah caught the look on Phoebe's face. "Have you known Asim long?"

"Four days. He came in last Friday morning and hired us to truck Mabel up here. We were bringing up that load of lumber anyway, so it worked out for everybody." She nodded at the mountain of building supplies.

"Do you do much of that kind of thing? I mean trucking animals around the country?"

Phoebe looked uncomfortable. "We're a small company, just my father and me. We can't afford to be too choosey in this economy."

Sarah wondered if McTavish Transport had been hired for that very reason. She gave Phoebe a friendly, conspiratorial look. "Did Asim make the arrangements to bring Mabel up here?"

"I think so. At least he's the one who made the arrangements with Kermit and me, and he had keys to get into the zoo."

"So the zoo will know about the latest problem."

"How could they help but know, considering all the cops around here?" Phoebe replied sharply. "I'm sure they'll talk to the zoo."

Sarah looked at Mabel's corral. "Have the police said anything to you about the attack?"

Phoebe seemed relieved to be on a different topic. "They say it happened near the fence, down by the shore and the grave site—that's where they've been working, anyway," Phoebe said somberly. "She may have cornered him as he tried to run away. Asim says that elephants are a lot quicker than they look."

"What do you remember about last evening when you were there? Did you see anybody?"

"I'm not sure if I should talk about it."

"It's not as though this was a murder investigation, and I won't tell anyone."

Phoebe looked doubtful. "Pastor Briskin said that you'd helped other people in the past."

"Oliver and I have helped people a few times," Sarah replied modestly.

"Do you think you can prove that Mabel didn't kill Bernie?"

Sarah watched Asim as he talked to one of the detectives while they stood where the enclosure had been roped off. "Maybe," she said doubtfully.

The two men walked over to Mabel's food and water trough. Mabel watched for a moment before she shambled over to Asim and reached over the wire with her trunk to snuffle his face.

"You don't sound very encouraging," Phoebe said.

"It's a police investigation, really. All Oliver and I can do is ask around."

Asim gave Mabel a carrot to distract her while the detective swabbed her tusk.

"Trying to get another blood sample off her tusk," Phoebe commented with a shudder.

"They must have done that earlier, didn't they?"

"They tried a little while ago, but the poor thing was cringing in the back of her pen, and too upset for them to get a good sample."

Sarah nodded. "It must be upsetting for her to have all those people wandering around, not to mention a dead body in her pen. She looks a lot calmer now then she did earlier, though."

"Who knows about elephants?"

"She's a wild animal, beneath the surface, like all of us." Ziggy had arrived unannounced to deliver this gloomy observation. "It was a dark day when Mabel arrived on our doorstep, and Pastor Briskin feels the weight of guilt sitting heavily on his shoulders."

"Your precious Pastor told Asim that you had a zoo," Phoebe said accusingly.

"Pastor Briskin is remarkably devious for a man of the cloth," Ziggy replied.

"Yes, but why did he invite Mabel up here, when he knew there wasn't any zoo?"

"He was trying to do somebody a favor—a trade of some sort. The man is a well-meaning religious octopus," Ziggy replied.

"Religious octopus? Do you mean the way he has of gathering in new members?" Sarah said.

"I was thinking more about the many connections he has with other churches, and his skill at horse-trading." Ziggy contemplated the trees as they swayed gently in the morning breeze. It was blowing from the northwest today, a fair weather direction in Maine, which meant the air would be warmed and dried after coming in over the land. "I seem to remember an old saying about good intentions, pavement, and roads to various unpleasant places."

A chickadee darted out of the woods, singing its spring song. Sarah admired the busy and feisty little birds who were hardy enough to survive Maine's winters, and quick to celebrate spring.

Phoebe frowned at Ziggy's mangled metaphor, and Sarah gave her a that's-just-Ziggy-being-Ziggy shrug.

"Does anybody know what's going to happen to Mabel?" Sarah inquired. "Will she go back where she came from, or will she stay here?"

"Asim says that she'll be killed if she goes back to the zoo," Phoebe replied.

Sarah got the feeling that Asim had already settled the question in his own mind, even though Mabel didn't belong to him.

"The police say that she has to stay here for now," Ziggy said. "There's no other choice after what happened." He glanced at Mabel, who was destroying another bale of hay. "It really boils down to a question of karma," he added.

Phoebe rolled her eyes.

"You're spouting all this karma rubbish just to torment Pastor Briskin, aren't you?" Sarah said. "Well, as far as I'm concerned, you can save it for when he comes back."

Phoebe scowled at Ziggy. "How do we know you don't want to keep her here at your imaginary zoo, just so you and Briskin can collect on her room and board?"

"I can't speak for the holy octopus," Ziggy replied coolly, "but that elephant has brought nothing but trouble to me."

Chapter 10

Ziggy took off on his bicycle around midmorning, presumably to hunt the wily soda can. With Phoebe and Asim elephant-tending, Sarah wandered down to the shore to see what the young archeologist was up to.

Bert had laboriously dug half-a-dozen shallow pits, each about two-feet square, in a rough grid along the piece of shoreline that would soon become the town's new park. The holes more or less surrounded Gerhard Burndt's grave, giving the area a somewhat pockmarked look. Sarah could see that the dirt from each hole had been run through a sieve.

Last fall, a group of volunteers from the town historical society had cleared the brush from the grave, trimmed the grass, and reset the broken headstone. Their tidying efforts had been somewhat marred by Bert's digging.

Bert seemed delighted for an excuse to stop and say hello to one of the few friendly faces around.

Sarah quickly discovered the reason for his willingness to put the shovel aside. Being sheltered form the wind, his work area was infested with black flies.

"Have you found anything interesting?" she said, swatting fruitlessly at a great cloud of the carnivorous insects.

"Not yet, unless you count the spearhead that Mister Borofsky found. But this is only the second phase."

"The second phase?" Sarah pictured weeks of Pastor Briskin's precious time slipping by.

"Yes. The first phase started with documentary research." He wiped a handful of black flies from his sweaty brow. "I've gone over old maps, early records, old deeds, aerial photographs, and so forth, to see what might be known of early Native American and Euroamerican settlements in this area. Now, I'm digging test pits to see what might be here." He swiped another handful of black flies off the back of his neck.

"It looks like hard work."

"It is, in spots. The amount of topsoil varies a lot. There's about three feet here in this hollow, but only a foot or so further up-slope."

"Is your work likely to slow down construction on the camp?"

Bert looked surprised by her question. "I can't see why, where I'm working on the piece that will be going to the town. That's where the artifact was found."

"Oh. I assumed it was on the part where the camp is going to be."

"Not quite, though it's close to the line. See where the soil was eroded back from the ledge by last winter's big storm?" Bert pointed with his shovel to where the sea had cut a chunk of soil down to bedrock, leaving a raw edge. "It was found right there, lying on the rock—a nicely made spearhead. My first guess is that it's about eight-thousand years old, but we'll need to do more research to get a better estimate."

Bert paused. "I suppose my work might have some effect on

Mr. Breener developing the rest of his property if signs of a major site turn up, but that seems very unlikely at this stage of the game. Frankly, the documentary records weren't very promising to start with, and the field work hasn't turned up anything, either. If it wasn't for the artifact that Mr. Borofsky stumbled on, and the fact that he's provided funding..." Bert shrugged.

"Is there any chance that it came from somewhere else?"

"Somewhere else?" Bert echoed blankly.

"I'm thinking about the gold-rush days when unscrupulous people would salt a mine to make it look like there was gold."

"Why would somebody do that?"

Bert was more naive than she thought. "Just to make trouble," she said.

Bert gazed at her through a black-speckled, blood-sucking cloud. "Ah. So that's why your Pastor Briskin and his work crew have been so unfriendly."

"I think they blame Anton Borofsky more than you."

"The town only has his word that he found the artifact here, and history is full of fraudulent claims." Bert shook his head sadly. "He seems very sincere, and as I say, he's been funding my work here, and the town planning board is supporting the research, too. I suppose they're hoping to find something interesting as a public attraction..." Bert ran down.

"This may sound silly, but has your research turned up any record of buried treasure around here?"

Bert laughed. "Buried treasure? God, no. Of course, there are legends of pirate treasure being buried all over coastal Maine, but nothing that I've heard of in this area." He looked at Sarah. "Is that why Briskin's people are upset about my metal detector? I've told them all that it's just to look for Euroamerican artifacts—just to cover all the bases."

"I'm only asking because there's a local legend about some

Huggard family treasure being buried around here."

For just an instant, the Harry Potter face disappeared and Indiana Jones took its place. Not so naive, after all, she thought.

"As I say, nothing like that came up in my research. But fanciful thinking can produce all kinds of legends." Bert swatted at the air. "Someday they'll invent a bug repellant that really works against these things," he grumbled.

Bert swatted at his tormentors again. "I'm not trying to say that there isn't any buried treasure, because anything is possible." He smiled. "There's something almost magical about stories of buried treasure that gets people to daydreaming."

"It does inspire magical thinking."

"A bit like the appeal of buying a lottery ticket."

Sarah nodded. Myra Huggard's mythical treasure was certainly capturing the imagination of Pastor Briskin's workers. She looked around and realized that the lower end of Mabel's enclosure was only a few yards from Bert's test pits. "Are you going to dig up Mabel's enclosure when she leaves?"

"I don't see any need, based on what I've found—or rather haven't found—here. I'll probably give the area a quick once-over with my metal detector after the elephant leaves to check for any Euroamerican artifacts: trash, utensils, and so on. Gerhard Burndt may have been the first settler to build here, but earlier European trappers and hunters may have passed through, and maybe traded with Native Americans."

"And buried some treasure?" Sarah said with a laugh.

"I wouldn't get my hopes up on that score," Bert replied.

* * *

Sarah left Bert with his shovel and black flies, and walked slowly along the shore towards the Borofsky's property line.

A crow, startled by her approach, squawked and flapped heavily out of a large, malformed multi-trunked pine tree—a "wolf pine," in local parlance. The bird gave a raucous warning call before lumbering off to find a safer perch. Sarah wondered if the tree was doomed to fall victim to Harvey's chainsaw.

Somewhere, not far from the pine, Evan Huggard had thrown together a lop-sided fishing shack. That must have been close to sixty years ago and there hadn't been much left of it when she was here last spring—just the collapsed walls buried under the tattered, tar-papered remains of the roof.

Harvey and Dudley hadn't quite gotten to the rotten boards and bits of junk that marked the spot, which made it the last untouched remnant of Sarah's youth in Maine. She stood over the decaying pile.

Some of the rotted boards had been moved recently. Curious, Sarah shifted a few of them to see what treasures might be underneath.

What she saw was the rear wheel of a bicycle, its old-fashioned balloon tire frayed by age. Somebody must have partially uncovered it, lost interest, and covered it up again. A disappointed treasure hunter?

She shifted a few more punky bits of wood and pulled the bike free from its resting place. It was a girl's bicycle of the type Sarah had ridden as a child. The paint had long-since been eaten away by the sea air and replaced by a coating of rust—with one exception. A vampish sticker of the cartoon character, Betty Boop, clung tenaciously to the rear fender. Sarah looked around, but nobody was in sight.

The Huggards never had any children of their own, nor did they seem to like children, though Myra's mysterious gift of *Owl* to the camp suggested some ambivalence on her part.

Evan had died—was murdered, Sarah corrected herself—the last year she attended Migawoc.

Sarah's blood ran cold as she imagined the possible reasons for hiding a girl's bicycle underneath Evan Huggard's fishing shack. The most benign possibility was that he'd stolen the bike and hidden it there, planning to sell it later for beer money. But there were more sinister explanations. She comforted herself with the possibility that somebody else put it there after Evan died.

The bicycle resisted her efforts to return it to its former resting place, so Sarah left Betty Boop on the ground. Leaving it out in the open could hardly cause much more damage.

Unfortunately, she didn't think to wonder why the last person to uncover the bike had gone to the trouble of hiding it again.

Chapter 11

The crime scene van edged its way out the driveway just as Oliver walked in. A growing crowd of newspeople were gathering, kept back by several state police officers.

"Mabel doesn't seem to be all that traumatized after killing Bernie last night," Oliver said to Sarah, as he looked at the enclosure and its inhabitant. He had just come back from his visit with the Borofskys, and he and Sarah moved to one side while Phoebe started the water pump and refilled Mabel's trough. Asim was still in a huddle with the police near the crime scene.

"*If* she killed Bernie," Sarah said. "We're supposed to be proving that she was framed, remember?"

"Mmm."

"Phoebe and I were talking about Mabel a few minutes ago. It's a big turnaround from this morning, when she was standing way off in the far corner."

"A resilient beast."

"Maybe all the visitors this morning have cheered her up. There were a couple of police detectives going over the crime scene earlier," Sarah said.

"There's still a little of the blood stain left on her tusk," Oliver observed. He looked around. "Where's Pastor Briskin and his crew?"

"He left in a big rush about an hour ago, right after Harvey went away to take Bernie's belongings to his widow. Dudley is in Myra's cellar, doing something under the excavator. I think he's checking to see if Bernie got it fixed last night."

"People are spending a lot of time working on that thing," Oliver said.

"He seems to think he can run it, assuming it's fixed."

"Let's hope he's right."

"At least it's keeping them busy. As near as I can tell, they're all either out of work or retired, and they seem to enjoy having a project like this to occupy them. Speaking of working, how did your visit with the Borofskys go, and what was Sasha wearing?"

"Why do I have the feeling that's a loaded question? As a matter of fact, she was wearing a beach towel."

"A beach towel?"

"She'd been swimming in the pool," Oliver explained.

Sarah nodded. "A string bikini, I presume."

"Your psychic powers astound me."

"The woman is nothing if not predictable."

"Yes, well," Oliver said briskly, "as far as the boat goes, they were leaning towards a lobsterboat yacht at first. It would have that Maine mystique they seem to like, and the type is popular."

"Sasha is going to pull lobster pots in her string bikini?"

"I doubt that she'll pull lobster pots at all. Nautical things aren't her forte when you get right down to it. She knows that the pointy end of a boat tends to be at the front, but the rest is pretty vague. Anyway, they ended up deciding on a Friendship Sloop."

"A string bikini would be more practical for sailing than pot-hauling," Sarah murmured.

"What's with the bikini thing?"

"I'm just curious about what the other half wears around the house, to business meetings, and the like."

"I wouldn't have called it a business meeting, exactly. It was more like a keeping-up-with-the-Vincents discussion. The boat is just for decoration, after all. Besides, neither of them know how to sail. From a decorative standpoint, the Friendship Sloop is as much a Maine icon as a lobsterboat."

"The whole business is decadent, if you ask me," Sarah groused.

"Decadent? Do you mean decadent, as in Sasha wearing a bikini to a business meeting? Or are you thinking about her third-storey swimming pool?"

"I mean having a boat built just to one-up your neighbor, wise guy. At least the Vincents use the Whitehall you built for them."

She checked her watch. "Brian Curtis called while you were at the Borofskys," she said tentatively.

"What did he want?" Oliver said, thinking about Sasha's comment.

"A 'luncheon date' is the way he put it."

"Sounds posh." Competition, or business, Oliver wondered. "According to Anton, Brian is trying to sell the lot next door, and is unhappy about Mabel being there."

"What does that have to do with anything?"

"Nothing, except that you have some influence with Ziggy, and you know what's going on here, first hand."

"Or," Sarah snapped, "it could be that he just wants to have lunch with me. After all, you've been down here spending the last few mornings with Lady Godiva—"

"—and her husband."

"—so I don't see any reason why I can't have lunch with one of the most respected men in town."

Perhaps it was fortunate that their conversation was cut short as an official-looking vehicle was ushered in the driveway.

"That looks like trouble," Oliver said as the SUV parked in the spot recently vacated by the crime scene van.

"Double trouble," Sarah added. The Golden Arms of Faith Full Gospel Church van was tailgating the SUV, and it muscled its way through the police cordon, parking next to the SUV. Dudley appeared from under the excavator to see what was going on, and Mabel waved her trunk at the newcomers.

How was it, Oliver wondered, that most black SUVs looked innocuous, while others seemed to radiate a sinister, black-helicopter aura. He made a note to consult with Ziggy on the aura phenomenon. Sure enough, the SUV disgorged three sinister-looking officials, just as a horde of Pastor Briskin's fervent followers tumbled from their van and enveloped the startled newcomers with hugs and hosannas.

"Don't you just love a parade," Oliver said to Charlie Howes, who had elbowed his way out of the crowd and made his way over to them.

"What is all this?" Charlie said.

"Haven't you ever been to one of Pastor Briskin's sing-in-and-revival meetings?" Oliver said.

"Pastor Briskin's what?" Charlie said.

"Shouldn't you be going back to help the police with crowd control?" Sarah asked.

Charlie looked at the growing turmoil while he thought about her question. "No way," he replied, as two more carloads of revelers ran the undermanned police blockade and released another battalion of true believers, this group laden down with placards. "I know too many of those people."

"You're in for a rare treat," Oliver assured Charlie as one of Pastor Briskin's crew began to torture *Nearer my God to Thee* on an out-of-tune banjo.

"I can't imagine God wanting to be anywhere near that banjo," Charlie commented.

Pastor Briskin's flock totaled almost twenty enthusiastic, albeit tone-deaf people, all of them dancing and singing loudly. At this point, the revelers outnumbered the police by more than three-to-one.

"Who are the people in the SUV?" Sarah asked.

"State mucky-mucks, come to evict Mabel from a residential area," Charlie said. The newly arrived officials were vainly trying to say something that sounded threatening, but their words were drowned out by Pastor Briskin's raucous choir.

"Exactly how do they plan to evict her?" Oliver inquired.

"That's their problem. I'm just a part-time deputy sheriff, remember? My guess is they'll try to serve papers on Ziggy, since he's the property owner."

"But Ziggy's not here," Oliver pointed out.

"He's no dummy," Sarah commented.

"How long is this likely to go on?" Charlie said nervously.

"Until the SUV leaves, or God strikes down the banjo player," Sarah replied.

The crowd was waving their newly-arrived placards, which proclaimed, "Save Mabel!" "Peace to elephants!" "We love Mabel!"

"Pastor Briskin's bunch are certainly fast workers," Sarah said as she admired the placards.

Charlie looked on with dismay.

Suddenly, silence descended.

"What happened?" Sarah said, craning her neck in an effort to see through the crowd.

Oliver, who happened to stick up in the air higher and therefore had a better view, replied, "It's more like who happened."

A tall, slender figure dressed in black jogging shorts and a spandex top appeared at the end of the driveway. Her ash-blond hair blew in the freshening breeze. "Leave the elephant alone!" she yelled, her voice cutting like a knife through the wind.

"What in the world is she doing?" Charlie said in awe.

"Being Pastor Briskin's secret weapon," Sarah replied.

"It looks like he took your advice about talking to Sasha, and it worked."

"We're responding to a complaint, ma'am," one of the officials replied. "I must ask you to move along."

"I withdraw the complaint!"

The crowd remained silent, frozen in place as though hypnotized by the unfolding drama. The term, "pillar of salt" flashed through Sarah's mind. She scolded herself for spending too much time around Pastor Briskin.

"It's not that simple, lady," one of the officials replied, his voice reflecting uncertainty.

"Then make it simple!" Sasha said, her voice dripping menace. "How dare you threaten this group of God-fearing people just so you can take away their pet elephant?"

"Look, lady—"

"I'm Sasha Borofsky from next door, and my husband has a lot of influence in this town, and I'm telling you to leave the elephant alone!" Sasha's threat wasn't lost on the SUV's officials.

"Are you rescinding your complaint?"

"What did I just tell you?" Sasha replied disdainfully.

Sarah could see the authorities huddled in a conference.

"I think she's done it," Oliver said in awe, a few moments later.

"I'll be damned," Charlie said.

Sarah leaned close to whisper in Oliver's ear. "I'll require a full report and an explanation for Sasha's behavior the next time you go over there."

"I hope you've noticed that she isn't wearing her bikini."

* * *

Thanks to Pastor Briskin's love-in, Sarah barely made it to the Squirrel Point Inn on time. The inn was a classic of its kind—a vast, rambling Victorian-era hotel, perched on the rocky tip of Squirrel Point where it overlooked the sea.

It was too early in the season for the inn to be crowded, so they were able to get a table next to the window, with its picture-postcard view of the water.

The Inn's restaurant was justly famous for its seafood, and the prices reflected its reputation. Sarah was glad that Brian was picking up the tab.

"I was thinking yesterday that it's just about a year ago that we first met," Brian said after they'd ordered. "You were standing in Myra Huggard's driveway, looking a bit preoccupied, as I remember."

"Standing there brought back a lot of memories. It had been almost forty years since I was there last, and so little had changed, except for the house having burned down."

Brian nodded. "Myra didn't change the place much. I'm afraid I startled you though, pulling in the driveway like that."

"I was afraid I might be trespassing, and you were going to chase me off."

Brian laughed. "You weren't the first person to trespass on Myra's land. A lot of people were curious about her house burning down."

"Morbid curiosity."

He shook his head sadly. "It's still hard to believe the old woman is gone. I knew her all my life, growing up. It's like Old Mother Huggard had been there forever—a real force of nature. Of course a lot of people thought she'd been murdered, right from the start." Brian smiled at Sarah. Brian Curtis, she reflected, had a smile that would melt a tax auditor's heart.

Lunch arrived, and they made small talk over the meal. It wasn't until dessert was served that Brian returned to serious matters.

"It's terrible about Bernie being killed," Brian said, "and what a bizarre way to die. I don't suppose you've heard anything about the investigation?"

"I expect that you know as much as I do, what with your connections."

"It'll take a couple of days to tie up the loose ends, but they'll probably decide it was an accident. What else could it be? Bernie shouldn't have been in the pen at night, but he was an odd duck."

"I suppose you must have known him pretty well, where he grew up in town."

"Oh, sure. Bernie, Dudley, Harvey, Bernie's sister Betsy, and I used to help Sam Merlew get the camp set up each spring. I was just a kid then, but we had a great time horsing around."

Brian gave her another smile. One could get a sunburn from too many of those, Sarah thought. "I had a teen-age crush on Betsy Knowles back then." He laughed. "Of course, I was much too young for her, and all the other boys in town had their eye on her, too. She was quite a looker." He turned solemn. "It was too bad, her running off like that."

"What happened?"

"She up and left one spring, and hasn't been heard from since. Of course, her parents died years ago, so Bernie and his family are all that's left. And now Bernie's dead." He shook his head sadly. "The Knowles family had a lot of problems. Her father was abusive, used to get drunk and beat up her mother. He beat up Harvey, too, when he tried to step in. Anyway, I think Betsy just had enough of it and ran off. Harvey certainly left town as soon as he got out of school."

"He did mention having a hard time growing up," Sarah said.

"He was a troubled kid, that's for sure. He had a short fuse and used to get into fights at school."

"Not surprising, considering his home life. Did he have anybody to turn to?" For some reason, her mind turned to Oliver. He'd be putting another coat of varnish on *Daisy Mae's* mast before long. Alone, since she was here, talking to Brian Curtis about Harvey Cassell, a man she hardly knew.

"I remember that he and Bernie were pretty close when they were kids, and the two of them got together after high school to start a construction company over in Damariscotta."

Brian was seated with his back to the window, and Sarah's gaze wandered over his shoulder to a lobsterboat as Brian talked on. The boat was pulling a string of pots close by the rocks in front of the inn, and a swell was rolling it violently. A submerged ledge further out tripped up an occasional swell, which hurled a tower of broken water into the air.

"I'm probably boring you silly, babbling on like this," Brian said apologetically, his words breaking into her reverie.

"Oh, no," she replied, flustered. "I just got distracted by watching that lobsterboat. It looks so close to the rocks."

"There's a pretty good sea running today; a big storm offshore is bringing it in. A man could get rolled right over the side on a day like this, if he wasn't careful."

"The water looks cold."

Brian nodded. "You wouldn't last long in it without a survival suit this time of year." He'd owned a lobsterboat in his younger days, before becoming a Realtor, a job that tended to be less strenuous and more lucrative.

"My boat's going into the water next week," Brian said. He owned a power cruiser now, built on lobsterboat lines, and he'd taken Sarah out a few times for day trips when she first arrived, last year. "I really enjoyed our excursions last spring," he said wistfully.

"They were fun, and the picnic lunches were great. Not to mention the wine."

Brian laughed. "I can't take credit for the picnic; Borealis Bread put that together."

"Well, they did a good job."

"We could go out again this spring, if you like," Brian said tentatively. "Or, you and Oliver could come out. We could run down to Pemaquid."

Sarah suppressed a sudden guilt pang. "Maybe later. We're pretty busy trying to finish up a boat that Oliver is building."

"Busy tends to happen in the spring. Speaking of busy, I hear that Oliver is going to build a boat for the Borofskys."

Word certainly got around in a small town. "It's not a sure thing yet. The boat is mostly for Sasha."

"I didn't think she knew anything about boats, or cared."

"It's mostly for decoration, as near as we can tell."

"Keeping up with the neighbors?" Brian nodded. "I guess they can afford it."

"Oliver's not too happy about the idea of designing and building a boat just for show, though he may be able to sell the design to somebody else afterwards."

"He'd better watch his step with Sasha Borofsky," Brian said casually. "That woman is trouble."

"So I gather."

Brian gave her another blinding smile. "On different subject, I was wondering if you could do me a favor."

So this wasn't just a social event, a casual date. Sarah suppressed her irritation. "What is it?"

"It's about Ziggy's elephant—"

"Pastor Briskin is responsible for Mabel being here, not Ziggy."

"Yes, but the elephant is on Ziggy's land, and that's the problem."

Brian hadn't gotten to where he was in the real estate business by being oblivious to nuance, and he could tell the conversation was starting to go badly. He soldiered on, regardless. "The trouble is that people don't like the idea of buying land next door to a zoo."

"It's one elephant, not a zoo, Brian."

"My client's property smells like a zoo when the wind is wrong. I know it's only supposed to be for a little while, but I don't know what that means. Is it a week? A month? Six months? What can I tell a potential buyer? And it'll be worse when word gets out about poor Bernie's death. That sort of notoriety can destroy property values."

"You want me to find out when Mabel is leaving? Strange as it sounds, I'm not sure anybody knows for sure."

"The sooner she leaves, the better. The kind of person who can afford land like that isn't interested in being told that the neighbor's elephant will be gone 'soon.' He'll buy somewhere else, where he doesn't have to worry about neighbors with elephants."

"There's no way I'm going to persuade Ziggy or Pastor Briskin to evict Mabel, even if I could. I'm not even sure why she's here in the first place, except that they're being paid to board her."

"How about moving Mabel up to Oliver's place? There's a lot more room up there."

"Why would Oliver want to do that, and what makes you think Pastor Briskin would go along? I really don't have that kind of influence over either one of them."

"Anything you can do would help. This is the time of year when people start to look for a place to buy. I can't afford to put customers off for months, and the owner of the property is already giving me hell as it is."

Chapter 12

While Sarah was enjoying her seafood lunch, Oliver was lingering at Ziggy's place as the last of Pastor Briskin's party-goers drifted away, along with the disillusioned SUV. Oliver hoped to squeeze whatever information he could from Charlie before returning home to a late lunch and *Daisy Mae*'s mast.

"Does all that stuff mean the police are done with the investigation?" Oliver asked his quarry, indicating the heap of rope and yellow tape, which was piled outside the enclosure.

"I doubt it, but the state cops don't take me into their confidence when it comes to that sort of thing."

"Do they know if Bernie was alive when he got skewered?"

"Skewered?" Charlie rolled his eyes. "I couldn't say either way. This isn't like one of those cop shows where the autopsy is done while the body is still warm. These things take time. I expect old Bernie is lying in a cooler somewhere, waiting his turn."

"So, you don't know if they thought about the possibility that somebody killed Bernie and framed Mabel for the crime?" Oliver said.

Charlie looked incredulous. "Somebody framed the elephant? Jeez, I wouldn't think it. Anyhow, you're talking way over my pay grade." Charlie shrugged again. "All I know is they took a ton of pictures, wiped some of the blood off the elephant's tusk, and spent a lot of time poking around the spot where Bernie died."

"A lot of time?"

"You saw them. They were down there from sunup, almost until Briskin turned up with his hootenanny. Seemed like a long time to me, but there's always some little question, some inconsistency with a thing like this. I expect they were just being thorough. Let's face it, they don't get to investigate a death-by-elephant case very often." He glanced at Mabel. "You've got to be extra careful when you're investigating an elephant," he deadpanned.

"So you think they'll decide it was an accident?" Oliver said.

"Most likely. Like I say, what else could it be?"

With impeccable timing—which Oliver suspected was intentional—Ziggy rattled his bicycle in the driveway, having neatly avoided the state officials and Pastor Briskin's party, though not the holy man himself.

The exuberant cleric hurried over, having sent the last celebrants on their way. "Hallelujah, Brother Charlie," Pastor Briskin crowed as he embraced the deputy in a bear hug that lifted Charlie's feet off the ground. Returning the disconcerted lawman to earth, Pastor Briskin added, "A glorious morning! We've saved Mabel!"

Ziggy raised his eyes skyward for a moment before lowering his gaze to the gleeful clergyman. "You've saved Mabel? Does that mean she has a soul, like a person?"

Pastor Briskin scowled at his troublesome companion. "Your attitude troubles me, Brother Breener. I pray that someday you may see The Light and come to accept Jesus in your heart. Until that wondrous hour, I refuse to get into a debate with you about whether the beast does or does not have a soul. In any case, God made the oversized creature, and as a believer in His mercy, I feel compelled to protect it from harm."

"Does that mean I have to accept an elephant into my heart?"

"Elephants have a hallowed place in scripture Brother Breener."

"In scripture, maybe, but this elephant has been a curse to my backyard," Ziggy retorted stubbornly.

A great wall of wind suddenly blew in off the sound, swept through the decimated line of trees, and overwhelmed them with a blast of cold air. "Myra is not happy," Ziggy said gloomily.

* * *

"How was your lunch?" Oliver said, when Sarah arrived at his boatshop later in the afternoon. He had finished varnishing *Daisy Mae's* mast, and was starting on the boom—a job she had been planning to do.

"It was fine," she replied curtly, as she absentmindedly scratched Wes on the back. "Do you want me to do anything?"

"There's the tiller and some small stuff on the workbench that need another coat of varnish."

They worked in silence for a while. Finally, Sarah said, "At least Brian didn't take his clothes off."

It took Oliver a few seconds to recover from the image her words had created in his mind. "Wise of him. A bikini isn't his style, and I suspect the Squirrel Point Inn would frown on nudity in their diningroom; it might shock some of their older clientele."

"He wants me to use my influence to have Mabel removed from Ziggy's place."

"He took you out to a fancy restaurant so you'd work on Ziggy and Pastor Briskin?"

"Don't rub it in."

"I'm just thinking that nobody can budge those two, especially the good Pastor. Surely Brian knows that."

"He's desperate," Sarah said. "Nobody will look at the land next to Ziggy with Mabel there. Especially when word gets out that she's a killer."

"Actually, I'm not so sure that Pastor Briskin has the final word on where Mabel goes. Something more is going on there."

"Do you think Asim is running the show?" Sarah said.

"He's Mabel's handler, and he could be something more than that, or he could be taking orders from somebody higher up the food chain."

"So, you think I should be sweet-talking Asim instead of Pastor Briskin?"

"I think Asim will be an even tougher nut to crack than Pastor Briskin. Besides, where would he move Mabel?"

"Interesting question. As a matter of fact, Brian suggested that she could come here and stay with you," Sarah replied, giving her brush a dainty flip over *Daisy Mae's* tiller.

Oliver stared at her with horror. "Here? What do you mean, here?"

"He figures that she'd be out of the way—"

"And he wants you to use your wiles to make me go along with this foolishness?"

"Should I go get my bikini?"

"Not until you've finished varnishing that tiller."

* * *

They ended up spending most of the afternoon working on the countless minor jobs that were needed to get the boat ready for her her launching, in less than two weeks.

They took a break from *Daisy Mae* around four o'clock and

brought out the spars for *Owl*, Sarah's sixteen-foot sailboat, so they could sand them down for their spring varnish. The mast, like the rest of *Owl*, was over ninety years old, and the spruce had collected an assortment of nicks and dents which the varnish couldn't entirely hide. Despite the marks of wear and tear, *Owl* was still a thing of beauty to Sarah's eyes. Looking at the boat and feeling the way she moved through the water made Sarah appreciate the genius of Nathaniel Herreshoff, the "Wizard of Bristol," who designed the boat in 1914.

Owl also reminded her of Myra Huggard, who for reasons nobody could fathom, had bought the boat, loaned it anonymously for the camp's use, and ultimately left the vessel to Sarah in her will.

Oliver placed the mast on a pair of padded sawhorses, which happened to be at a convenient working height, and they started sanding, one at each end of the spar. "The varnish is in pretty good shape, so I don't think it'll need more than a light sanding before we put on a coat or two."

The job was familiar to Sarah, since she had spent the winter repairing *Owl* before coming to Maine last year. It was the same winter that her marriage was disintegrating. At the time, the project had been a form of therapy, a way of getting back to her working class roots.

"Penny for your thoughts," Oliver said after the silence had gone on for a while.

"I was just thinking that each of the mast's dents and scars must have its own story to tell, a story that's been lost in time. A lot like Myra's story."

Oliver put aside his sandpaper. "You're beginning to sound like Ziggy, brooding over an old woman who's been dead for more than a year."

Sarah thought about blackened pots and kettles. She knew perfectly well that Oliver still brooded at times over his dead wife,

killed by a drunk driver more than a decade ago. In all fairness, she
still brooded over her one-year-old divorce from Claude, her
philandering ex-husband. Why shouldn't she and Ziggy brood over
Myra Huggard? Some wounds never completely heal.

She would have challenged Oliver about all this a year ago.
Instead she said, "The difference is that Ziggy talks as though she's
still haunting the place and running things, and maybe she is, in a
way."

Oliver ran his fingers over a stained spot on the mast. "Just
because she manipulated people when she was alive doesn't mean
she's still doing it now that she's dead. That's just Ziggy-talk."

Sarah frowned. "I've always suspected that she left *Owl* to me as
a way to lure me back to Maine."

"Something I approve of, by the way."

"This last year has certainly been interesting," Sarah admitted.
"I know it's just Ziggy being Ziggy, with his astral planes, and
whatnot, but still..."

Oliver went back to his sandpaper. "The trouble with Ziggy's
train of thought is that it leads to the idea of elephant-possession."

"Elephant-possession? As in Myra's ghost got mad at Bernie for
trying to dismantle her house foundation, so she had Mabel kill
him? I'll go for something more concrete, thank you."

"Such as?"

"Buried treasure. When I was at camp, some of the girls used to
tease Myra when we walked by her driveway. They'd chant things
like, 'Old Mother Huggard went to the cupboard to fetch her pot of
gold. I didn't do it, but—"

"—which is probably why she left the boat to you," Oliver
interjected.

"We knew she didn't have two nickels to rub together. It was
just another little cruelty aimed at an unpleasant, eccentric old
woman. Teenage girls can be vicious."

"So can teenage boys," Oliver commented. "I don't like where you're going with this, though."

Sarah went on, regardless. "Suppose there really was a pot of gold, or something like that, squirreled away down in the cellar, or buried in the yard. Suppose Bernie started taking the foundation stones apart with his excavator and spotted a cache of some kind. Suppose the excavator wasn't really broken, and he was under there rooting out Myra's treasure instead of fixing the hydraulics."

"And somebody killed him to get the treasure, whatever it was, and framed Mabel for the crime? I don't like this theory at all."

"Why not?"

"Okay, suppose Myra did have some canning jars, or whatever, filled with gold coins, and they were tucked away among the pickled beets in a corner of the basement. Then what?"

Sarah scowled. "Pickled beets? You're not taking this as seriously as I'd like."

"You have a paint smudge from *Daisy Mae* of the tip of your nose." He offered her a piece of paper towel. "Wouldn't she have mentioned this cache of treasure in her will?"

Sarah scrubbed her face with the towel. "Why bother? After all, the house and its contents were going to Ziggy anyway. How does my nose look now?"

"Your nose looks beautiful. But Ziggy would need the money to pay the property taxes, so why wouldn't she tell him about the stash? More important, why didn't Myra use it herself to pay the bills? Why take a chance that he wouldn't find this mysterious treasure?"

"Okay, suppose Myra didn't know about the hoard of gold. You know the way stuff can accumulate over the years in an old cellar, and that place dated back to the 1700's, when the Huggard family settled this area. Myra didn't move into the house until after she married Evan Huggard, and I doubt if she would have spent much time poking around the cellar's foundation stones."

"So your hypothetical treasure got lost in the Huggard family history?"

"Things can get lost when you rely on oral history," Sarah said, picking up her sandpaper. "Look what happened to Gerhard Burndt's grave. Nobody knew where it was for hundreds of years before it finally turned up." Sarah refrained from reminding Oliver that people had died during the turning-up process.

"So, what was Bernie doing in Mabel's pen instead of Myra's cellar?"

"Maybe he got tired of poking around in the cellar and decided to go treasure hunting in her pen that night."

"And he scared her, so she gored him?" Oliver said. "Wouldn't he have had his metal detector? What why wasn't it with him when he was killed?"

"I'm still working on that," Sarah grumbled. "Speaking of metal detectors, I talked to Bert Farley this morning, and he has one."

"Why wouldn't he?"

"No reason, but it was bothering Bernie. He thought Bert was looking for the Huggard treasure."

"Do you think they got into a fight over it?"

"I thought Bert was too academic for that, at first. But I did get a flash of Indiana Jones when I mentioned the buried treasure legend."

Oliver groaned. "That's all we need: Indiana Jones and the Killer Elephant. And all this is over an imaginary treasure. I told you Ziggy would get us into trouble."

"Why don't you blame it on Myra? It's her treasure."

"Because she's dead, though nobody seems to believe it," Oliver muttered in frustration.

Sarah still wasn't ready to give up. "How about this? Suppose somebody, maybe Bert, saw Bernie lying there dead, and took the metal detector away."

"Why?"

"Maybe he took it to discourage the other would-be treasure hunters. The whole bunch of them have gold-fever, and Bert wouldn't want the competition. In fact, it's entirely possible that Bert killed Bernie and framed Mabel."

Oliver sighed. "It's no wonder that Ziggy calls you Ditch Lady Sarah."

"I don't really search out the worst in people," she said defensively. "These things just seem to happen."

The worked in silence for a while before Sarah said, "Of course, Bernie could have been killed for some other reason that has nothing to do with hidden treasure."

"Mmm," Oliver said, refusing the bait.

"Maybe the Borofskys are behind it. Anton has threatened to have Ziggy killed if he built next door, and there Ziggy is, building next door. Maybe Bert is plant, a hit-man in disguise. Maybe he was lurking down by Gerhard Burndt's grave, waiting for a chance to strike. A murder or two might be just be enough to sink the schedule for Pastor Briskin's camp. We know that he needs to have it all built by late June or his backers will pull out their support."

"Are you trying to get a rise out of me?" Oliver grumbled. "Think about it: if the camp project dies, Ziggy will go broke and he might turn whole place into a public park, complete with rock concerts every Saturday night."

"Anton might figure he could buy Ziggy out at the last minute."

"Maybe," Oliver agreed. "But why kill somebody just to delay construction when there are easier ways, like sabotaging the excavator? The problem with your murder theories is that there's no proof that Bernie was actually murdered. Except by Mabel, who doesn't care about stashes of gold, or camps for troubled teens."

"You're right. This is all just conjecture. We need to get more information to make any real headway," Sarah concluded.

"True," Oliver said, looking at her suspiciously. "I was hoping that Charlie would tell me something useful when I talked to him earlier today, but he doesn't seem to know much."

"I'm not sure he'd tell us what he knew anyway."

"Probably not. On the other hand, Charlie talks to Pearly occasionally."

Parlin "Pearly" Gaites was a local boatbuilder, and a friend of Oliver and Sarah. He also happened to be the deputy sheriff's uncle. Family connections matter in a small town like Burnt Cove, so Charlie often shared information with Pearly. Confidentially, of course.

"You could talk to Pearly and see what he's heard," Sarah suggested.

"I am not going to try to weasel any confidential information out of Pearly again," Oliver announced. "He was pretty irritated the last time I did that."

"You're right," Sarah agreed. "We should do it together. After all, two weasels are better than one."

* * *

Sadly, the amateur weasels were derailed by Sarah's cell. The call was from Sam Merlew.

The Merlews had a two-room apartment attached to their barn. Sarah had spent last summer in this granny flat, and it had worked well for both Sarah and the elderly couple.

The Merlew's were in their eighties now, and Sarah thought of them as her second parents, especially with her birth parents gone.

"I just wanted to let you know that Kate took a tumble down the stairs yesterday and broke her right arm pretty badly," Sam said.

"Oh, no. How is she doing? Is she home?"

"She's home, but pretty uncomfortable; it was a rough night for her. She's taking a nap right now, but I think she'd love a visit later this afternoon if you happen to be free.

"How about four o'clock?" Sarah said.

"Perfect. I'll tell her you're coming. She's feeling mighty low, and seeing you will perk her up no end."

"How are you holding up?" Sarah asked.

"Making do."

Sarah could hear the worry and fatigue in Sam's words. "I'll bring an overnight bag just in case. I can make supper for you to give you a little break."

Chapter 13

May in Maine can be like a fickle lover, full of warm, soft caresses and the promise of a sultry summer one minute, and a blast of cold, harsh despair the next. Oliver was thinking about these things, and the forecast of a possible frost tonight, as he knocked on the Borofsky's door Tuesday morning.

"Anton has gone off until tomorrow," Sasha said, as she answered the door. "A minor crisis down in The City. Some of his business rivals can be downright ruthless. Anyway, it's just me and Nika this morning." She was wearing what looked to his uneducated eye like a filmy dressing gown. She caught his glance. "I dressed informally this morning, since we're good friends."

"Why don't I come back another day, when Anton is here," Oliver suggested.

"Don't be silly; I won't bite. Besides, Anton trusts my judgement completely, and it is my boat, after all." Sasha took Oliver's arm and led him across the expanse of marble flooring towards the study. "I had Nika bring some coffee into the study before she went up for her morning rest, in case you want some.

The poor woman is getting older, and she has to have her morning nap or she's useless for the rest of the day."

Sasha seemed relieved when Oliver declined the coffee, and she directed him to a love seat in front of the massive fireplace, where a small blaze struggled to soften the damp chill of the morning's northeast wind. She sat against him with her arm on the back of the love seat behind his shoulders.

"I'm glad to see that Mabel didn't get evicted," Oliver said. The elephant's name is Mabel?"

"Yes, and I'm sure Pastor Briskin appreciates having you go to bat for her."

Sasha patted Oliver's knee. "I didn't do it for him. I did it for me. Personally, I'll be sorry to see her go. I like elephants, and she's only supposed to there for a week or so. That doesn't seem terribly long, does it?"

"Of course not," Oliver agreed. On the other hand, it would seem like a long time if Mabel ended up in his back yard, as Brian had suggested.

"Anyway, Anton figures that we'll be rid of that man and his rowdy friends before then." She shrugged. "Anton can be a bore about things like that."

Oliver wondered what made Anton Borofsky think that he'd be rid of Ziggy and his crew so soon.

Sasha went on. "They were certainly noisy over there yesterday—most inappropriate in a residential neighborhood."

Sasha turned her attention to the folder in Oliver's lap. "Let's see what you've got," she murmured, as he took out a collection of drawings and photographs. It was difficult to maneuver with Sasha pressed against his right arm, but he managed to lay the papers on his lap at last. "Wouldn't it be more comfortable to spread these out on the table?" he suggested.

"But it's so cold over there and the fire is nice and warm." Sasha stretched like a cat, luxuriating in the fireplace's miserly heat.

He could feel the heat radiating from her body where it pressed against him. He noticed that the sash of her gown had come untied.

It was clear from her comments that Sasha's mind wasn't on the subject of boats, about which she knew next to nothing, and cared less. It was also clear where her mind appeared to be. Once again, Oliver thought about Sarah and her sharpened stake.

"Here's a picture of a 28-foot Friendship Sloop," he said, trying to ignore the aroma of her freshly washed hair. "It would be a good size for two people to daysail, or take out overnight."

"A Friendship sloop? I like the name." Her hair brushed his ear as she leaned in to study the photograph.

"They were originally built in Friendship, Maine for fishing and lobstering."

"Oh," she said, disappointed. "Is it a friendly town?"

Oliver was beginning to wonder how many conversations they were having. "It must be. After all, they built a lot of these boats."

"Could you take it out overnight? Would it have bunks?"

"Yes."

"Did you build this one?"

"No. These pictures are just to give you an idea of some possibilities."

"Bunks," she murmured. "It would be so romantic to spend the night on our little boat and be rocked to sleep in our bunk." She wriggled closer, her arm brushing the nape of his neck. "It would have to be bigger than the Vincent's boat for that, wouldn't it?"

"It would be about ten feet longer, a bigger boat all around."

"And our boat would have sails." She gazed into Oliver's eyes. "Would you teach me how to sail?"

"You and Anton?" He shrugged away her hand, which was toying with his left ear.

Sasha's eyebrows arched. "Don't be so stodgy and uptight.

You're positively prudish. Where's your spirit of adventure? You need to learn how to relax, and try new things. We're just friends, good friends, enjoying each other's company. Who knows where friendship can lead?"

"How about friendship leading to a new boat?"

"Your trouble is that you don't think like a hunter," she scolded. "You don't think about the thrill of the chase."

"When will Anton be back?"

"Tomorrow. I told you that." She leaned forward. "Don't you find me desirable?"

"Very desirable. That's the problem."

Sasha leaned back against the sofa. "It's just as well. Anton would kill you if he caught us."

Oliver looked at her, and sensed the excitement in her voice. Was having Anton kill her lover a part of the thrill for Sasha?

"Sarah is a very lucky woman," Sasha went on. "No wonder I hate her. She certainly keeps you on a short leash."

"There's no leash involved."

"Don't you think she's a bit possessive? She strikes me as being very insecure; I'm surprised she lets you come over here at all."

"Her ex-husband was a philanderer. It makes her sensitive."

"Do you think I'm a philanderer?" Sasha asked coyly.

"I wouldn't know anything about that, or about your marriage."

Sasha got up abruptly. "I'll have Anton call you when he gets back."

Without another word, she ushered him out the door and into the cool, blustery morning air.

* * *

While Oliver was being entertained by the scantily clad and free-spirited would-be yachtswoman, Sarah was sitting down with the

Merlews over after-breakfast coffee.

Sam happened to be on Burnt Cove's planning board, and Sarah took the opportunity to question him.

"Why did the town hire an archeologist to look at the new park?"

Sam smiled. "I get a kick out of calling that little fifty-foot-wide strip of land a park, but it does have Gerhard Burndt's grave, so I guess it qualifies. The fact is that we haven't gotten approval from the voters to accept it for a park, and I'm not sure they will approve, not where it would cost the town money for upkeep, not to mention the lost tax revenue."

"So the town doesn't actually own it?"

"Like I say, the town may never own it, unless the voters decide it's worth the cost. Anyway, we didn't hire Bert to look over the proposed park; Anton Borofsky did that and he's paying him handsomely for the job. Who were we to complain, and who knows, maybe he'll come up with something. After all, the voters would be more likely to approve taking the land if it had some archeological significance in addition to the grave."

"It sounds like Anton Borofsky wants the town to take it."

"Oh, yes," Sam replied. "I expect he figures it's that much less land for Ziggy to clutter up."

"He's not the only one who wants that land to be a park, either," Kate said. "Brian Curtis has been lobbying the planning board to take it, too."

"It sure would be a lot easier for Brian to sell the lot next door if it was a park, no matter how small it might be." Sam drained his cup and leaned back with a contented sigh. "Who knows? Maybe Bert will find the Huggard treasure, or pirate treasure, whichever it is. That would put the cat among the pigeons, for sure."

"You told Bert about the treasure legend?" Sarah said.

Sam laughed. "Of course. Why not?"

"You should be ashamed, spreading silly rumors like that," Kate scolded.

"We were just joking around, mother. The whole planning board was laughing about it. He knew we were kidding. Besides, he's more interested in the stone spearhead that Anton found."

"Does Bert have any way to prove it's authentic?" Sarah said.

"You don't trust Anton Borofsky?" Sam said.

"He's much too rich to be trustworthy," Kate said, in a fine display of class prejudice.

"On that note," Sam said, rising, "I'll let you two hold the fort while I run into Rockland and pick up some groceries."

"Don't forget the shopping list," Kate said to his retreating back.

Sarah and Kate sat with their second cups of coffee after Sam had left.

"Thank you for staying over last night," Kate said. "It made Sam feel better to have some help. He's such a worrier." She smiled at Sarah. "You're being a worry-wart yourself, dear. I love having you visit, but I'll be fine once some of these bruises and sprains get better. There's no need for you to spend the another night in our guest room."

"You were sleepwalking last night," Sarah commented. "Are you sure you aren't going to do that again? Sam was terrified that you'd wander around in your sleep and fall down the stairs again."

"I was wide awake the first time I fell."

"That's my point. Walking around in your sleep is worse, for heaven's sake. Sam was lying awake half the night trying to keep an eye on you. One or two more days would let him get some rest."

"It was that pain medication, or sleeping pill, or whatever it was, that had me sleepwalking, and I'm not going to take any more of that stuff."

"Have you talked to the doctor? There are other medications

that wouldn't have that side effect."

Kate gave Sarah an exasperated look that made it clear she was done talking about medications and doctors. "What have you been up to the last few days?"

Sarah filled Kate in on *Daisy Mae's* progress and the goings-on at Ziggy's place. She paused and drank more coffee before going on. "There was an old bicycle hidden under the remains of Evan's fishing shack."

The coffee cup hovered at Kate's lips. "A bicycle? In Evan's fishing shack?"

"Underneath it. A girl's bike."

"Somebody probably tossed it under there after he died, and forgot about it."

Maybe it was her imagination, but there was something about Kate's expression. "It looked pretty old, and it was very rusty, as though it had been there for a really long time."

"Probably not all that long, what with it being right next to the salt water." Kate shifted uncomfortably in her chair, perhaps trying to ease her bruises.

"It had a Betty Boop sticker on the rear fender."

"Did anybody see you down there, looking at it?" Kate's voice turned sharp.

All the workers were gone at the time, except Bert and Dudley who were both out of sight, and Sarah had checked to make sure she couldn't see the Borofsky's windows from the shack. "No, but somebody must have dragged it out from under Evan's shack. Dudley, Harvey, and Bert were all down there at various times. And Bernie, too, before he died. Why do you ask?"

"Betty Boop. That goes back a long way," Kate said, half to herself.

"Do you know who it belonged to?"

Kate returned the cup to its saucer. "Bernie's sister, Betsy, had a bicycle with a Betty Boop sticker on it," she said reluctantly. "It might have been hers."

"Brian said that she ran away from home."

"She left a note on the kitchen table, saying she was leaving. Everybody assumed that she rode her bicycle into Waldoboro and caught the afternoon bus to Boston. Nobody was all that surprised, considering what her family life was like. Anyway, she was never heard from again. Of course, there was no Amber Alert system in those days." Kate glanced at Sarah. "Obviously, that can't be her bicycle, though."

"Why not?"

"Because she must have used it to get to Waldoboro, of course," Kate said.

"It's a long bike ride from Burnt Cove to Waldoboro."

"Not if you're a teenager who happens to be desperate enough, and she was a very strong-willed girl."

Sarah thought Kate was trying much too hard to deny the obvious. "How would Evan Huggard end up with her bicycle under his fish shack, if she rode it to Waldoboro?"

"If it was her bicycle," Kate said.

"If she ever got on a bus."

Kate grimaced as she reached across the table and rested her hand on Sarah's arm. "I know you had a problem with Evan when you were in camp, but that doesn't mean—"

"*A problem with Evan?* The man attacked me!" Sarah snapped. The memory still tied a knot in her stomach, even after all those years. "He might have killed me if Myra hadn't come along and stopped him. Do you think it makes me feel better to know that attacking me ended up getting him killed?"

Kate lowered her head and Sarah noticed that her white hair was thinning on top. "No, I'm sure it doesn't," Kate said softly. She looked up, her eyes meeting Sarah's. The deep wrinkles coursing down the old woman's face made her look every minute of her eighty-three years. "Believe me, what happened that afternoon has haunted Sam and me ever since the day Myra called to tell us about it—just as I'm sure it's haunted you. Evan was a dangerous man, especially when he got drunk, but that doesn't mean he did anything to Betsy."

Kate removed her hand from Sarah's arm and gazed across the room. "If that bicycle did belong to Betsy, which I doubt, then it must have been put there years before you started coming to camp. Wouldn't you kids have seen it in your wanderings?"

"None of us dared to spend much time anywhere near Evan's shack."

"I'm glad to hear it. We did tell you kids not to wander around the Huggard's land, not that it did much good." A frown wrinkled her brow as she sipped more coffee. "I don't understand how somebody could manage to fit a bicycle underneath the shack."

Sarah conjured up the structure in her mind's eye. "The ground slopes down towards the water there, so the land side, with the door, was pretty much sitting on the ground, but the water side had a couple of stone blocks, one on each corner, so that side was a couple of feet off the ground. Betty Boop could have just fitted underneath."

"Wouldn't somebody have seen it?"

"There were half a dozen broken lobster traps piled up on that side of the shack. It would only have taken a few minutes to move them out of the way, slip in the bicycle, and put them back."

"You still don't know for sure that it was Evan who put it there," Kate said.

"I don't know that it wasn't, either."

Kate sipped more coffee in thoughtful silence. "I think it would be better if that bicycle disappeared before anyone else finds it."

"Wouldn't most of Betsy's friends recognize it?"

Kate shook her head sadly. "Yes, in which case the cat may already be out of the bag."

Chapter 14

Sarah left the Merlew's house right after her coffee with Kate. Ziggy's new place was just a few miles further down Squirrel Point road, and Sarah stopped in to see what was going on while she waited for Oliver to finish talking to the Borofskys, next door.

A state police cruiser was parked at the end of the driveway, probably to fend off the news media. She walked around the vehicle, feeling the officer's eyes on her back.

Mabel was standing forlornly at the rear of her pen, apparently unmoved by the bright sun, land-warmed northwest wind, or the big clump of daffodils, refugees from Myra's defunct garden, which were blooming just outside her fence. There was no sign of Asim.

Harvey Cassell and Dudley Tibbs, who had been hard at work clearing brush along the shore, were glad to have an excuse to take a break, and they came strolling up to say hello. Viewed close-up, Sarah could see that both Dudley and Harvey had the muscular physique of men who were well used to manual labor. She decided to take Kate's advice and not mention Betty Boop. Why stir up painful memories for no good reason? Instead, she said, "How much more clearing are you planning to do?"

"Just a little more down along the water," Dudley replied. "Not too much though, because there are laws about how much you can cut along the shore. Mostly, we'll just be clearing the small stuff."

"That crazy elephant has cleared out most of the brush in her pen," Harvey said.

"More like she made a mess of the place, rooting stuff up," Dudley grumbled as he scowled at Mabel. "We'll have get out all the junk she knocked over."

"It can wait," Harvey said. "The town will be taking over the land where her pen is, anyway." He looked disapprovingly towards Gerhard Burndt's grave, where Bert was kneeling over one of his test pits with a sieve. "Damn fool archeologist."

"Treasure hunter is more like it," Dudley said. "The sooner we get rid of him, the better."

"What makes him think there's buried treasure here?" Harvey said.

"The guy's an archeologist. He must have done a lot of research: old records, maps, and stuff; that's what archeologists do. If an expert like that thinks there's buried treasure around here, then I believe him."

"Believe what you want, but I think the whole buried treasure story is a bunch of baloney."

Dudley frowned. "You've heard all the talk. I'm just saying, where there's enough smoke, there's gotta be fire. Finders-keepers is the rule when it comes to buried treasure, but it's not right for some stranger to come in and take what isn't his."

Bert's presence was obviously becoming more and more unwelcome. "It's good of you to come over and do all this work," Sarah said, trying to deflect their attention.

The two men looked self-conscious for a moment before Dudley said, "When Pastor Briskin asked for volunteers last month,

Harv, Bernie, and me talked it over, and figured it might be fun to come back to our old stomping ground and do some good, and see what the place is like now."

"The town sure has changed over the years," Harvey added.

"Too darn many out-of-staters, now," Dudley grumbled, shooting a look in Bert's direction. He caught himself and glanced at Sarah with mild embarrassment.

Harvey turned to her. "I hear you used to know Myra in the old days."

"I went to Migawoc Camp, back in my teens, and I knew her that way."

"Bernie and I had moved to Damariscotta, and Dud had moved next door to Newcastle by the time you were going to the camp, I imagine. There was more construction work down there." He paused. "I remember Myra used to be pretty hard on the camp kids, though—didn't care for having all the rich flat-landers next door."

"She could be pretty unpleasant if she took a dislike to a kid, but she wasn't too bad with me," Sarah said.

Harvey looked at her skeptically. "She liked you?"

"As well as Myra liked any of the campers, I guess."

Harvey considered this. "Well, she sure took a liking for Ziggy, leaving him all this land. Of course, that was only five or ten years ago, and maybe she'd softened up by then. Or gotten even more batty."

"We all knew Myra, seeing as how we grew up in Burnt Cove," Dudley said.

Harvey nodded. "Burnt Cove wasn't a friendly town, as far as I was concerned..." He let the words hang in the air for a moment, before going on. "Myra's husband, Evan, was a piece of work, too. Was he still alive when you were at camp?"

"Yes," she said.

Harvey's eyes seemed to be looking right through her. "Evan

could be a tough customer when he got drunk," he commented off-handedly. "Yes, a person wanted to steer clear of old Evan when he was on the sauce."

* * *

Sarah went over to Oliver as he walked in the driveway and looked around. Mabel shambled up to the fence and waved her trunk at him. "I see Mabel is here, being the welcome wagon."

"She's cheered up a lot since this morning," Sarah said. "Speaking of welcome wagons, was Sasha wearing her bikini, again?"

"Less, in places. Has Pastor Briskin and his crew been around?"

"Pastor Briskin was off with Asim when I got here. He went to get his pulp truck, and find a pickup for Asim to borrow while he's here. Harvey and Dudley were down by the shore, piling up brush until a few minutes ago. They went off to get something to eat, and Bert is eating a sandwich down by the shore."

"Nice and quiet," Oliver said.

"That won't last. They're coming back after lunch. Dudley is all psyched up to run the excavator and is going to give it a try."

"Maybe we should get some lunch ourselves, before those lunatics come back," Oliver suggested.

"Sasha was wearing less than a string bikini? How is that possible? What does Anton have to say about having his wife prance around the house naked?"

"She wasn't exactly naked, and he wasn't there."

"Anton wasn't there? Where was he? And why did Sasha stop the police from taking Mabel away?"

"Anton was away in 'The City,' on business. As for Sasha, she just likes elephants."

"That's all she had to say about Mabel?"

"She says that Anton is being a 'bore' about Mabel. The two of them obviously don't see eye to eye when it comes to having an elephant next door. He thinks about it as a way to get rid of Ziggy, and she thinks about Dumbo."

Sarah paused. "So it was just the two of you, talking about boats, which is a subject she knows nothing about?"

"The maid was in the house."

"Doing what?" Sarah asked.

"Taking a nap."

"Interesting. Does the maid know anything about boats?"

"I didn't see her. And we weren't just talking about boats."

"What else were you talking about?"

"Besides Mabel? According to Sasha, Anton expects to be rid of Ziggy and his zoo soon."

"I wonder how he plans to do that."

"The bare-naked lady didn't say," Oliver replied. "Maybe you should come with me next time, so you can observe her dress code first-hand."

"It sounds like an un-dress code, to me. Admit it, she's a temptress."

Oliver frowned. "I'd have to be pretty much dead to deny that, but there's a big difference between being tempted and giving in to it. As I've said before, she's not my type. You're my type."

"I'm glad to hear it. The thing that gets me about Sasha is this creepy relationship where she seduces men, and then has Anton knock them off."

"Or has them beaten up. I suppose it fulfills her need to be protected, and his need to protect her."

Sarah shivered, partly from the cool, northeast wind. "Nice arrangement for both of them, but not so nice for her victims."

"I told her that I wouldn't go back unless Anton was there."

Sarah gave Oliver an enthusiastic embrace and a lingering kiss.

"Careful, the Spider Lady may be watching us from her boudoir," Oliver said.

"That's the whole idea. Well, partly, anyway. How did she take it when you told her Anton would have to be there before you went back?"

"She was irritated, and announced that I was too uptight and prudish. Then she escorted me to the door."

"Be careful. You know what they say about a woman scorned."

"She also said that you're too insecure, and you're keeping me on a leash."

"Are you telling me that just to be aggravating?"

"How is Kate doing?" Oliver said, moving to safer ground.

"She's still in a lot of pain, between the broken arm and all the bruises. They think she cracked a rib, too."

"Not good for somebody her age."

Sarah nodded agreement. "Remember the bicycle I told you about?"

"Betty Boop?"

"It might have belonged to Betsy Knowles."

"And it was under Evan's shack?" Oliver said. "That could be bad."

A gust of wind whipped through the trees, bringing with it a scattering of big, wet snowflakes. "I just called Charlie, and told him about Betty Boop. He's coming over to look at it."

"Let's go take a look ourselves before everybody gets back from lunch," Oliver suggested.

"What about contaminating the crime scene?"

"Crime scene? It's just an old bicycle." Oliver set a brisk pace towards the water.

"It's gone," Sarah said a moment later. "It was right here yesterday morning."

They walked around the area, searching to no avail. Oliver half-heartedly shifted a few rotten boards and peered under them.

"What are you doing now?" Sarah said.

"I'm just checking to see if there's another bicycle underneath this mess."

"Is there?"

Oliver shook his head.

"Kate thought the bike should disappear."

"It looks like somebody else felt the same way," Oliver said. "Whoever it was must have waited until after dark when nobody was around and Asim was asleep. Maybe we should ask him," Oliver said.

Charlie came striding up just then, looking mildly irritated at having his lunch hour interrupted. "So where is this mysterious bicycle?"

"Somebody's taken it away," Sarah replied, "since yesterday."

Charlie sighed. "So what makes you think it belonged to Betsy Knowles?"

"It had a Betty Boop sticker on it, just like Betsy's bike."

Charlie looked at Sarah skeptically. "She must have run off about forty-five years ago, before I was born. I don't see how you can tell who it belonged to after all those years, anyway." He shrugged. "And with it gone, there's not much anybody can do."

"But what if it was her bicycle?"

"It wouldn't necessarily mean anything. I didn't know the man very well—I was pretty young when he died—but from what I've heard, Evan Huggard was a scrounge. He probably spotted the bike lying around somewhere, probably at the bus stop in Waldoboro, and took it home, figuring he could sell it for beer money."

"Then why *didn't* he sell it?" Sarah snapped.

"Probably because it dawned on him who the bike belonged to and he didn't dare try to unload it, what with all the publicity. He might not have been a genius, but he wasn't that dumb."

Oliver put a restraining hand on Sarah's arm and turned to the doubting deputy. "It wouldn't have taken Evan long to peel Betty Boop off the fender if he wanted to sell it. Or take it into Rockland where it wouldn't be recognized."

"Maybe she never got to Waldoboro," Sarah said angrily. "Maybe Evan snatched her up before she got there."

Charlie gave her a pained look. "Look, I know you guys have been involved in a couple of murders, and maybe even helped solve them, but that doesn't mean everything that happens around here is a murder. Most times an old bicycle is just an old bicycle."

Sarah and Oliver watched as Charlie drove away amid the scattered snowflakes.

"He didn't take Betty Boop very seriously," Sarah grumbled. "And why in the world is it snowing in May, for God's sake?"

"I know what Ziggy would say."

Sarah looked disgusted. "He'd say Myra was calling down a blizzard, of course."

"Luckily, it's just a few stray flakes. They'll stop in a couple of minutes. And an old bicycle doesn't prove that Evan is responsible for Betsy's disappearance."

"Do you think I'm dreaming things up, too?"

"I think you have a very good reason to suspect Evan, but there isn't any proof."

"I know what he was capable of." She was silent for a while, shivering. He took her in his arms. "First Evan and then Claude—I've had some bad luck with men...I'm so lucky to have met you...What am I going to do about Sudbury?"

"I don't know the answer to Sudbury, but I'm not going anywhere."

Sarah leaned back in his arms. "I can't explain it, but I have to know what happened to Betsy, and if Evan was involved."

Oliver nodded slowly. "Just remember that Charlie could be

right. Most times Betty Boop is just a rusty old bicycle."

"And sometimes she's a vulnerable teenager."

"Yes," Oliver said. He glanced up at the Borofsky's house. "Bernie and Bert both had metal detectors. Probably one of them was prowling, looking for the treasure, found the bike, and dragged it out to look at."

"I found the bike Monday morning, and Bernie died Sunday night, so if he'd found Betty Boop, it must have been before then. Bernie would probably recognize it and assume the same thing I did, that Evan killed Betsy and hid the bike."

"Yes," Oliver agreed, "but why didn't he call the police, like you did? More important, why would somebody take Betty Boop away after Bernie died? Unless it was to protect Evan's good name, though I don't see why anybody would bother to do that."

"Okay, maybe Bert found Betty Boop while he was looking for treasure, and dragged it out to look at."

"But why would he take it away? I can't see him having any use for it," Oliver said.

"Maybe somebody else saw it lying there later and took it away." Sarah sighed. "We can't prove that Betsy was murdered, or even Bernie, for that matter. All we have are possible motives."

Oliver nodded. "Evan could have attacked Betsy and killed her. His motive is pretty clear— sick, but clear."

"And somebody could have killed Bernie to stop him from hunting for Myra's treasure," Sarah said.

"Somebody like Bert?"

"I don't know," Sarah said. "Maybe Bernie's death was an accident, after all. Maybe Mabel did kill him by mistake."

"I thought you were trying to prove she didn't kill Bernie," Oliver said.

"I can go either way on that."

"You already have gone either way, several times, as I recall,"

Oliver replied.

"I try to be flexible. Do you suppose Ziggy found the bike and took it away, without knowing who it had belonged to?"

"Ziggy? Tidying up?" Oliver said incredulously. "That's not the Ziggy I know. His old place on Meadow road is a monument to junk. Come to think of it, a lot of his neighbors are the same way."

Whereas Squirrel Point road ran along the water and was home to a number of immaculately kept mansions, Ziggy's former shack was on Meadow road, which ran up the center of the peninsula and was much less pretentious. The two byways represented two different worlds, even though only a mile or two separated them physically.

"Ziggy can't have known Betsy, or her bicycle, because he's only lived here for the past ten years or so." Sarah said.

"Maybe Ziggy added Betty Boop to his collection. Another lawn ornament, like the Borofsky's new boat, only cheaper," Oliver suggested.

Sarah punched his arm playfully. "If we knew who took Betty Boop, we could probably figure out what happened to Betsy. I'm freezing. Let's get out of here and find someplace warm before the crew comes back."

Chapter 15

Pastor Briskin's workers converged on Ziggy's estate after lunch, ready to do some serious work before any new disaster could put a crimp in their efforts. The wind was still blowing, but the snow flakes had vanished, at least for the time being.

Dudley Tibbs was one of those rare Maine natives who happened to be an idealist—an almost unheard of trait in such a pragmatic state. His quixotic idealism caused him to firmly believe that May meant spring, so he had ignored the cold and dressed in a T-shirt, which strained to contain his muscular torso.

"Are you sure you can run that thing?" Pastor Briskin asked Dudley, nodding at the late Bernie's excavator.

"No problem. Bernie showed me what all the levers do back when he first got it." Dudley settled his John Deere cap firmly on his head, glanced up at the cab, and considered matters. "I'll experiment with the old foundation stones first, just to get a feel for it before I start digging out any of those big tree stumps."

Pastor Briskin turned to Ziggy, who was standing with his bicycle at the ready. "I have a feeling that things are going to go well this afternoon, Brother Ziggy." He looked with mild disapproval at the Can Man's bicycle. "Aren't you going to stay and watch? After all, this marks a new beginning, the time when we break ground and Myra Huggard's dream starts to become a reality."

The two men stepped back as the excavator roared into life amid a black cloud of oily smoke.

Ziggy turned his baleful stare away from Pastor Briskin's eager face and gazed up at the sky, where the sun was playing a game of peek-a-boo with the clouds. The cool northeast wind toyed with his beard. "There's bad karma in the air this morning." He glanced at Mabel, who was cowering at the back of her pen. "Even your elephant feels it."

The ground shook as the excavator's jaw crashed into a piano-sized slab of foundation granite. Dudley glanced at his startled audience apologetically. Harvey, sensing excitement, abandoned his brush gathering and joined the onlookers. Even Bert put down his shovel to watch.

Pastor Briskin frowned as they moved further away from the racket. "You don't seem to be savoring the excitement of this new beginning, Brother Ziggy. Surely you aren't still mourning Myra Huggard?"

"I mourn the loss of her way of life."

"Your grief is understandable, but we can't escape change."

"Myra could."

"I say this out of love and compassion, my friend," Pastor Briskin said, placing his hand on Ziggy's shoulder. "But you need to bail your bilge, Brother Breener," he advised, waxing poetic. "You must rid yourself of these noxious thoughts. Put the past behind you and look to the future."

"When will your elephant be a part of my past?"

"The authorities have agreed that she should stay here under police supervision until they've finished their investigation," Pastor

Briskin replied stiffly. "And while we're on the subject, I would appreciate it if you stopped referring to the animal as 'my elephant.' I've told you many times that the church is being paid handsomely to board Mabel for a few days, or maybe a week or so. That's the limit of my involvement."

The excavator roared as its arm waved erratically in the air before crashing to the ground.

Pastor Briskin took the opportunity to offer another pearl of wisdom. "Myra may have avoided change, but only during her lifetime. She knew change would come with her death. And she selected you to bring about that change. Think of it: thanks to you, all these people are coming together to make the old woman's dream become a reality."

There was a screech of metal-against-stone as the arm clawed spastically at the foundation.

"Perhaps," Ziggy said doubtfully, "but what was her dream, exactly? And what is reality, really?"

"I'm not going to be sucked into another of your Zen-like discussions. The point is that Myra selected you because she trusted you to do the right thing with her legacy."

The excavator rocked alarmingly as Dudley struggled to control the beast.

"Perhaps," Ziggy repeated, even more doubtfully.

"It distresses me to see you talking this way. You should be rejoicing, after all the months of legal wrangling and delays, that at last—"

Pastor Briskin's cell phone chimed a few bars of the *Hallelujah Chorus,* and he walked away to find some privacy and quiet.

Harvey and Ziggy watched the excavator's arm thrash ineffectually for a few moments.

"Dud is going to need a lot more practice with that thing," Harvey observed.

"Bad karma," Ziggy replied as he started to wheel his bicycle towards the driveway. He was stopped by Pastor Briskin's frantically waving arm. He walked reluctantly over to the agitated cleric.

"We are ruined, Brother Breener!" Pastor Briskin said in a voice of despair. "The NGTS Bank and Trust has withdrawn its financial support for the Spruce Cone Center. Worse, our sister churches in Pennsylvania have also withdrawn their support. No more building supplies. No more funding."

"Does that mean they're going to take their elephant away?"

The bereft clergyman scowled. "Here we are, facing total disaster, and all you can think about is an elephant? Mabel is the only source of funding we have left after this catastrophe."

Ziggy's beard bristled with irritation. "So now our future depends on harboring a murderous elephant, a serial killer? What cruel twist of fate has led us to this horrific state of affairs?"

With an earth-shaking thud, Dudley managed to drag a foundation stone into the cellar hole.

"The man is supposed to be piling the stones *outside* the cellar, not *inside* it," Pastor Briskin muttered.

"To coin a phrase," Ziggy persisted, "What did your zoo know about murderous Mabel, and when did they know it?"

"I keep telling you that's not our concern. We can only hope that your two friends will prove her innocence, but in the meantime, Mabel's fate is up to the police."

"Don't you mean 'Sister Mabel?'"

"This isn't a good time for you to start toying with me. Do you have any idea what this means?" Pastor Briskin's voice was loud enough to bring Harvey over to listen in. "It's the end of Myra's dream for a youth camp. It's the end of your dream of fulfilling her wishes. I will pray that you may learn to take your mission more seriously."

Ziggy frowned. "Your divine holiness may remember that I

didn't ask to inherit Myra Huggard's land. The old woman sprung that trap on me posthumously."

"It's an opportunity, not a trap."

"It's a nightmare, not an opportunity."

"Let's not quibble over this." Pastor Briskin glared at Borofsky Castle. "It's obvious who pulled the financial plug on our work. We have a common enemy lurking behind that wall."

"Borofsky and his wife spend half their time watching us out their window," Harvey commented. "Though I think he's been away for the last day or two."

"Away in Pennsylvania, sabotaging our efforts," Pastor Briskin said darkly.

"I've only met him a few times," Harvey said, "but Borofsky seems like a nice guy. For a foreigner and a millionaire. Do you really think he'd do something like that?"

"He threatened to kill Brother Ziggy last year," Pastor Briskin informed him.

"You've met Anton Borofsky?" Ziggy said to Harvey, surprised.

"He's wandered over here a few times when there weren't too many people around. I surprised him a couple of times when I was here alone, and he walked in the driveway. I don't think he expected anybody to be here."

The excavator reared up like an enraged tyrannosaurus rex and pounced ferociously on another slab of granite.

"I must escape this madness," Ziggy said, mounting his bicycle.

"I shall pray that you may find peace in this matter, Brother Breener."

"Pray that I find a vast mountain of empty soda cans before the property tax comes due," Ziggy retorted as he pedaled out the driveway.

The excavator wound itself up to a suicidal pitch, which ended with a loud, metallic bang.

Silence abruptly descended.

Ziggy did not look back, or slacken his pace.

* * *

Dudley's T-shirt had accumulated an assortment of grease stains by the time he stepped to the ground, his face grim.

"What's the verdict, Brother Dudley," Pastor Briskin said.

"She's dead as a haddock." Dudley half-heartedly wiped his hands on a rag. "Engine threw a rod right through the crankcase. Nobody's going to fix that."

"It was a piece of junk to start with," Harvey said solemnly.

"It's our piece of junk," Pastor Briskin pointed out.

"I thought it was Bernie's piece of junk," Asim said.

"It's Bernie's widow's piece of junk, now," Dudley concluded.

"Why can't it be fixed?" Pastor Briskin asked. "Can't you do anything to get the thing running again?"

"Easier to show you than explain," Dudley replied. "Climb up and see for yourself."

Pastor Briskin sighed as he peered at the ruined engine, from which a jagged piece of metal protruded.

"It'll take a while to replace the engine, assuming the excavator's worth fixing. The whole thing's pretty much worn out," Dudley said.

"We don't have much time to spare," Pastor Briskin said. "Not with our schedule. We'll have to rent another machine."

"With somebody to run it," Harvey murmured.

Dudley gave Harvey a murderous look. "Do you know how much an excavator operator charges?"

"I'm just saying it might be worth it—"

"Let's cross that bridge when we come to it," Pastor Briskin intervened briskly.

"I imagine the neighbors will be glad to see us being shut down like this," Dudley commented, glancing over at the Borofsky's mansion.

"Maybe the excavator was sabotaged," Harvey suggested.

"Where's that so-called archeologist?" Dudley asked, looking down towards Gerhard Burndt's grave. Bert was nowhere to be seen.

Harvey nodded. "He's more of a Judas than we think, if you ask me."

"Why would anybody sabotage the excavator?" Asim asked.

Dudley gave him a pitying look. "You haven't been around much, but our neighbors next door would love to shut us down, permanently."

"They think of us as an eyesore in the making," Harvey added. "And to have somebody murdered here only makes it worse. I hear that Borofsky tried to buy Ziggy out last year, and threatened to kill him when he wouldn't sell."

"Brother Breener wisely included a poison-pill clause in his will, which would make his untimely death very disadvantageous for his neighbors," Pastor Briskin explained.

"So Breener isn't as spaced out as he seems," Harvey said.

"He marches to a different drummer," Pastor Briskin replied tactfully. He glanced over at the Great Wall of Borofsky. "I suppose we shouldn't be too quick to pass judgement on them. There are others who would like to prevent Ziggy from building a camp for troubled teens here. There could be a conspiracy in the neighborhood."

Chapter 16

Having left the exploding excavator for others to deal with, the
Can Man pedaled his bicycle slowly down Squirrel Point road
with one eye on his quarry, which lay silent and still amidst the dead
leaves and brush beside the road, and the other eye on the out-of-
state drivers who sped by erratically and fast. The season was early
yet, and the weekend was long gone, so he had gleaned less than
three dollars worth of refundables so far this afternoon.

Ziggy meditated on many things as he rode along: elephants and
excavators, Myra and murder, foundation stones and the future,
mansions and money, pastors and policemen, past and present. The
list went on in endless combinations and permutations, all of which
churned ceaselessly in his head.

No wonder the Can Man was irritable.

It began to get dark after a while, thanks to a cloudy sky, and it
became hard to spot Ziggy's prey in the shadowy ditches, so he
decided to drift over to his new estate. He figured that everybody
was likely to be gone, except Mabel and Asim, who pretty much
kept to themselves. The solitude would give him one last chance to
look over the place before Dudley and the excavator went to work

tomorrow and swept most of it away—assuming the decrepit machine hadn't swept itself away.

Ziggy rattled into Myra's driveway—it would always be Myra's driveway as far as he was concerned. He set the bicycle on its stand in front of the old house site, still largely hidden behind the wounded excavator, which seemed to have bled a large quantity of oil onto the ground while Ziggy was away.

Mark Twain once said, "If you don't like the weather in New England now, just wait a few minutes." The truth of that saying was demonstrated by the wind, which had swung around to the south during Ziggy's absence and was now wafting warm air and the scent of elephant up to his nostrils. He turned away to face the house foundation, the excavator, and the stink of engine oil.

Between the aroma of elephant on one side, and excavator on the other, the place smelled even more alien. Once again, he wondered what Myra would think of the changes. He glanced around, half expecting her to appear and share her opinion.

Ziggy didn't consider himself to be a superstitious man, in spite of what others might think. On the other hand, the strength of Myra's personality seemed to defy death, relentlessly seeping through the barrier between this world and the next.

The old woman had always been rooted to this place and to her house. If Myra Huggard's spirit was anywhere, it would be here, Ziggy thought. He cleared his mind and knocked on the door—figuratively of course—as he had so many times, back when Myra had been alive and there was a door to knock on. In his mind, he asked to come in for a chat.

There was no answer to his psychic rapping.

Ziggy sighed. It was foolish to think that she would reply, what with the excavator sitting on the doorstep and stinking up the place. God, how Myra would have hated that. No wonder she wasn't speaking to him, not that she had spoken to him since her death—at least not directly.

Perhaps he'd have better luck at the chicken coop. Myra had loved her hens. The coop was long-gone, of course, but at least the spot was clear of machinery, though with all the brush and trees cleared away, and her ancient Studebaker sold to an antique car collector in New Jersey, there weren't any landmarks to show where the hen-pen had been. Ziggy made his best guess and cleared his mind.

Sarah Cassidy swam into his consciousness.

Ziggy pondered this. What was Myra trying to say, if anything? The old woman told him once that Sarah had been looking at the hens when they first met. Of course, the Ditch Lady had been in her teens back then, and a camper at the Migawoc Camp for Girls.

"What are you trying to say?" Ziggy murmured.

Behind him, a pickup roared by on the road, drowning out his words. It occurred to Ziggy that a pickup truck had nearly run Sarah down when they first met, and that she was clambering out of the roadside ditch only a few yards away from where he stood.

A crash and the sound of a woman's scream galvanized Ziggy into action.

Ditch Lady Sarah. That was Myra's message. Or, more accurately, her warning.

He grabbed his bicycle and raced out to the road, to the ditch where he'd first met Sarah.

He saw a body a little further along, its ash-blonde hair fanned out on the ground like a halo. It was laying half in the ditch not far from the spot where Ziggy had first seen Sarah, almost exactly a year ago. He dropped his bike in the middle of the road, scattering his hard-earned treasure across the pavement.

Sasha was lying on her back, the left side of her head matted with blood. Three puncture wounds in her abdomen oozed blood, and a fourth wound was pulsing a steady stream of red from her upper leg.

Ziggy Breener, connoisseur of soda cans, roadside ditches, and other arcane matters, knew right away what had happened and who was responsible.

Burnt Cove had hired Eubie Fiske and his ancient Ford 8N tractor to mow the roadside brush in this part of town last fall. Sadly, Eubie, who was even more ancient than his tractor, had poor eyesight and had failed to drop the cutter bar low enough to trim the brush short—perhaps it had been a cloudy afternoon like this one. As a result of Eubie's cutter bar misadjustment, half-a-dozen pencil-sized stubs jutted up from the bottom of the ditch. Since they'd been cut at an angle, the ends were sharp and Sasha had landed face-down on this impromptu bed of nails.

Somehow, she'd managed to crawl out of the ditch before passing out. Ziggy figured that she was lucky the damage hadn't been much worse.

Ziggy knew all about Eubie because the bat-eyed gentleman had managed to slice the ball of his thumb quite badly while sharpening his tractor's cutter bar last fall, and had turned up at the Can Man's shack to have it bandaged. Eubie dribbled quantities of blood on Ziggy's kitchen table, and complained loudly while the wound was being cleaned of assorted bits of chaff and dirt. Ziggy finally managed to silence his querulous patient by offering to stitch up the gash instead of just bandaging it.

These thoughts percolated through Ziggy's brain while he pulled off his shirt and pressed it against the leg wound. He felt around Sasha's waistband, looking for a cell phone, but found none.

"I was attacked by a moose," Sasha mumbled in a semi-conscious way.

Ziggy looked around and saw what appeared to be a deer print. Probably a buck, judging from the size. Not a moose, though, or Sasha would have been tossed a dozen feet into the woods and trampled as well.

Sasha's eyes opened and rolled around for a moment before focusing on Ziggy's face as he leaned over her. She screamed, an inarticulate banshee howl.

"You've been hurt," Ziggy said reassuringly. "Try to stay still."

"Get your filthy hands off me, you pervert!" Sasha tried to sit up and push his hand away from her wounded leg, only to fall back with a gasp of pain.

"You may have a concussion," Ziggy said, trying to peer into her eyes.

"Get away, you horrible creature!" Sasha howled.

"Where's your cell phone?"

Her eyes opened in horror. "Why are your clothes off? What are you doing to my leg?"

"I'm using my shirt and belt to put a tourniquet on your leg," Ziggy replied patiently. "You've damaged an artery, and are bleeding profusely."

"Get your filthy hands off me. You're hurting my leg." Sasha weakly tried to push his hands away from the tourniquet.

"Where's your cell phone? You could bleed to death without medical attention."

"Bleed to death? What do you know about medicine, you quack?"

Zigfield Follies Breener, M.D., and former ER trauma specialist, was beginning to lose his patience even faster than Sasha was losing her blood. "Cell phone!" He barked.

Sasha was startled by Ziggy's uncharacteristic outburst, and she pawed around her waistband without success. "It's gone... You stole it... I'll have you arrested for this... Anton will have you killed..." her speech was getting slower and more slurred.

"Perhaps, if that is my destiny, but meanwhile I want you to stay still," Ziggy replied distractedly as a Cadillac Escalade with New

York plates stopped at his impromptu road block. A middle-aged woman with heavily permed blond hair looked down into the ditch from her perch on the passenger seat.

"My God, Rudy, that hobo just killed a woman," she said to the driver.

"Call 911!" Ziggy yelled up at the SUV.

"Close the window and lock your door, Jenine," Rudy said. "We haven't got time to stop for this. Clear the road!" he shouted down to Ziggy.

"PQ5787!" Ziggy yelled back.

"The man's talking gibberish, Rudy. He must be stoned, and he's probably dangerous."

"That's not gibberish. The lunatic has our license plate number."

Jenine peered more carefully into the ditch. "Call 911, Rudy! I think the woman's alive!"

* * *

"That was a wonderful meal," Sarah said appreciatively. She and Oliver were seated at a dim corner table in Marcel's restaurant in Rockland.

"The best is yet to come," Oliver assured her, as their waitress appeared with chocolate cake. A single candle burned in the middle.

"Happy anniversary," Oliver said.

"I can't believe it's been a whole year."

"I marked my calendar."

"Yeah, right."

"One year ago today, at ten-thirty in the morning of May fourteenth, you drove up to my house with *Owl* on your trailer. I haven't had a peaceful minute since."

"Me either." She smiled at the memory. "I thought you were

pretty obnoxious when we first met."

"First impressions are very important."

"It wasn't until that time on Pemaquid Point when you almost took a bullet to protect Pearly and me that I realized how wrong I'd been." A tear on her cheek glistened in the candlelight.

He took her hand. "It never occurred to me not to take that chance."

They sat for a while as candle wax began to drip onto the cake.

"Anyway," Oliver said, breaking the silence, "I got something to mark the occasion." He took a small, gift-wrapped package out of his pocket.

"You're a constant source of amazement," Sarah said, pulling at the bow.

The silver earrings were in the shape of sailboats. Sarah held one up to the candle, turning it, and watching the delicately hammered surface glint in the light. "It's *Owl*."

"I gave the silversmith a drawing. It seemed appropriate, since *Owl* is how we met."

"They're beautiful, thank you." Sarah leaned over the table to kiss Oliver, nearly setting fire to her blouse in the process.

Sarah fingered the earrings. "A lot has happened in the last year," she said in a small voice.

Oliver looked at her solemnly as she toyed with the bits of silver.

"A lot has happened that I didn't expect." She spoke slowly. "And I guess the earrings brought it all to a head." Her eyes glittered in the candlelight. "When I came here last spring, it was to get over Claude and my divorce. I was just going to stay in the Merlew's granny flat for a couple of months to sail *Owl*, and get my head straight. And then I met you, and everything changed." A tear ran down her cheek, and she rushed on. "And then I rented the Carnell's cabin for the winter. I hadn't planned to do that, but I did because it seemed like the easiest thing at the time. And then Ziggy's shack burned down, and I let him have my cabin, and moved in with you. I didn't plan to do that, but I did because it seemed like the easiest thing to do at the time."

Oliver watched her fingers turning the earrings over and over.

"All those things just happened. I've been living out of a couple of suitcases for the past year," she went on, "...well, plus a few things I've bought along the way. I've been drifting from one place to the next for the past year, because it was easy. It's like I'm being pushed by circumstances into doing things because they're easy. I want to do them because I'm sure they're right."

She reached out and took his hand. "I didn't plan to fall in love with you, either, but I did."

"Is this about Sasha? Because I—"

"No, it's not," she said a fraction too quickly. "At least not exactly. I know in my mind that you're not a womanizer, like Claude. I know in my mind that I can trust you, but—"

"Once burned, twice shy?"

She nodded slowly. "I know it's silly, but the scars are still there, deep down inside." She wiped her eyes impatiently. "I promised myself that next time I'd be in control; that I'd look before I leaped; that I'd never let another Claude sweep me off my feet; that I'd never be vulnerable again."

"How can anyone live a life, a real life, without being vulnerable?" Oliver said, anger in his voice.

"I don't know," she replied, her voice just above a whisper. "But don't you see that we're both carrying the same scars? We were both cheated, me by Claude and his bimbos, and you—"

"Arlene was killed, murdered, by a drunk driver. How is that the same?"

"You and I were both cheated," she repeated, "robbed of our marriages. We're both scarred, Oliver. I need to trust the future again. I need to trust myself."

She let go of his hand and ran her thumb over the textured surface of the earrings. I love these, and I love that you gave them to me."

"There aren't any strings attached."

"I needed to hear that. There are times when it feels as though I'm on a runaway train. And I'm afraid of where it's going."

"Like Ziggy?"

Sarah looked at Oliver, startled. "Yes, like Ziggy. The three of us all have ghosts from our pasts haunting our futures."

They sat silently for a while, holding hands.

"The Realtor from Sudbury called this afternoon. I guess that's part of it," Sarah said at last, "Anyway, she has a couple who may be going to make an offer on my house down there."

"Do what you have to do," he said quietly.

She gripped his hands tightly. "There's another thing; it may be a while before Kate is able to do much."

Oliver nodded.

"They're both kind of shaky right now, and I think it might be a good idea to see if they'd like to have me stay with them for a day or two, at least until Kate's a little better."

Oliver watched silently as Sarah put on her new earrings.

Chapter 17

Wednesday morning was cool when Oliver got up, but the sky was clear, and warmer weather was forecast by midday. Since Sarah was staying at the Merlew's, Oliver called her after breakfast and they arranged to meet at Ziggy's place after Oliver had stopped in at the Borofsky's.

Anton, looking distracted, greeted Oliver at the door and escorted him into the livingroom where Sasha was reclining on the sofa amid a sea of pillows. She wasted no time regaling him with a dramatic account her accident and sufferings.

"It was a huge moose," Sasha said melodramatically. "He leaped out of the woods, and crashed right into me. A pickup truck had just gone roaring by and I was riding right at the edge of the ditch to let him pass when the moose jumped out and hit me."

"It must have been terrible, my dear," Anton said soothingly. "People drive much too fast on these back roads, and it probably startled the moose. Would you like another pillow?"

"It wouldn't help," she grumbled. "Everything hurts, no matter how I lie. You wouldn't believe some of the places that were bruised, Oliver," she murmured.

"You're very lucky to be alive," Anton said.

"No thanks to that awful man."

"Now, dearest, you know what the doctor told you at the hospital. If Breener hadn't arrived to provide first aid, you easily could have bled to death." There was a catch in Anton's voice as he spoke the words.

"He assaulted me while I was lying there, helpless. He was taking his clothes off when those people stopped to help. I shudder to think what could have happened if they hadn't come to my rescue."

Anton gave Oliver an embarrassed glance. "Perhaps you were confused, my dear. That's not what that nice couple from New York said. According to them, he was using his shirt to put a tourniquet on your leg when they stopped to help."

"It may have looked like that to them, but *I* was there! I want the man arrested!"

Anton patted her hand. "I'd like nothing better than to do that, but we have to have proof. The police can't do anything without proof."

Sasha pouted. "Then you could teach him a lesson, the way you've taught the others."

"I am not going to resort to physical violence over this. Never fear, he'll get his comeuppance soon enough."

"What does that mean?" Oliver said, bristling.

"You have a saying in this country, 'There's more than one way to skin a cat.' As I've told you before, there are a number of influential people in town who aren't happy with the idea of some sort of youth camp for delinquents being set up in this area. Steps will be taken."

"Ziggy saved your wife's life. You might think about cutting him some slack."

"One good deed doesn't give him the right to run rough-shod over the rights of his neighbors."

"There was a girl's camp here for years, before you arrived," Oliver pointed out.

"Times have changed since then. Now there are permits, regulations, environmental considerations, many things that are required today. I don't think Breener and his friend, Briskin, have all the paperwork in hand. Brian Curtis has an interest in this, and he's agreed to look into it."

Anton shrugged. "But you're here to talk about our new boat, not our neighbor's problems."

"Have you had a chance to look over the drawings I dropped off?" Oliver said, reining in his temper.

"They look perfect," Anton said.

"Do you think it will be big enough?" Sasha said. "We want to have plenty of room for entertaining."

"It's about the right size for two people who haven't had a lot of sailing experience," Oliver said. "You can always get something bigger later on."

"Why don't you give us a quote," Anton said briskly, "so we can get started right away."

"You don't have any changes or questions before I start drawing up the lines?"

"The boat's perfect, just as it is," Anton assured him.

"The sooner you can start, the sooner it will be finished," Sasha said.

"Can you have it ready for us this summer?" Anton inquired.

"This summer?" Oliver said in a strangled voice. "How about next summer?"

* * *

Sarah was about to pull into Ziggy's driveway when she spotted Bert's pickup parked by the roadside nearby. The archeologist was loading the last of his equipment into the truck as she walked up, and she could see an assortment of plastic buckets, trays, trowels, and sieves all jumbled in the truck's bed.

"You're leaving?" she asked.

"I don't like being used," he replied angrily. "And I don't like being blamed for everything that happens here." He dropped his shovel and pickaxe in the truck bed with a loud clatter. His metal detector was propped up in the passenger seat.

"I don't blame you for feeling picked on."

"Picked on? They won't even say hello when I walk by. All I get are threatening looks, or smart remarks."

"They think you're a threat, Bert."

He looked at her disgustedly. "Like I'm going to dig up their precious treasure?"

"According to Sam Merlew, you knew about the treasure legend all along. Why did you tell me you didn't?"

There was also a legend that if you lived in Maine long enough, and were bitten by enough black flies, you'd become immune, and the bites wouldn't turn into big, itchy red spots. Clearly, Bert hadn't been in Maine very long. Even so, his blush nearly obscured the bites.

"I was afraid you'd think I was secretly looking for it, like everybody else," he said ruefully. "You were right, by the way," he added, changing the subject.

"Right about what?"

"The spearhead was planted. I had it examined by an expert, and the stone didn't come from Maine, or anywhere close. Borofsky all but admitted that he'd planted it when I confronted him."

Sarah nodded. "He was probably hoping to delay the construction."

"He can do whatever he wants, but I'm not going to be a part of it. I quit yesterday afternoon."

* * *

Sarah watched Bert drive away before walking in Ziggy's driveway, where she was immediately accosted by Pastor Briskin, who was bursting with news about the Can Man's exploits.

"Brother Ziggy is a hero," Pastor Briskin began. He went on to tell Sarah, Dudley, Harvey, and Asim about Sasha's accident in breathless detail. The others had already heard the news, but Pastor Briskin was a skilled narrator who could make the story new and more dramatic with each retelling.

Ziggy stood to one side, holding his bicycle, looking uncomfortable, and staring into space while Pastor Briskin described Sasha's accident and Ziggy's rescue.

"I didn't know she rode her bicycle every day," Asim said.

"She goes out every afternoon, around four o'clock," Dudley replied. "I see her crane her neck to look in the driveway as she goes by."

"Like she doesn't see enough staring out her upstairs window," Harvey added caustically.

"She's quite a sight wearing those spandex tights, though," Dudley added appreciatively.

"Let's not speak unkindly about the poor woman," Pastor Briskin said. "Remember that God loves her, just as He loves all of His children. And we should also remember that He chose to send Brother Ziggy to use his medical skills in order to save her life."

"It was Myra who sent me," Ziggy muttered.

Pastor Briskin frowned at his troublesome friend.

"Are you a doctor of some kind?" Harvey said.

"So people say," Pastor Briskin replied peevishly.

"He's a brilliant doctor," Sarah said to the doubting group.

Just then, Anton Borofsky strode in the driveway and approached them. He was wearing a short-sleeved Polo shirt and Bermuda shorts in spite of a cool southeast breeze, which was blowing in off the water. Looking at the pelt of hair on his arms and legs reminded her of the term "Russian Bear."

Sarah wondered if that meant that Oliver was alone with the vampire-lady. She scolded herself. She really needed to stop obsessing over Oliver and Sasha.

As it happened, Anton looked like an unusually good-natured bear as he approached Ziggy. "I'm sorry to hear that your funding has dried up," he said smoothly.

"It has?" Ziggy managed to look innocent and unconcerned.

An ominous rumble sounded in Pastor Briskin's chest.

Anton forged ahead. "In view of your financial reverses, I'm prepared to make a generous offer for your land."

"You are?" Ziggy said.

"Yes, I am, and in consideration for the work you've done to improve the lot, clearing the brush and thinning the trees..." Anton glanced at the trampled and rooted ground inside Mabel's pen. She waved her trunk at him hopefully. "And other things, I am willing to raise my last offer considerably." He paused, wrinkling his nose at the aroma of elephant. "I assume that animal will be gone before I buy the land."

Sarah wondered if Abner Haskins was right about the Borofsky's finances. Could Anton really afford to buy out Ziggy?

"We have a Judas in our midst, Brother Ziggy," the irate pastor growled.

"I have an obligation to Myra," Ziggy said woodenly.

"The woman is long-dead," Anton retorted with exasperation.

"I suppose that might possibly be so," Ziggy replied after due consideration. "Or she may just be on another astral plane, looking down on us as we speak. If that's the case, then it would be dangerous for you to buy the place." Ziggy shook his head sadly. "I don't think she likes you, and I wouldn't want to burden you with her anger."

Anton Borofsky didn't like to be baited, and he was sure Ziggy Breener was doing just that. His face reddened. "Did it ever occur to your drug-fried brain that the town will take the place for back taxes, and you'll end up with nothing?"

"I had nothing before Myra died, so it makes no difference if the town takes it away," Ziggy pointed out. He stroked his beard thoughtfully. "On the other hand, if I can't keep the land, then I'd want to sell it to somebody the old witch would approve of. It's the only way to keep her out of our hair."

"I was a good neighbor to the old lady," Anton lied piously.

"I'm thinking the place should go for something beneficial to the town," Ziggy went on dreamily. "A general store, an open-air theater for rock concerts." He smiled as inspiration struck. "A drive-in theater for those who are older and miss such things. That would be perfect. Myra loved watching old movies on her TV." His gaze rested benignly on Anton Borofsky's purple face. "There are so many choices, and many of them would save you from Myra Huggard's wrath."

Gathering his last reserves of patience, Anton turned to Pastor Briskin. "You seem to be the only person around here who has any grasp of reality. Explain to this idiot that the money is gone, and you're broke."

"God will provide," Pastor Briskin replied, echoing Ziggy's apparent serenity.

"And just how will that happen?" Anton sneered.

"I'm not so sure about God providing," Ziggy commented, "but Myra will."

Pastor Briskin opened his mouth to address this latest outrage, but Ziggy cut him off. "Or perhaps she won't. Either way is of no matter."

Anton Borofsky was nothing if not persistent, and clamping down firmly on his temper, he tried to reason with Ziggy again. "Do you have any idea of the regulations and permits that you'll need to run a camp here?" Anton pointed to Pastor Briskin. "You're a fool to let yourself be taken in by this religious huckster. All he cares about is building his camp for teenage hoodlums."

Pastor Briskin's bushy eyebrows looked as though they were about to burst into flame. "Hoodlums?!" he thundered. "You would deny troubled youth from across the country the chance of redemption?!" He paused for breath. "I see great evil here," he went on, struggling with his fury, "and your wife is a Jezebel. Take care that you don't reap what you sow."

"Don't you dare threaten my wife!"

"Perhaps your wife's accident was a warning from God!"

The cleric and the tycoon were both big men, and they stood nose-to-nose. For a moment, Sarah feared the two would come to blows.

Ziggy coughed discretely and Anton Borofsky took a step back before saying, "If you're trying to make some kind of a crazy threat, then you'll be meeting Jesus a lot sooner than you think." He unclenched his fists with a conscious effort.

"My flock are people of God. We don't resort to violence, unlike some," Pastor Briskin retorted. "I will pray for your souls, that you may come to see Jesus."

Anton ignored the barb and turned to Ziggy. "I'm offering you enough money to live the rest of your life in comfort. You'd be smart to take the offer."

Ziggy turned away wordlessly, mounted his trusty steed, and pedaled off.

* * *

"That pair doesn't have a clue about boats," Oliver said to Sarah as they stood in front of Myra's old foundation later that morning. The dead excavator had been dragged away, which gave them a better view of the partially dismantled stonework. "Even worse, they don't care. Sasha's only worry was that the boat might not be big enough to impress all their friends."

In typical Maine fashion, a front had raced through and the wind had swung into the northwest, blowing away the smell of diesel fuel from the oil-soaked ground in front of them.

"It's not much fun building a boat for somebody who doesn't take any interest in what's going on," he concluded.

"A lot less fun than working with Abner."

"Abner is a gem. If it weren't for the money, I'd say no to the Borofskys." Oliver looked around. "Where is everybody?"

"Dudley is clearing more brush by the shore and Pastor Briskin is off somewhere, trying to rent another excavator for Dudley to play with this afternoon, God help us. Harvey has gone off to rent a wood chipper, and Ziggy rode away to pick up cans. I think can-hunting is a kind of therapy for him."

"The man needs every bit of therapy he can get," Oliver said. "Especially with Mabel still here," he added as she wandered up to the fence and waved her trunk at them.

"I think Ziggy's convinced that she's a killer."

"Don't say that in front of Asim," Oliver murmured as the man in question appeared carrying an armload of brush from the clearing operation down by the shore.

Sarah turned away from the pen. "Pastor Briskin told everybody about Sasha's accident. How is she feeling today?"

"Sore and mad."

"Clothed?"

"All her bruises were covered. Besides, Anton was there, at least until he came over here."

"I suppose there'll be scars. Not good for her bikini collection." Oliver gave her a look.

"Sorry," she said. "That was catty. The woman is lucky to be alive. One of those stakes could have stabbed her in the—" Sarah caught herself. "I feel guilty now about those things I said earlier, about vampires and stakes."

"It was a freak accident."

"Yes, and I'm sorry it happened. I really am."

"Plastic surgery can do wonders," Oliver said. "I doubt if anything will show."

"According to Pastor Briskin, Ziggy saved her life. I hope she's appreciative."

"She wants him arrested for trying to molest her. According to Sasha, he was taking his clothes off when the tourists came along to stop him."

"Ziggy was going to molest her?" Sarah said. "He was taking his clothes off? The man saved her life, for crying out loud. Is she nuts?"

"She's a very troubled woman right now."

"Mmm."

"Not even Anton is buying her foolishness over Ziggy," Oliver added. "In fact, he referred to Ziggy by name, the first time I've ever heard him do that."

"By name? Not 'that man,' or 'that bum,' or something worse?

He must be reevaluating things."

"He called him Breener, not exactly friendly, but it's a start. He also refused to press charges for attempted molestation, or even have Ziggy beaten up. Sasha was peeved."

"Sasha is a very unpleasant woman. Speaking of unpleasant, Anton just offered to buy out Ziggy, now that funding for the camp has dried up."

"Interesting," Oliver said. "He gave the go-ahead for his new boat, too. Abner may be right about Anton struggling with competition in the fish preservative business, but he still seems to have money to throw around. According to Sasha, he was away in 'The City' yesterday. Maybe he got rid of his competition, and cut off the camp's funding at the same time. Killing two birds with one stone."

"Pastor Briskin certainly thinks he's responsible for turning off the money spigot."

"Which is bad news for both him and Ziggy," Oliver replied. "Ziggy has no way to pay the taxes if the Spruce Cone camp doesn't lease the land, and the camp is a very important project for Pastor Briskin."

"He said some quite un-Christian things about both Borofskys. I thought the two of them were going square off for a minute."

"Do you think Pastor Briskin would retaliate against the Borofskys over the funding?" Oliver said. "What would he do, burn down the Great Wall?"

"Briskin called him evil, and her a Jezebel."

"Strong words for Brother Briskin, and not entirely inaccurate, either," Oliver commented. "The good pastor must have been on a tear, but I still don't see him resorting to physical violence."

"Agreed, but his outburst might inspire one of his flock."

"Anton is pulling some strings closer to home, too," Oliver said.

"He has Brian Curtis checking to see if Pastor Briskin has all the permits he needs to run a camp."

"Why Brian?"

"He does have an interest in protecting land values in this area, especially where he's trying to sell the lot next door."

"I know all that. I'm just wondering why Borofsky doesn't hire a lawyer to do that kind of work, instead of a Realtor."

Oliver was beginning to feel the ice thinning under his feet. "I got the impression that Brian volunteered, probably as a favor to Anton."

Chapter 18

Pastor Briskin's energetic crew got a lot of work done Wednesday afternoon. Harvey and two other workers chipped a truckload of brush, setting aside the choicer pieces for Mabel's enjoyment. For his part, the church's spiritual leader put on his trucker's hat and hauled away a load of pulp wood to sell for some much needed cash. Dudley, meanwhile, made headway with the newly rented excavator and managed to do a passable job of piling up the foundation stones and clearing the way for loads of dirt to fill in the hole.

If Myra disapproved of all this activity, she thankfully refrained from interfering.

Ten miles away, at the Hound Hill Boatworks, Sarah and Oliver were putting in a fruitful afternoon spreading paint on *Daisy Mae*.

And so it was that all the various workers went off to their homes at dusk, tired and a bit sore, but happy with the progress they'd made, and relieved that no catastrophe had befallen them and their work. Yet.

Pastor Briskin had come up with a tiny tag-along camper for

Asim to use so he could stay near Mabel for the night. The camper's teardrop profile limited the interior headroom, and its length wasn't much greater than Asim's height. Even so, it was a big improvement over the pup-tent and sleeping bag on the ground that he'd used last night.

Maine's weather gods, apparently embarrassed by yesterday's cold snap, decided to turn up the heat Wednesday afternoon by bringing in a steady flow of warm air from the southwest.

The result of this climatic shenanigan was that where Asim had shivered in his sleeping bag last night, he was now sweltering in the eighty-degree heat tonight. Worse, there was only the faintest of southwest breezes wafting through the camper's open door.

Ah, spring in Maine.

Asim dozed restlessly in the overheated bunk, which happened to be a good four inches too short for his frame. A vehicle passing by on the road wakened him from his half-sleep. It was after ten o'clock and traffic was usually scarce at that hour.

Also, he wasn't sure if it had passed by. He lay still, straining to hear any further noises.

A gunshot shattered the quiet and Mabel gave a squeal of terror.

With a shout, Asim charged out the door, saw a figure standing in the driveway, barely visible in the faint moonlight. Asim sprinted up to the driveway, not thinking about the possible danger.

He made it half way up to the driveway before hearing a vehicle roar off into the night.

Chapter 19

Weston Farmer, Esquire, wasn't a dog who suffered trespassers gladly. Especially trespassers who drove eighteen-wheelers. And even more especially when said trespassers arrived at five o'clock in the morning. Not being a bashful animal, Wes made his disapproval known to the world as well as Oliver Wendell, who happened to share his dog's opinions concerning nighttime trespassers.

Oliver rolled over with a groan to wake Sarah, but she wasn't there, having decided to spend another night at the Merlews.

As a result, he dressed hastily and confronted his uninvited guests in a dark mood which matched the pre-dawn gloom.

His visitors were, in fact, behaving more like invaders when he emerged from the kitchen door. Phoebe was backing her rig around behind the house, while Pastor Briskin, Ziggy, Asim, and a handful of others, who's faces weren't familiar, stood next to the Golden Arms of Faith Full Gospel Church van. Oliver guessed that yesterday's workers couldn't be lured from their beds in the wee small hours after having put in a full day at Ziggy's place.

"No, absolutely not," Oliver growled as the delegation approached.

"You haven't even heard our tale of woe," Pastor Briskin said.

"If it has anything to do with elephants, the answer is no."

"I'm disappointed in you, Brother Oliver," Pastor Briskin said sadly.

Oliver rolled his eyes and sighed.

The mournful cleric was not a person who could be discouraged by a mere eye-roll, or even a sigh. "I've always considered you to be a Good Samaritan, a man full of compassion and love for his fellow creatures, of God's creation. A man who is always ready to step into the breach, to—"

"We need to get Mabel away from Myra's place," Ziggy interrupted. "Somebody took a shot at her earlier tonight. The gunman missed, but we need to find a place where she'll be safe."

"We need a place where she'll be out of sight," Asim added.

"Somebody took a shot at Mabel?" Oliver said. "Do you know who?"

"We have a Judas in our midst," Pastor Briskin said grimly.

Sarah had told Oliver about the fact that Pastor Briskin referred to Bert Farley as a Judas. Judas or not, the young man had become a scapegoat among Pastor Briskin's crew, even after his departure. "I assume the police are investigating?"

"Yes," Pastor Briskin replied, "but you can see why it's important to move her. She was lucky this time, and fortunately Asim was there to chase the gunman away before he could get off a second shot. She'll only be here for a few days. Or until you can prove her innocence."

"What if she *did* kill Bernie?" Oliver said.

"Negative thinking isn't helpful," Pastor Briskin replied.

"Neither is fanciful thinking," Ziggy commented.

"I'm amazed that you, the master of fanciful and bizarre

thinking, would say such a thing," Pastor Briskin countered.

Once the sun rose, it promised to be one of those rare spring days of the sort that is especially coveted by someone who wants to apply varnish to boats, and Oliver had planned to put in a full day of work on *Daisy Mae*. He looked at his unwanted guests with dismay. This motley bunch was ready, willing, and more than able to chop at large chunk of time from his precious morning schedule. "What's to keep this big game hunter from coming here and blasting away?"

"Secrecy," Pastor Briskin replied. "And Charlie Howes. He'll be discreetly guarding Mabel until the police finish their investigation and Mabel is proven innocent."

"If she's proven innocent," Ziggy muttered.

"It's been a very long night," the haggard clergyman said, "and I'm in no mood to debate this with you. I have been told, however, that the fact the investigation is taking so long suggests the police may have doubts about Mabel's guilt." He turned to Oliver, adding, "I also have faith that God will reveal the truth to you and Sister Sarah."

"Do you have permission from the police to move Mabel here?" Oliver said.

"I've already checked, and it's fine with the police to move her. Apparently, some Realtor in town pulled strings."

"A Realtor?" Oliver said.

"He's trying to sell the land next door and wants her out of there."

Wes watched with growing suspicion as Mabel was backed out of the truck. She looked groggy and unsteady on her feet, but otherwise unharmed.

"Is Mabel all right?" Oliver said as soon as Asim returned from unloading Mabel.

"I gave her a tranquilizer for the trip," Asim said.

"A tranquilizer? Is that usual?" Ziggy said.

"I thought it best. This has been a very stressful time for her, and she didn't like being shot at."

Oliver thought that was understandable. "She won't go berserk in my back yard when she comes out of it, will she?"

"Certainly not," Asim said stiffly. "Besides, Pastor Briskin has loaned me a camper, and I'll be staying right here with her."

Oliver felt a headache coming on.

"Bless you, bless you, Brother Oliver," Pastor Briskin said, wringing Oliver's hand. "God never forgets a Good Samaritan. You're truly a life-saver."

Admittedly, it was early in the morning, but Oliver couldn't remember giving permission to have his back yard turned into an elephant hideaway, in spite of Pastor Briskin's profuse thanks.

"You make it sound as though I'm putting up the Queen Mother," Oliver grumbled, extracting his hand from the cleric's vise-like grip.

"Er, yes," Pastor Briskin said, momentarily derailed. Rallying quickly, he said, "Would you like to show us where you want Mabel's enclosure?"

"She'll be out of sight if we put her behind the house," Asim suggested.

"Or maybe in the livingroom," Oliver muttered.

Asim was above such pettiness. "A place that has a few trees for shade would be ideal."

"She's not going to bulldoze all the trees down, is she?" Oliver said.

"Just the small ones," Ziggy commented.

Asim scowled at this, but refused to take the bait and marched off to supervise Mabel's unloading.

Oliver hoped that all of this was some particularly noxious dream from which he could soon escape.

"It'll be a lot easier to finish clearing Ziggy's land without Mabel's enclosure taking up a good part of the property," Pastor Briskin said brightly.

With an efficiency born of practice, Asim, Phoebe, and four other nameless members of Briskin's flock, soon had Mabel and the parts for her pen unloaded.

Wes had never met an elephant, especially one in his driveway. Standing behind his master and protector, he barked ferociously.

Mabel waved her trunk at him and made faint snuffling sounds.

"Wes, hush," Oliver said above the racket.

Mabel trumpeted, which sent Wes scuttling into the shop.

"They'll get along fine," Pastor Briskin said reassuringly. "Elephants like dogs."

"So long as they don't get too close to her tusks," Ziggy added.

"How long did you say she'll be here?" Oliver said.

"Just a few days, Brother Oliver."

Ziggy snorted.

Oliver refrained from pointing out that Mabel had already been at Ziggy's place for almost five days. "Is the zoo paying you to board Mabel and truck her around like this?" he asked Pastor Briskin. "Isn't it getting kind of expensive?"

"Of course the zoo is paying," Pastor Briskin replied. "Their elephant is very important to them. They pay for her transportation, food, and a stipend for Asim." After a pause, he added, "Naturally, they pay our struggling church a small sum, a token gift, for our help." He brightened. "In fact, their generosity is providing enough money for us to rent the new excavator, so we are able to carry on our work at Brother Ziggy's property."

The heavy, eight-foot fence posts were being pounded into the ground at a surprisingly rapid pace.

Oliver doubted that he would be getting a token gift from the zoo.

* * *

The sun was climbing above the trees before Phoebe had a chance to confront Asim in private. She'd driven most of the night to get here, and she was bone tired. She was also out of patience. "You're darn lucky I happened to be in Portland when you called. Even so, I can't keep coming up here at the drop of a hat to move your fool elephant every couple of days."

"You know perfectly well that she's not my elephant, and I had no choice. It was too dangerous for her to stay there with all the news people hanging around, and somebody taking shots at her."

Phoebe looked over to where Mabel was standing groggily in her new enclosure while the work crew finished driving in the fence posts and stringing the heavy wire fencing. "Did you really need to dope her up again? Is it safe to keep doing that?"

"Mabel is getting the best of care," Asim replied coolly.

Just then Charlie pulled in the driveway.

"I don't like any part of this," Phoebe said as she watched Charlie getting out of his car, which he'd been forced to leave well down the driveway thanks to Asim's rusty pickup, the camper, the semi, and the church van.

"You didn't have a problem with moving her last time," Asim pointed out.

"I didn't know your crazy elephant was a serial killer last time—I told you that before. And now she's killed somebody else. That makes a total body count of three, so far. That's a problem for me, Asim. I never did understand why you brought the fool animal up here anyway. Surely you could have found a better place. At least a place with a zoo, where she could be kept away from people. What happened?"

"There wasn't a lot of time to line anything up, and I was

misled, okay?" Asim growled, glaring in Pastor Briskin's direction. "What more can I tell you?"

"Kermit and I should have realized something was fishy when there wasn't any zoo when we first got to Maine, and this place isn't a zoo, either."

"I'm doing the best I can on short notice. It's not as easy as you think to hide an elephant."

"There's too much going on that I don't understand." To Phoebe's relief, Charlie walked by them without stopping, and began talking to Ziggy and Pastor Briskin. "How much longer do you plan to keep up this shell game?"

"She'll be safe here, and this place is away from prying eyes, unlike a zoo; that's what counts."

Phoebe looked at her companion, well aware that he hadn't answered her question. Actually, she thought, knowing the truth about what was going on was what really counted, as far as she was concerned. And she wasn't hearing the whole story, not by a long-shot.

"What in the world did you think you were doing, running after a gunman in the middle of the night?" Phoebe said.

"Don't start in on me. The cops have already bawled me out. I was mad, all right?" Asim looked at her ruefully. "Besides, I figured having a half-naked Zulu yelling and charging out of the darkness would be enough to scare anybody away."

Phoebe laughed in spite of herself.

"The man was a lousy shot," Asim went on, "All he did was put a hole in Mabel's watering trough."

"How do you know Mabel wasn't standing next to the watering trough? He might have been a pretty good shot, considering how dark it was."

"Give it a rest," Asim grumbled.

"Besides, you were a lot closer to him than Mabel, or the

watering trough." Phoebe rested her hand on Asim's arm. "I'd just hate to see you get hurt over this."

* * *

After breakfast, Oliver spent an hour calling various zoos in Pennsylvania, looking unsuccessfully for the erstwhile home of Mabel-the-murderous-elephant. Finally, he reached the Hart's Ridge Zoo, a small establishment in the northern part of the state. The place was represented by the hearty voice of one Wilbur Dennis, who's official title remained unclear.

"What can I do for you this fine spring morning, Mister Wendell?" Wilbur said.

"I wanted to ask about your elephant exhibit. Our kids have been watching *Dumbo* cartoons on TV, and they're anxious to see an elephant in the flesh."

"I'm sorry to say our exhibit is closed for renovations right now," Wilbur replied mournfully.

"That's too bad," Oliver said, thinking that he might have hit pay dirt at last. "When will the elephant be back?"

"That's a little hard to say for sure, Mr. Wendell. We're a small zoo, as you may know, and funding is always tight, but we hope to have our new enclosure finished by mid-summer."

Oliver's kitchen dated back to the era when such spaces were designed to meet the needs of large farm families with hearty appetites, and it extended the full width of the house. As a result, he could sit at the kitchen table and see the driveway—where Charlie's car blocked the entrance—from the front windows, and Mabel's enclosure—which filled the back yard—from the rear. He was hemmed in by unwanted guests—guests who saw fit to invite themselves in and take over.

"Not until mid-summer? That long?" Oliver said. He watched Asim spreading some sort of lotion on Mabel's forehead. "I was hoping it would be a lot sooner."

"Our zoo has a lot of other animals for you and your children to enjoy. I'm sorry about the inconvenience, but we want our new enclosure to provide the best possible environment."

It seemed unlikely that the apologetic gentleman fully appreciated the level of Oliver's inconvenience. "How many elephants do you usually have?"

"We only have the one. In fact that's part of our reason for remodeling. We'd like to get a second animal. As you may know, elephants are very social, and a single elephant by itself can get lonely and unhappy. Unfortunately, they're very expensive to obtain, as well as expensive to feed and care for, and our finances are quite limited." Wilbur caught himself just short of making an appeal for money.

Oliver saw Wes sitting outside Mabel's enclosure, his head cocked to one side as he watched her toying with a lobster pot buoy which had a length of line attached to it.

"What are you doing with your elephant during the renovations?"

"We're boarding her at another zoo. Why do you ask?"

"I'm just curious. Our kids are bound to ask. You know how youngsters are," Oliver said, trying to sound like an indulgent parent.

"Of course. Kids do have endless curiosity. Actually, our elephant is on a sort of tour, out of state. It's a chance for other, smaller zoos to have an elephant, at least temporarily."

Bingo, Oliver thought. This must be Mabel's elusive home. "I understand there are two varieties of elephants? Besides *Dumbo*, of course."

Wilbur laughed politely. "Yes, there are. Our animal happens to be an African elephant. As you may know, African elephants tend to be bigger than the more common Indian elephant."

"I understand that they can be more aggressive than Indian elephants?"

The heartiness in Wilbur's voice faded. "I wouldn't say they're more aggressive, Mister Wendell. They can be harder to train than Indian elephants—a bit more stubborn—but that's all. Also, like a great many animals, they can become aggressive if they're mistreated."

"I think it's great that you're sharing your elephant. It must be a wonderful opportunity for a zoo. Is your elephant named Mabel, by any chance?"

There was a tell-tale pause on the line. "No, it's not. I think you must have the wrong zoo." Wilbur's voice took on a wary tone. For Wilbur's sake, Oliver hoped the man didn't play poker.

He watched Mabel flip the buoy onto her back, much to Wes' delight. Had Mabel flipped Bernie onto her back before she killed him?

"My mistake," Oliver said lightly. "Where is your elephant now, by the way? Just so I can tell our kids when they ask."

"We're boarding her at a private zoo, at the moment," Wilbur said coolly. "Now, if you'll excuse me, I have a lot of work to do."

"Did you arrange that through a Pastor Leonard Briskin in Maine?" Oliver said "Are you sure you know where your elephant is?"

"Who are you?"

"I am the person who happens to have Mabel living in my back yard."

"In *your* back yard?"

"She's tossing around an old lobster pot buoy at this very

moment. She seems quite contented."

"Are you the owner of Ziggy's Zoo?"

"Not exactly," Oliver replied "I'm more like an annex to the zoo."

"I see," came the disapproving reply.

"You said that you'd owned her for three years. Where did she come from before that?"

The line went dead.

Chapter 20

Sarah arrived at Oliver's house around mid-morning to work on *Daisy Mae*. The boat was at that deceptive stage of her construction where she looked completed, yet still lacked a myriad of little details, all awaiting their turns. Oliver had written a list, but for every item he crossed off, two more materialized, a boatbuilder's version of kudzu.

Oliver filled Sarah in on Mabel's arrival while they worked.

"Do the police have any idea who took a shot at her?" Sarah said when Oliver had finished his tale of woe.

"No. The gunman had a pickup truck parked on the road and got away before Asim could get a good look."

"I can think of several reasons for wanting to kill her, revenge being the most likely one," Sarah said.

Oliver nodded. "Bernie's family certainly has a motive. He was a deer hunter, and he must have guns in the house. Also, Charlie let slip that Bernie's son was being questioned. Of course they didn't find the bullet, so there's no way to prove anything."

"I doubt if there are many people who would blame Bernie's family."

"I think Pastor Briskin also suspects Bert Farley, at least he talked about Judas being the shooter."

Sarah nodded. "That's shorthand for Bert with Briskin's crew. They see him as Anton's hired man. Or gunman in this case."

"So Anton paid Bert to shoot Mabel, just to get rid of her?"

"Her room and board are Pastor Briskin's last source of income for building the camp," Sarah said.

Oliver nodded. "Mabel's big, galvanized watering trough might look a little like an elephant in the dark, from a distance, or if Mabel was standing next to it. If Asim is right, and the shooter was standing in the driveway, the range would have been about sixty, or seventy yards—not all that long a shot."

"But in the dark?"

"Good point. On the other hand, the shooter had plenty of time," Oliver said.

"Do you think he missed on purpose?"

"There are people who just want Mabel moved, but not necessarily dead."

"I know what you're thinking," Sarah said coolly.

"You do?"

"You're thinking that Brian tried to use me to get Mabel moved when he invited me to lunch the other day, and when that didn't work, he took a shot at Mabel to get her out of there."

"I'm not thinking anything of the sort," Oliver said impatiently. "Those are *your* words. I've know Brian Curtis for years, and I can't see him doing something like that. On the other hand, what about the owner of the land? How desperate is he to sell? What if he got tired of having Mabel discourage potential buyers?"

They were her words, Sarah thought. Did she trust Brian? Did she trust herself? Did she trust anyone?

They worked in silence until lunchtime, which they ate hurriedly, while discussing what to tackle next on *Daisy Mae's* to-do list.

Marsha Pruit, the Realtor in Sudbury, called Sarah just as she and Oliver were finishing their sandwiches.

"I have good news on your house," Marsha said.

"Another nibble?" Sarah said.

"A bite. An offer, with earnest money. It's a young professional couple, thinking of starting a family. She's an investment adviser, and he's lawyer."

Claude was a lawyer, Sarah mused. It had taken him nearly six months to recover from the outrage of learning that Sarah had put 'their' house on the market, no matter that it came to her in the settlement. Oh, well. "What's the offer?"

Marsha hesitated. "It's on the low side. You know how the market has been the last year or two."

"How low?"

Marsha gave her the figure.

"That's a lot less than I'd hoped. Was there something they didn't like about the place?"

"They're excited about it, Sarah. They made an offer, after all. Sure, they had a few little gripes. There always are; that's how it works when you're haggling over a house. There was some comment about the diningroom being too big, for example, and they're worried about the cost of redecorating—"

"Lawyers like big diningrooms, so they can have big parties. And what's wrong with the decor?"

"Anybody who buys a house is going to make changes. They do it to make the house fit their own lifestyle. They want to make it their house, after all, not somebody else's. There's nothing personal.

Remember, this is strictly a business transaction. It's their job to find little faults, just like it's my job to talk up the good points. Try not to take any of this personally. It's strictly business, but I don't need to tell you that."

"What about making a counter offer?"

"I think they'd be expecting one. They know it's a low-ball, so they may be hoping that you'll split the difference."

"That's still less than I was hoping to get for the place."

"Make a counter offer that you're comfortable with, then. You don't have to sell the place for less than you think it's worth if you don't want to. Someone else, who's willing to pay more could come along tomorrow, for all we know."

"Or maybe not," Sarah said.

"Or maybe not," Marsha echoed.

Wes had been staring up at her hopefully, and he nudged her leg with his nose. She dropped the last soggy corner of her BLT into the waiting maw.

"Another buyer always comes along sooner or later, Sarah. It's just a matter of time, and your patience. Think about the offer, and call me back in a day or two." With that, Marsha was gone.

She was right, Sarah thought. It was just a business transaction. And yet, how much were her memories of the place worth to her? There had been a lot of good years, and two children, in that house, before things turned sour. Was she really ready to let them go?

So long as she owned the house, Sudbury had been kind of refuge, a place to retreat to if her adventure in Maine turned out to be nothing more than an adventure, a passing thing. Was she ready to let go of the security blanket? If she wasn't, then what did it say about her relationship with Oliver?

Wes, in a prime example of fickle love that would have made Sarah's ex proud, transferred his attention to Oliver. A sucker for big brown eyes, he sacrificed the last of his sandwich to canine lust.

Oliver had been listening to Sarah's half of the conversation, and must have guessed what it was about. "An offer on your house?" he said.

"Yes."

Oliver nodded. "That could be good news or bad news," he mused.

"It's a low-ball offer."

"Take your time."

Sarah looked out the window to where Mabel was demolishing another bale of hay. "I feel like Mabel, bouncing around from place to place. Even elephants have more luggage than I do. And don't tell me that elephants have trunks."

"What do you take me for, Milton Berle?" Oliver said, offended.

"I could see the words forming in your brain, Wendell. You should be ashamed."

* * *

One of the advantages of painting something is that it almost always looks better when you've finished. The other advantage is that when you're done, you're done. Too much fiddling only makes matters worse A few final licks at the last holiday, clean the brush, and sit back to admire the result. So it was with a sense of satisfaction that Sarah finished painting *Daisy Mae's* cockpit and clambered down the ladder to the ground.

Oliver hadn't had such a satisfying experience. He'd been attaching fittings to the mast and found to his disgust that the box of 2-inch, #10 bronze wood screws was empty. With much grumbling, he and Wes had gone off to Rockland in search of more.

Feeling at loose ends, Sarah wandered out of the shop to check

on Mabel. It was almost four o'clock in the afternoon, and both
Mabel and Asim appeared to be snoozing in the sun. Rather than
disturb them, she decided to drive over to the Merlews, see how
Kate was doing, and hash over Sudbury. Yes, a cup of tea and a
little conversation would be good.

Sarah called to make sure Kate was free, left a note for Oliver,
and set out.

Chapter 21

Like *Owl's* mast, the old-fashioned wooden tabletop in the Merlew's kitchen had collected its own assortment of dents and stains from decades of use, each imperfection telling its own story of mishap, inattention, joy, anger, and a myriad of other human emotions.

"I suppose you've heard that Bert Farley quit," Kate said.

"I saw him yesterday morning as he was leaving."

"Did he tell you that somebody had left a threatening note on his windshield? It called him a Judas."

"He didn't mention that," Sarah said, "but the Judas thing sounds like one of Briskin's crew."

"Or maybe it was somebody pretending to be one of them. The note was a quote from the bible about Judas falling headfirst, and 'bursting asunder.'"

"Echoes of Bernie, not that he burst asunder, exactly."

"Being gored is close enough for me," Kate commented.

"Pastor Briskin's crew will feel happier with Bert gone—less competition in the treasure hunting derby. All of them, except maybe Harvey, have gone treasure happy and they saw Bert as competition."

"Harvey always was the sensible one in that bunch, for all his other faults."

"It's too bad about how they treated Bert; he seemed like a nice guy."

Kate looked disgusted. "I can't believe any of them take that treasure foolishness seriously."

"They might not have at first. It's almost like a mob thing, where they pile one rumor on top of another and egg each other on. I wonder why nobody got the fever before."

"Probably because there never was a bunch of them right there in Myra's back yard to encourage each other."

Sarah ran her fingers over a dent in the tabletop and wondered once again if somebody was taking things seriously enough to kill. She saw Kate's expression and decided to change the subject. "It looks like I may be selling my house in Sudbury. I've finally got an offer, after more than a year of waiting."

"Isn't that a good thing?" Kate could see the doubt and uncertainty on Sarah's face. "Are you selling, or having to sell?"

"I know that I don't want to live there anymore. On the other hand, it's not as though I need the money. Claude was actually pretty generous with the alimony."

"But why not sell the place if you don't want to live there? Wouldn't selling it give you cash to buy something else, somewhere else? Are you keeping it as a security blanket, just in case?"

Sarah wondered if she was really that transparent. "What's wrong with security blankets?"

"Nothing, I suppose, unless you cling to it too long and it keeps you from moving on to new things."

"Thank you, Doctor Phil." Sarah caught herself "Sorry, that's unfair. It's just that so much has happened in the last year that I'm not sure where I am. I need a little space to figure things out." Now that she said it, the words seemed inadequate.

Kate ran her fingers absentmindedly along the edge of her cast, gazed at Sarah, and waited for more.

"Sudbury is a whole different world compared to here," Sarah went on. "Maybe you're right and I'm hanging on to Sudbury when I should be moving on. Damn. Now I sound like Doctor Phil."

Kate smiled. "I know it's a truism, but you have to come to terms with the past before you can face the future."

Sarah scowled. "Calling the house a security blanket makes it sound as though the past year in Maine—"

"—and Oliver," Kate put in.

"—was just a trial balloon that I could let go of if things didn't work out. It's not that easy, dammit."

"I should hope not. Letting go of the past is never easy. And in some ways, it shouldn't be." She paused. "For what it's worth, your relationship with Oliver over the past year has done good things for him. And I think he's been good for you, too. At least it looks that way from where I sit."

Sarah nodded slowly.

Kate shifted in the chair to ease her bruises. "The point is that you've both changed a lot in just a year, and that's bound to be hard. You can't stop change from happening, but you can adjust to it."

"That doesn't mean I have to like it."

"That's true, but you can think about the choices you do have. You could get a place here. That would be my first choice, and probably Oliver's, too." Kate sipped more tea, taking her time. "You could be a snow bird, with a place here and another in Massachusetts. How about moving to New York? Your son is there."

"That's already too many choices." Sarah played with her teaspoon.

Kate gave her an impatient look. "I can make suggestions, but I'm not going to tell you what to do with your life. Only an enemy would do that. You need to start trusting yourself, though, before you can think clearly about the future."

"That trust business is the hard part for me." Sarah took another swallow of tea. "Have you seen what's happened to Myra's place?"

"You know how Sam and I feel about Myra Huggard. The woman was vicious, and her husband was worse, as you know perfectly well. I didn't go over there any more than I had to when the Huggards were alive, and I'm certainly not going there now that Briskin and his crew have ripped the place apart."

"It had to happen, I suppose, ripping the place apart, I mean."

"That's one break with the past that you're better off making as soon as possible," Kate said coolly.

"Ziggy seems to think that Myra is haunting the place, and there are times when even I wonder."

Kate looked at her, irritated. "You and Ziggy make a pair. For heaven's sake, can't either of you let go of anything? What was it about Myra Huggard that has you two so hung up on her?"

Truisms galore. Sarah smiled in spite of herself. "Are you going to tell me that I have to stop looking back at Myra Huggard before I can look at the future?

"Looking back at Myra Huggard, of all people," Kate muttered. "She was the most backwards-looking person I ever knew."

"She had her good side."

Kate eyed Sarah over the rim of her teacup. "I'm not going to dignify that comment with a reply." She put her cup down. "Would you like me to hot that up a little?"

"I'll get it," Sarah said. She went over to the stove and poured for Kate and herself. "Did I mention that Betty Boop is gone?" she said casually.

"So what? I thought it was all settled that Bernie's death was an accident; he just got too close to the elephant. Surely you aren't still thinking that he was murdered."

"I was beginning to think that it probably was an accident, until Betty Boop turned up and then disappeared. I'm not so sure anymore." Sarah was quiet for a moment, before returning to the treasure hunt. "Bernie had a metal detector stashed away in the excavator."

"Bernie?" Kate frowned. "He should know better."

"According to Dudley, Bernie was using it to find the water pipe from Myra's well to the house."

Kate's frown deepened. "Myra didn't get running water until five years ago."

"You mean she was still using that outhouse five years ago?"

Kate nodded. "Eldon's girlfriend, Cathy, got money from the welfare people to pay for the plumbing. Eldon put in the pump and hooked it up to the house. You could ask him, but my guess is that he used plastic pipe."

"Maybe Bernie didn't know that."

"That's possible," Kate said. "He wasn't exactly a genius."

"He spent a lot of time in the old cellar hole, supposedly working underneath the excavator. Maybe he was really—"

"I thought we were done talking about the treasure foolishness," Kate interrupted sharply. "Myra might have squirreled away some cash under her mattress, but the Huggards never had a stash of gold coins, or silver ingots, or pirate treasure, or strong boxes, or anything like it, hidden in their cellar, or anywhere else." She gave Sarah a meaningful look before adding, "And certainly not under Evan's fishing shack."

"Yes, but if Bernie *thought* there was something hidden away, and he checked out Evan's shack with the metal detector, he would have found Betty Boop."

"On the other hand, you don't know when the bicycle was found. Maybe somebody else found it after Bernie died," Kate said.

* * *

One of the advantages of living ten miles from the coast was the peace and quiet, things that Oliver valued. Another advantage was that property taxes were much lower, which was important to someone who relied on boatbuilding for a major source of income.

The disadvantage of living where Oliver did was the need to get *Daisy Mae* from his shop, perched on the side of Hound Hill, down to the water. For this reason, Sarah and Oliver stopped work around mid-afternoon and made their way to Parlin "Pearly" Gaites' boatshop, a place which was on the water, having been planted there half a century ago when waterfront land was just waterfront land and not an almost priceless commodity.

There was also the chance that Charlie had let drop some tidbit of information that they could weasel out of Pearly.

Unlike Oliver, who used modern techniques to build wooden boats, Pearly Gaites stuck with the traditional ways of building. As a result, the two often traded good-natured jabs.

Sarah and Oliver parked in Pearly's rutted dirt parking area. A seagull, perched on a piling at the end of Pearly's pier, eyed them mistrustfully for a moment before flying away.

Being May, a time when boat owners start to think about spring and the process of putting their boats in the water, Pearly and his mountainous young assistant, Eldon Tupper, were busy getting said boats ready to launch, as well as finishing a thirty-six foot yawl, which they'd been building over the winter.

"Looks like we're a little ahead of you," Oliver commented as he admired the yawl.

"My boat is bigger than yours," Pearly countered.

"We're faster workers," Oliver replied.

"Now, now, children," Sarah said.

"We have a question," Oliver said.

"Two questions," Sarah corrected him.

Pearly looked at his visitors suspiciously. "Are you two planning to take a big chunk out of my workday?"

"Not if you say yes," Oliver replied. "We need to put *Daisy Mae* in the water, and I figure that she'd look really good on your launching ramp."

Eldon Tupper, all 6-foot 6-inches and 300 muscular pounds of him, tiptoed over to listen.

"What do I get out of it?" Pearly said, frowning at Eldon.

"You get to rub shoulders with Abner Haskins, a genuine multi-millionaire."

"Multi-millionaires are a dime a dozen, nowadays," Pearly grumbled.

"This one likes boats," Oliver said.

"When do you want to put her in?" Pearly inquired.

"A week from Saturday."

"Have to be early in the morning, when the tide's high." He eyed them in much the same way the seagull had a few minutes ago. "You're not going to sit on my launching ramp all day, playing with lengths of rope, are you?"

"We'll be gone before you know it," Oliver assured him. "I'll have the rigging all set up before we get here."

"Daisy Mae was quite a beauty in the comic strip," Pearly commented.

"Speaking of beauties," Sarah said. "I was wondering what you remember about Betsy Knowles."

Pearly shook his head sadly. "Bad business, her running away like that, but things were pretty tough at home, from what I heard. Her father was pond scum. Rumors were that he abused her."

"A good reason to run away," Oliver said.

"Which she did, as soon as she was old enough, and had the money to buy a bus ticket," Pearly said.

"I found her bicycle underneath the remains of Evan's fishing shack," Sarah said.

Pearly shook his head. "I know where you're going with that, and you're wrong. Evan couldn't have had anything to do with Betsy disappearing."

"Why not?"

"Because he and his boat were stuck on a ledge all that day, and half the night."

Pearly put his foot up on a convenient saw-horse and settled himself into his story-telling mode. "The damn fool went out in his lobster boat, drunk as boiled owl, probably taking a swig of booze every time a pot came up. Anyway, he managed to run onto a ledge outside New Harbor. I got a call on the radio about two in the afternoon to go and pull him off, but the tide was falling and he was high and dry when I got there. Hell, the damn fool was so stewed he hardly knew he was in a boat, much less on a ledge. It's a good thing Bernie Knowles was there or Evan might have fallen over the side and drowned."

"Bernie was there?" Sarah said.

"He was Evan's stern man. A good worker. Of course he was just a teenager back then, but he was a strong kid, and he could handle pots with the best of them."

"How long were they stuck?" Oliver asked.

"According to Bernie, they'd been pulling pots since about dawn and were heading back to Burnt Cove when they ran aground. Like I say, he landed on the ledge when the tide was about half out, so it was evening before it came in far enough for him to get off. It must have been close to midnight before he got back to his mooring."

Oliver knew all about small town rumor mills. "Why didn't everybody know about that?"

"Evan was scared to death that Myra would find out he was drunk and give him hell, so he swore me to secrecy. And Bernie didn't want anybody to know that he'd cut school to make a few extra bucks pulling pots." Pearly looked mildly guilty. "Of course I'd have piped up if the cops started asking around and accused Evan of anything, but nobody ever did." He looked at Sarah suspiciously. "Don't tell me that you're playing Sherlock Holmes again. The whole business with Betsy Knowles happened some forty-five years ago."

"We're not playing Sherlock Holmes," Oliver said emphatically. "We're just curious."

"Just curious is why you two keep getting into trouble."

Thwarted on one front, Sarah turned to Eldon. "What about Myra's plumbing? Did you put in metal pipe from the well to the house?"

Eldon gave her an incredulous look. "Who uses metal pipe anymore? I used PVC, like everybody else."

"So a metal detector wouldn't work if you wanted to find the pipe?"

"Hell, no," Eldon replied. "Why bother anyway? The line runs straight from the well to the house, and the pump is right there in the corner of the cellar, so you couldn't miss the water line."

"What's with the metal detector? Where did that come from?" Pearly said.

"Bernie had a metal detector in his excavator," Oliver explained. "He told Dudley that he was going to use it to find the water pipe."

"Baloney," Pearly said. "He was looking for Myra's imaginary money box."

"Bernie did spend a lot of time in Myra's cellar, supposedly working on his excavator," Sarah said.

"What money box?" Eldon said.

"That's the whole point," Pearly said disgustedly. "She never had any money stashed away."

"Apparently Bernie thought she did," Sarah said.

"That's because they never filled his skull more than half way when they were pouring in the brains," Pearly replied.

Chapter 22

Sarah and Oliver ate supper at Rockland's Burger King. The setting wasn't as romantic as Marcel's, but Sarah was too busy brooding over Betty Boop to care. Who would take the bicycle away, and why? Why was she so disappointed to learn that Evan Huggard had an alibi for Betsy's disappearance? Why wasn't she relieved to think that Betsy was probably alive and well after all, and living a good life somewhere else? Why did everything have to change so fast, when she wasn't ready? Why wasn't she glad to be finally selling her house?

"Abner sent us a letter," Oliver said as they finished their meal. "I forgot to show it to you earlier." He pulled an envelope out of his pocket and handed it to her:

Hello to my favorite boat builders,
I have a business trip to the west coast over the weekend, so I can't come up and see how things are going with *Daisy Mae*. Anyway, now that we're nearing the end of this

marvelously enjoyable project, I wanted to say again how much I've appreciated your advice, patience, and friendship.

They say that having somebody build a boat for you is a lot like getting married—you get to know each other really well, for better or for worse. It's been a joyous marriage for me!

You'll be getting a final payment on delivery of *Daisy Mae,* of course, but I want you to have this bonus as a small token of my appreciation.

Cheers,

Abner

Tears blurred Sarah's eyes as she read the note, and at first she had trouble reading the amount on Abner's check. "That note is so sweet." She deciphered the check. "There's got to be a mistake. That's so much money..."

"Half of it is yours," Oliver said. "I could never have finished the boat in time, or done as good a job, without your help."

"I don't want to be paid."

"Why the hell not? You certainly earned it."

"Because it makes me feel like an employee, that's why not."

"I have never, ever thought of you as an employee," he replied, irritated. "You mean a lot more to me than that."

Abner had talked about building a boat together as being like getting married. Perhaps he was right, which only muddied her churning feelings.

"I love you, Oliver," she said, just above a whisper, partly in hopes of thwarting the flapping ears in the next booth. "The last year has been like a dream. I feel like Abner, and that's part of the trouble—I'm scared that it will end and I'll wake up, and it will have all gone wrong."

"I'm not like Claude, but I don't know any way to prove it,"

Oliver replied in despair.

"It's not you, it's me. Things have changed so fast in the past year, it's like being caught in an avalanche. I need time."

* * *

They pulled into Oliver's yard at dusk, and Wes greeted them ecstatically as they opened the kitchen door.

The kitchen's back door opened onto a tiny porch, just big enough to hold two folding chairs, which provided a view across a small hay field with the woods behind it. The delicate, haunting call of a hermit thrush came from deep in the woods.

Of course the hay field was now home to Mabel's enclosure and Asim's teardrop camper. Sarah and Oliver settled into the chairs, counting on a light northerly breeze to keep the black flies at bay, May having finally decided to settle in and act like spring.

While his two humans took their ease, Wes galloped over to Mabel's enclosure, where the pachyderm and the pooch greeted each other like old friends.

"It didn't take long for that pair to become bosom buddies," Sarah commented. "Asim says that elephants have a very good sense of smell, like dogs, so they do have something in common. Maybe that's why they get along so well."

"It must be a whole different world for them—a world of subtle aromas that talk to them on a totally different level that we can't understand."

"Yes," Sarah replied vaguely, looking distracted.

Oliver followed her gaze to Asim's camper, where a dim light glowed through the window. "The man certainly keeps to himself."

"Very secretive. Not even Phoebe seems to know much about him." She glanced at Wes and Mabel. "Do you think it's safe to let

Wes get so close?

"'Trust animal wisdom,' as Ziggy keeps saying. So far they're just sniffing to get acquainted."

"When does sniffing turn to tusking?" Sarah mused.

"That's not a good attitude for somebody who's trying to prove Mabel's innocence. Don't you trust your client?"

Sarah sat for a while. "I'm not sure I even trust myself."

Oliver took her hand.

"Do *you* trust Mabel?" Sarah said.

"I trust her to be an elephant. What more can one ask? Life is full of risks. She doesn't strike me as being malicious, though. Or possessed by evil spirits, for that matter."

Sarah noticed that the light had gone out in Asim's camper. "Early to bed, early to rise," she said. "Let's go inside; it's getting buggy out here."

They made a pot of tea and sat at the kitchen table while Wes kept Mabel company.

"I was just thinking," Oliver said, "that Ziggy's place is empty right now, for the first time after dark since Mabel arrived and Bernie died—a chance for some nighttime treasure hunting."

A vague idea had been crawling out of the muck at the edge of Sarah's mind. At Oliver's words, it hopped back into deep water, like a skittish frog. "You're right. We need to call the Borofskys."

Oliver reached for the phone. Even as he did so, an idea crept into his mind—not a skittish frog, but a toothsome alligator.

Sarah watched, bemused by Oliver's sudden sense of urgency as he punched in the numbers.

The phone rang for some time before a sleepy-voiced Sasha picked up. "Do you know what hour it is, Oliver?"

"I'm sorry to wake you up, but this is important. Is Anton there?"

"He's gone back to The City for a few days. What do you want him for?"

"Are your doors locked?"

"Of course. We always lock the doors before going to bed, especially with our disreputable neighbors wandering around." Sasha was wide awake now. "Why do you ask?"

"I wonder if you'd do me a favor."

"What do you want?" she replied, sounding curious.

"Are your lights out upstairs?"

"That's a strange question."

"Are they?"

"Of course they're out. I was fast asleep until you woke me up."

"Good."

"Good that you woke me out of a sound sleep?"

"No. Good that your lights are off. You'll be able to see outside better. I want you to look out your dressing room window, and tell me what's going on next door."

A hint of coyness crept into her voice. "But I don't have any clothes on."

Oliver ground his teeth. "All you need to do is look out the window—"

"With the lights out?"

"Yes. Please. It could be important." Or he could be making a fool of himself, Oliver thought glumly.

"You'll be sorry if I trip over something while I'm hobbling around in the dark," she said peevishly. Oliver could hear Sasha muttering as made her way to the dressing room window, her cell phone in hand.

"There's nothing out there. Wait...I can see a light."

"Where is it?"

"Next door, of course," she said impatiently.

"Where, next door?"

"Where the elephant pen used to be. I can see a light moving around there, like somebody is looking for something."

"Call the police, and don't let anybody in, especially not any of Pastor Briskin's people."

"You sound very mysterious, Oliver. I'm all a-tingle. It's just Nika and me here. What if someone tries to force their way in?"

"Call the police, *now,*" Oliver repeated. He figured the Borofsky's massive doors would require some time, and an almighty-great battering ram, to break down. On the other hand, Nika, a small, mousy woman, wouldn't be able to put up much of a fight if an intruder did get in.

"Could you come over and stay for the night?"

"I'll be over tomorrow morning to talk."

"I thought you wouldn't do that unless Anton was here. You must be loosening up."

"I'm making an exception, because there may be a killer out there, and I think it would be best not to let anybody in."

"Not even Pastor Briskin?"

"Not even Pastor Briskin." Oliver wished that he knew who to trust. "Call the state police and tell them there's a prowler."

"I'll call that cute-looking sheriff, Charlie Howes."

"The state police would be better at this time of night." Poor Charlie was just a part-time deputy who wouldn't be happy to be called out so late.

"But I don't know the state police, and I do know Charlie."

"Fine. Call Charlie. Just do it now."

Sarah gave Oliver a questioning look as he put the phone down.

"I feel sorry for poor Charlie," Oliver muttered. "He's in for a long night."

Meanwhile, Sarah had captured her skittish frog. "I think I

might know who killed Bernie."

Oliver listened as she talked.

"I know it's thin," she concluded.

"Your theory may be thin, but it's the best we've got, especially where we don't even know for sure why Bernie was killed." Oliver thought about his alligator and added, "Though I think I know how we may be able to narrow down things down."

"It sounds like we need to make some plans," Sarah said when he'd finished talking.

Chapter 23

Once again, May tried to drive Maine's residents mad. Having sweltered yesterday, a cold front was due to sweep through later today, and tonight would drop into the forties.

At least the black flies would be held at bay.

These thoughts weighed on Oliver's mind as he knocked on the Borofsky's door Friday morning.

Nika wordlessly escorted him to the study, where Sasha sat on the sofa in front of the fireplace.

The lady of the manor wore a baggy sweatshirt and baggy sweat pants. She looked at him coldly through baggy, bloodshot eyes. The lack of any make-up made the facial disaster complete.

To Oliver, she seemed to have aged a decade in the last twenty-four hours. The "term beauty sleep" was obviously more than an abstract notion in Sasha Borofsky's world. If only Sarah could see her now, he thought. He sat down in a nearby armchair. "How are you doing this morning?"

"You're like a ghoul at a traffic accident," Sasha snarled. "How does it look like I'm doing?"

A cold front had already swept through Borofsky Castle.

Oliver assumed the question was rhetorical. "I could come back later, if you like."

Sasha wasn't about to let him off the hook that easily, however. "Thanks to you, I was up most of last night, being abused by your precious sheriff. I'm not accustomed to being bawled out by some hick cop."

"You didn't call the state police?" Oliver said tentatively.

"I certainly did. I filed a complaint against the sheriff for his rudeness."

"So the police didn't find any sign of the prowler?"

"Of course not. The idiot sheriff told me to turn on all the floodlights when I called him, 'for my safety,' he said. It was all I could do to get him to come over at all."

Oliver scolded himself. He should have realized that Charlie would have her turn on the outside lights. It was the sensible thing, after all. "He was probably in bed when you called," Oliver said mildly.

"So what? It's his job to come when he's called. On top of that, all the running around last night has made my leg worse."

"I'm sorry to hear that."

"Anton is going to be furious with you when he gets back," Sasha said venomously.

"When does he get back?"

"The day after tomorrow, and I'm sure he'll deal with you harshly for stirring up all this trouble."

"Would you rather have had a killer wandering around your back yard?"

"Anton wouldn't have bothered with those worthless cops. He'd have gone out and nabbed the prowler, or whatever he was, all by himself."

"I'm sure he would have," Oliver replied soothingly.

"I should have gone out myself. And I would have if my leg was better."

"Confronting him would have been very dangerous."

"So *you* say."

"You didn't catch a glimpse of him yourself?"

"It was too dark over there, and he must have run like a rabbit the minute the floodlights came on."

Sasha grumbled for a while before saying, "You talked about having some questions when you called?"

"I was wondering if you might have seen anything unusual at Ziggy's place earlier, like—"

"Unusual?" Sasha broke in. "You mean besides Breener, babbling nonsense behind his Gabby Hayes beard, or Briskin the truck driver who pretends to be Moses, or the homicidal circus elephant?"

Oliver wondered morosely why nobody seemed willing to let him finish a sentence lately. "Sorry, I didn't phrase that very well—"

"I should say not."

Oliver tried again. "What I meant to ask was if you had seen anybody with an old bicycle over there."

"You mean besides Breener's bicycle?"

"This one would be much older and rustier."

"I don't make a habit of spying on the neighbors," Sasha said primly, "but I do glance out the window occasionally, especially since I haven't been able ride my own bike after the accident."

"This would be down by the shore."

"You know perfectly well that I can't see down that way. The angle is wrong. I did have a good view of the elephant before she was taken away, though," Sasha grumbled. "I don't see why somebody shot at her. There are too many would-be Daniel Boones around here."

"So you didn't see anybody carrying an old bicycle past your window to the road?"

"Not while I was looking. I don't watch all the time, for heaven's sake, and somebody could have taken it away along the shore where I couldn't see." Sasha paused. "I did see the archeologist, but he didn't have a bicycle."

"You saw Bert last night?"

"Yesterday evening around dusk, after everybody had left."

"What was he doing?"

"He went down to the shore, where I couldn't see."

"I thought he quit Wednesday." Oliver wondered what Bert was doing here two days after he'd quit.

"I suppose."

"Did he stay down there very long?"

"Not too long."

"Was he carrying anything when he came back?"

"He might have had a shovel."

"A shovel?"

"Or something in his hand."

"You couldn't tell for sure?"

"It was getting dark."

Prying anything useful out of Sasha was starting to be heavy going as she rapidly lost interest in Oliver's questions.

"You're not making any sense," she said. "Why would anybody care about Bert Farley, or a rusty old bicycle?"

Had Sasha mistaken Bert's metal detector for a shovel in the semi-darkness? "It's probably nothing, but still—"

"I'm tired of talking about all the sordid business next door," Sasha announced. "I need to take a nap after last night."

"I have one more favor to ask before you do that," Oliver said.

"*Another* favor? After last night's fiasco?"

* * *

The mood at Ziggy's estate was a lot more upbeat than the climate at Borofsky Castle when Sarah pulled into the driveway and parked. She was greeted by Ziggy and Pastor Briskin, who were watching Dudley work with the excavator. He seemed to have mastered the machine at last, and was tidily leveling the last traces of Myra's house foundation.

"Good morning, Sister Sarah," the cheerful cleric said. "I trust that Mabel and Asim have settled in?"

"Beware of the elephant," Ziggy warned in a low voice.

"Why don't you like elephants?" Sarah inquired.

"I don't like that elephant," Ziggy replied. "She has a bad aura."

"You've said that about Myra, too," Sarah pointed out.

Ziggy stared at her, goggle-eyed. "I have?" His eyebrows crept upward into his watch cap as he considered the implications. "Could the astral planes intersect...?"

Sarah cringed at the idea of Myra's ghost taking possession of an elephant. What had she just done to Ziggy's mind? What bizarre notion had she planted in the Can Man's fevered brain, and where would he go with it? She should never have mentioned Myra and Mabel in the same breath. "For heaven's sake, that's not what I—"

"I won't have any more of this heathenish talk!" Pastor Briskin exploded. "Mabel is a poor, harmless beast! She doesn't share *anything* with Myra Huggard!"

"There are things in the universe that are beyond our comprehension," Ziggy replied cryptically.

Pastor Briskin took a deep breath. And then another. "Perhaps, Brother Breener—and I say this in a loving fashion—Satan has an icy grip on your heart, and that is why you speak in this strange way."

Ziggy looked at his companion impassively, apparently too absorbed by thoughts of Myra and Mabel to worry about anything as trivial as mere Satanic possession.

Undeterred, Pastor Briskin went on. "There are people who don't come to our little church, Brother Breener; people who don't hear the Good News; people who don't accept Jesus into their hearts; people who don't seek salvation. Nevertheless, I welcome them all, unbelievers though they may be, for I know that someday Jesus will touch their hearts and they will see The Light." He glared meaningfully at the Can Man.

Ziggy's gaze swept over the newly cleared land—a patch of ground shorn of most of its trees, laid bare, transformed from the woodsy thicket of brush and saplings it had been a few short weeks ago. He gave no sign of seeing The Light, or hearing Pastor Briskin's words at all, for that matter. "Once again, oh Ditch Lady, you've offered a great insight. We must listen to the elephant, not the chicken coop, in order to hear Myra's voice."

"Ziggy—" Sarah began.

"I must do my morning rounds," Ziggy interrupted as he turned away and walked slowly over to where his bucket-laden bicycle leaned against a tree.

Pastor Briskin watched him go. "Our Brother is still grieving Myra's death, and this," his arm swept the construction site, "is difficult for him."

Yes, as Kate had said, change was difficult. "Myra was a bigger-than-life person." She put her hand on Pastor Briskin's arm. "We need to talk."

It took a while to explain, but Pastor Briskin looked at her thoughtfully for a moment when she had finished. "Your plan troubles me. Are you sure this scheme will work? Have you cast a wide enough net in your investigation of Brother Bernie's death?"

"Do you have any other ideas? Do you think Mabel killed Bernie, after all?"

"I'm beginning to be afraid that she didn't. Have you considered

Anton Borofsky, or Bert Farley, or Brian Curtis? What about Asim Okiro?"

"Yes, I have thought about them. They all wanted to see the last of Mabel, except for Asim, and who knows what he wants?"

"I know my flock, and I can't imagine any of them murdering Bernie Knowles," he said solemnly. "And I can't imagine any of them trying to shoot a poor, defenseless elephant, either." He shook his head sadly. "And yet imagination can fail us at times. It's a sin of pride to be too sure that you know what another person could or couldn't do."

Or what an elephant could do, Sarah thought. "We know that Mabel has killed twice before," She pointed out. "Bernie may be her third victim. It could be as simple as that."

"A comforting hope, but I'm afraid that your quest will bring us still more grief." He gave her a sad, haunted look. "I need to go and pray about this." With those words, he walked off.

Sarah wandered around by herself, feeling out of place, and looking halfheartedly for any relics from Myra's past.

She was relieved when Oliver walked in the driveway. She gave him a long hug.

"You look a bit lost," Oliver commented.

She felt more than a bit lost. "Ziggy and Pastor Briskin had another spat."

"It's always dangerous to put two idealists together, especially when they don't agree," Oliver said. "And Pastor Briskin is under a lot of stress, what with losing most of the funding for his camp."

"I hope he doesn't back out of our scheme. He was sounding mushy a minute ago."

Oliver smiled. "Describing him as being 'mushy' is a stretch for me. The man may be stressed, but I think he'll do the right thing in the end." Oliver paused "You didn't tell him about your elephant theory?"

"No. I thought that part might be too dangerous, and it's just a theory. He's already struggling with the possibility that one of his flock may be a killer."

"That's not only possible, but likely even, though Sasha saw Bert Farley prowling around just before dark, which makes him a promising candidate. He apparently went down to the shore and came back a little later."

"So we have to add another treasure hunter to the list? Was Bert carrying a treasure chest when he left?"

"He might have been carrying a metal detector, but it was too dark for Sasha to be sure," Oliver replied. "But hope springs eternal for treasure hunters and he might have come back later, after dark. Unfortunately, treasure hunting and murder seem to go hand in hand."

"Sad but true. Did you get anything else out of Sasha?"

"She didn't see the late-night prowler, or so she said. Charlie told her to turn on the lights when she called him."

"A sensible precaution, unfortunately. And it could have been Bert, back again to do some treasure hunting."

"Maybe he forgot something else."

Sarah nodded. "What about Betty Boop?"

"Nothing there, either."

"Speaking of nothing, what was Sasha wearing this morning?"

"A big, baggy sweater. She must have been pretty thoroughly banged up."

"I actually could feel sorry for her. What about the other thing?"

"I think she'll do it," Oliver replied uncertainly.

"You don't sound convinced."

"It took a lot of persuading."

"Luckily, you have a way with the ladies," Sarah said, giving him a kiss on the cheek.

"The woman is unpredictable in a lot ways, and she's been

acting strangely since her accident."

"Her looks are very important to her self-esteem."

"I just hope she doesn't go ballistic and come apart. I might have had better luck selling this scheme to Anton. He's a lot more stable than Sasha right now."

"Don't underestimate her. She's tougher than she seems. And smarter, too."

"Let's just hope this works, for Mabel's sake."

"Time will tell," Sarah said philosophically. "I'm going to stop and visit Kate for a bit to make sure she'll be okay for the rest of the day, and then I'll come up to help with *Daisy Mae* around lunch time."

Chapter 24

A cool north wind was rattling the doors of the boatshop when Oliver got back home around mid-morning—not a good situation when one wants to put varnish on a boat. Fuming over the unseasonable weather, Oliver puttered around *Daisy Mae,* doing odds and ends. Wes, picking up on his master's restlessness, trailed along behind.

Oliver wondered what summer would bring to his relationship with Sarah. Was she going to spend the summer at the Merlew's again? Would she even stay in Maine this year? He realized with a twinge that he'd assumed a lot, perhaps too much, about their relationship, and their future.

These gloomy thoughts were interrupted by Wes, whose infallible nose for trouble sent him leaping down the driveway, shattering the mid-morning air with his most piercing doomsday howl.

Oliver stepped out of the shop to see an all-to-familiar semi laboring up the driveway.

"What brings you here," Oliver said to Phoebe as she dropped down from the cab.

She looked surprised. "Didn't Asim tell you? I'm taking Mabel away."

"Taking her away? Again?" Oliver wondered if his call to the Hart's Ridge Zoo yesterday morning had triggered this latest move. "Where is she going this time?"

"Nobody's told me that little detail," Phoebe said peevishly. "This is no way do to business, I can tell you that much." She looked around. "Where is everybody?"

"Asim went off to run some errands about an hour ago," Oliver said.

"He'd better bring back a work crew soon. I'm supposed to be loaded up and on the road by one o'clock."

"One o'clock? It's after ten now. What's the rush?"

"I just take orders."

"Nobody told me anything about this," Oliver grumbled.

Just then, Asim rattled up the driveway in his loaner. "You're early," He said as he strode up.

"Where's your work crew? I haven't got all day."

"We can start without them," Asim replied.

"I hate to ask this," Oliver said, "considering how much I'd like to see the last of Mabel, but have you talked to the police? Have they given you permission to take her out of town?"

"What do the police have to do with anything?" Phoebe said sharply.

"According to what the sheriff told me, the investigation into Bernie's death is still ongoing," Oliver wondered where Charlie was. Wasn't he supposed to be "discreetly guarding" Mabel? The deputy's idea of discreet seemed a bit casual to Oliver. Perhaps some crisis, or pure boredom, had drawn him away from his sentry duty.

"Ongoing? What's to investigate?" Phoebe said, staring suspiciously at Asim. "I thought it was just another accident, another elephant oops-a-daisy. What's the problem?"

"She was framed," Asim insisted stubbornly. "That permission business is just a bunch of bureaucratic red tape. Move the truck around back so we can start taking down the enclosure."

"My rig isn't moving a goddam inch until I get a green light from the cops," Phoebe said angrily. "Do you know how much sleep I've lost, driving back and forth like a yo-yo every day, just to move your fool elephant around?"

Asim opened his mouth to speak, but she cut him off.

"And don't try to sweet-talk me about how much I'm being paid. This whole deal stinks, and now you want me to interfere with a police investigation? And to top it off, you don't even have a crew to help load up? I'm fed up with you and your damn elephant!"

Asim glared at her. "Do you think I enjoy this? I'm having trouble enough just trying to keep Mabel alive without you giving me grief."

"That animal is your problem. Do you know how much trouble *I* could get into, smuggling a hot elephant around the country?"

"Mabel is not a 'hot' elephant—"

"Look, McTavish Transport stretched the rules when you first came to us, but enough is enough. I'm not going to take a chance on having the state police impound our rig. Get permission from the cops." Phoebe crossed her arms with an air of finality.

"Mabel is the victim here," Asim pleaded. "Don't you care about that?"

"I care more about not turning into a victim myself."

"The zoo would probably be willing to pay you an extra bonus for the job."

"Just how much is an elephant worth?" Oliver inquired.

Asim scowled. "What? Are you trying to put a price on Mabel's head?"

"I'm trying to understand why a zoo would spend so much time and money to move an elephant around the country, and so far nobody seems to have an explanation."

Phoebe nodded. "I've been wondering that, too. How about it, elephant man?"

"This isn't any of your concern. Either of you," Asim said.

"It's my rig; it's my concern."

"Let me make a guess," Oliver said. "We know Mabel killed twice before—" He held up his hand to silence Asim. "I'm sure it was an accident, both times."

"Mabel was devastated each time," Asim said sadly.

Oliver wondered how one could tell when an elephant was devastated. Had she been devastated by Bernie's death? She had seemed moody, but what did that really mean? "I'm sure her previous victims' next of kin were devastated, too. One accident like that is understandable, but two accidents must raise alarm bells—"

"I told you Ray's death was because he violated the zoo's safety rules," Asim interrupted. "The lawyers and insurance people are in the process of settling all that."

"So your job is to keep Mabel out of sight until an agreement is signed?"

"Yes. It's only for a few more days. Lawyers are slow."

"What about the private eye?" Phoebe said. "Does he go away once the lawyers sign off?"

"Of course. I told you it would all blow over."

"Suppose the lawyers can't agree? Lawyers can be troublesome that way," Oliver said.

Asim looked impatient. "They already have an agreement. It's just a matter of putting it all in writing."

"What if the agreement falls through?"

Asim gave Oliver a sad, defeated look. "They'd probably have to put her down."

"It sounds like that might be for the best," Phoebe murmured. "Three deaths..."

They looked at Mabel silently for a moment. She stood by the fence looking back, unaware that her life was hanging by a thread.

"I suppose the Hart's Ridge Zoo bought Mabel from her previous owner after the first accident?" Oliver said, breaking the gloomy spell.

Asim nodded. "It was all done quietly. The previous zoo didn't feel they could keep her after the incident, and the Hart's Ridge Zoo was looking for an elephant. They even changed her name. It was best for all concerned."

"How long have you known Mabel?" Phoebe said.

"Since she came to the Harts Ridge Zoo—not that long, when I think about it now. I thought I knew her, and that she was just near-sighted and a little clumsy." He looked back at Mabel again. "People just don't understand. Elephants aren't like other animals. They're really smart, and they have human emotions: love, compassion, loyalty, a sense of right and wrong. Just look into an elephant's eyes, and you can see what I mean. She's like a daughter to me."

"The zoo is taking advantage of your feelings, Asim," Phoebe said gently. "They're using you to protect themselves. Don't you see that they're setting you up to take the fall, to be the bad guy?"

Chapter 25

Phoebe flatly refused to take Mabel away, despite a long and furtive phone conversation between her and, Oliver suspected, the Hart's Ridge zoo. The heated discussion between the dwarfish trucker and the towering elephant-keeper dragged on, fueled in large part by the absence of Pastor Briskin's work crew.

Oliver drifted off after a while and decided to pick up lunch in Rockland where he'd be free of the bickering. Besides, Wes loved car trips and he'd been neglected the last few days.

* * *

Thanks to a southwest wind, the afternoon had turned much warmer by the time Oliver and Wes got back from lunch. The first thing he noticed was that Phoebe's semi was gone, and so was Asim's rusted loaner, along with his camper. Wes rocketed around back to check on his new friend, but Mabel was gone as well. The quarrelsome duo had obviously come to an agreement, but where had they taken Mabel?

Stranger still, they had left her pen behind. Wherever she was headed must have an enclosure of its own. Was she going back to the Hart's Ridge Zoo to face possible execution?

Oliver watched for a moment while Wes snuffled around the empty enclosure, sniffed the air, and whined unhappily for his missing friend. Maybe they'd just gotten tired of waiting for Pastor Briskin's crew and left without the pen. If so, why the rush?

Oliver had picked up some groceries, and he called Wes away from his fruitless elephant hunt. The pair went inside to put the food away.

He and Wes were still inside when Sarah called.

"I managed to persuade Kate to take a nap, so she's pretty well settled for the afternoon," Sarah said. "Any news up there in elephant-land?"

Oliver filled her in, concluding, "I can understand why the zoo might want to move Mabel after getting my call yesterday, but how much longer can they keep up this game of hide and seek?"

"Moving her is getting to be as hard as hiding her," Sarah said. "I wonder why Pastor Briskin's work crew didn't turn up on schedule to help move Mabel."

"Interesting question. I've been wondering about that, too. Maybe he had trouble lining up anybody on such short notice."

"Or maybe he doesn't want Mabel moved," Sarah said. "It's money out of his pocket if the zoo takes her away, and it's hard to imagine that he'd want to be involved with moving an elephant that's on the lam. They could be taking her almost anywhere, so long as they stay one step ahead of the police."

"It would have to be somewhere that Phoebe approves of," Oliver concluded. "Maybe Asim persuaded her that you'd prove Mabel's innocence, as Pastor Briskin keeps saying."

"Stop reminding me about Pastor Briskin," Sarah grumbled.

"Anyway, I'm heading over to Ziggy's place in a little while to see how things are going."

"Why don't you pick me up at the Merlew's," Sarah suggested. "That way there won't be so many cars to deal with later."

* * *

Oliver had just hung up the phone when a black SUV pulled up to the kitchen door. Why, Oliver wondered, was his life suddenly cluttered up with black SUV's?

He went outside to speak with a rumpled looking young man who waved a card announcing that he was a private investigator. "Are you the owner of Ziggy's Zoo?" he asked.

"I am not, thank God," Oliver replied fervently. "Where did you get that idea?"

The gumshoe ignored Oliver's question. "Do you have an elephant here?"

"Not anymore. They took her away this afternoon while I was out."

Oliver's visitor looked decidedly unhappy with that piece of news. "Where is the elephant now?"

"First of all," Oliver said, irritated, "Mabel is not my responsibility, and second, nobody told me they were going to take her away, or where. Come to think of it, they didn't really tell me she was coming here in the first place."

"And you have no idea where the elephant went?" the detective said, his voice dripping with disbelief. "What about Asim Okiro? Do you know where he is?"

"He's probably with Mabel. Why don't you ask the zoo that owns her?"

The detective gave Oliver a threatening look. "That elephant is a material witness in a possible lawsuit, and I need to get a deposition from Asim Okiro."

"Are you going to get a statement from Mabel, too?"

"This is no joke, Mr. Wendell. You could be prosecuted for harboring a fugitive."

"Harboring a fugitive?"

"I know that the man who was trampled last week at the Hart's Ridge zoo was killed by the elephant you call Mabel. I also think the same elephant killed a man three years ago at another zoo. All we need is proof that it's the same animal."

"You want Mabel's DNA?"

The detective nodded. "My clients are angry that the Hart's Ridge Zoo apparently hid the elephant's past by changing her name when they bought her."

"I thought it was all settled that the maintenance worker was at fault for being in her pen alone."

"It was settled until she killed again up here. It's one thing to go into a harmless elephant's pen when you shouldn't be there, but it's quite another thing if that elephant happens to be a serial killer, and the zoo was hiding the fact."

"What makes a serial killer?"

The detective frowned. "Two deaths in two weeks, for starters. More important, it raises the question of whether the zoo is criminally liable for secretly harboring a dangerous animal. That throws any settlement out the window."

"And opens the door to a major lawsuit," Oliver murmured. It wasn't reassuring to learn that his guess had been right.

"My client has a right to see justice done. Three strikes and you're out, as the saying goes."

"Aren't you jumping the gun? The police haven't ruled that

Mabel killed Bernie. Maybe she was framed."

"And maybe pigs can fly. I plan to have all my ducks in a row when the police rule that the elephant killed your friend."

It looked like Mabel's visit to Maine might have started off as the zoo's attempt to keep Mabel out of the limelight while they negotiated a settlement, but Bernie's death had obviously raised the stakes. No wonder Asim and the zoo were so anxious to keep her out of sight.

Chapter 26

It was almost four o'clock when Oliver stopped by to pick up Sarah at the Merlews. He spent a few minutes visiting with Kate and Sam, who both assured Sarah that she didn't need to spend another night "baby sitting," as Kate put it.

"I don't think Charlie Howes likes me anymore." Oliver commented as he and Sarah got into his Honda. "He blames me for Sasha's phone call last night."

"I don't like Charlie all that much either, considering his attitude towards Betty Boop. What did he say about our scheme?"

"He's not a happy camper. At first he said no." Oliver paused. "Actually, he said a lot more than that, but it all boiled down to no. An emphatic no. I had to have Pearly talk to him before he agreed to go along. Unhappily, I might add."

"Good for Uncle Pearly."

"All of which proves once again that blood is thicker than water," Oliver said

"The important thing is that Charlie will go along."

"Don't expect any enthusiasm. I shouldn't have called Sasha last night. It would have worked out fine if the cops had caught the prowler, instead of letting him get away."

"Of course you should have called her, for heaven's sake. After all, there might have been a killer wandering around out there." Sarah paused. "Do you think Sasha might be in danger?"

"Only if somebody thought she saw too much. She didn't seem worried, though. Mad at me yes, worried about her safety, no."

"Sasha, Charlie, Phoebe, Asim, Mabel, and a gumshoe," Sarah grumbled. "You have altogether too much fun when I'm not around." She was quiet for a moment. "I made a counter offer on my house this morning."

"Does the Realtor think they'll accept it?"

"If they want the place badly enough. Or they might make a counter-counter offer."

"What's the least you can live with?" Oliver said.

"Here you are being practical about what I can live with, when I'm not even sure what I can live without."

* * *

Sarah and Oliver pulled into Ziggy's driveway, where Pastor Briskin and Ziggy stood watching while Dudley deftly uprooted a tree stump.

"You are a sad disappointment, Brother Oliver," Pastor Briskin said by way of a greeting.

"And how is that?"

"You had our poor, overworked sheriff wandering around last night, looking for some imaginary prowler."

"I told Sasha to call the state police."

"You didn't think our deputy sheriff was competent to deal with a simple prowler, if there was one?"

Oliver hated lose-lose conversations. "I didn't think it was fair to get Charlie out of bed, when the state police were available," he replied peevishly.

Pastor Briskin grumbled and turned to Sarah. "You were supposed to prove that Mabel was innocent, instead you're just stirring up trouble. I'm not sure you should go on with your investigation."

Sarah struggled to rein in her temper. "I thought we'd been through all that. A member of your church was murdered, and if Mabel didn't do it, then one of your flock is the most likely a killer. You can't have it both ways."

"There's a hawk amongst the flock of doves," Ziggy commented.

"Your words are not helpful," the disgruntled pastor informed Ziggy.

"It's very likely that the killer was right here last night," Oliver said.

"What have you done with Mabel?" Sarah said, going on the attack.

Pastor Briskin gave her a startled look. "She's at Brother Oliver's place, of course."

"Not any more," Oliver said. "Mabel, Asim, and Phoebe disappeared earlier this afternoon. The only thing they left behind is the pen."

Pastor Briskin looked him, appalled. "This is a disaster. The poor beast will be killed."

"Asim didn't call you about getting a work crew? You didn't know that she was going to be taken away?" Sarah said.

"I would have stopped them if I had known they were planning to kidnap her." Pastor Briskin turned to Oliver. "You should never have called the zoo. They called me and were very upset. I expect they feel threatened."

"They feel threatened, all right. And they have reason to," Oliver replied.

"Mabel knows who the killer is," Ziggy announced.

"Especially if Mabel happens to be the killer," Pastor Briskin grumbled.

"You figured it out, didn't you?" Oliver said to Ziggy.

Ziggy bowed to Sarah. "I saw the connection between Myra, money, and murder, but you showed me the connection between Myra and Mabel. You closed the astral loop."

"Astral loop? Why must I suffer this constant barrage of babble?" Pastor Briskin growled. "Your endless double-talk drives me mad, Breener.

"It's not double-talk," Sarah said.

"You saw it too?" Ziggy said delightedly.

"It came to me last night."

"What came to you?" Pastor Briskin said.

"It's simplicity itself," Ziggy said. "When you think back—"

"Explain it later," Oliver interrupted, looking over the Can Man's shoulder. "We've got company coming."

Pastor Briskin opened his mouth to object but stopped when he spotted Sasha Borofsky marching in the driveway while gamely trying to hide her limp.

"This does not bode well for the afternoon," Ziggy muttered.

Stalking up to Oliver, Sasha said, "I talked to Anton on the phone, and he holds you responsible for what happened last night."

"Me responsible? How is that? What did I do?" Oliver said incredulously.

"I warned you about this," Sarah murmured.

"He blames you, too," Sasha informed Sarah. "He'll deal with both of you when he gets back!"

Pastor Briskin, championing the underdog, stepped into the breach. "They were just trying to prove that Mabel didn't kill

Brother Bernie, though they haven't done a very good job, so far."

"Don't try to defend them, you bible-thumping fraud!" Sasha screeched. "You're the one who brought that murderous elephant into the neighborhood! You'll pay for this, along with the rest of them!"

"I thought you liked Mabel," Oliver said.

The remainder of Pastor Briskin's workers ambled over to enjoy the excitement.

"Now, Sister Sasha, Mabel isn't a—"

"I am NOT your sister!" Sasha, her face purple with fury, stamped her foot—the one at the end of her injured leg—gasped with pain and nearly fell to the ground. Ziggy caught her just in time.

"Get your hands off me you mangy bum!"

"I am not mangy," Ziggy replied stiffly. "You, however, should be more careful not to aggravate your injuries."

Sasha rounded on her tormentors like an enraged bull. "I will *not* be treated like a fool! All of you will regret this when Anton gets back!"

Pastor Briskin struck a conciliatory pose. "Surely we can avoid making threats, Sis—, er Mrs. Borofsky."

"Threats! You haven't seen anything yet! I'm not going to stay here and take any more abuse from the likes of you!" Ziggy reached for her arm as she raised her foot for another stamp.

Sasha caught herself and breathed heavily for a moment through bared, clenched teeth. "If I had my way," she said slowly, and with deadly malice, "and if I could do it, I'd have you all arrested for harassment, but Anton wants Nika and me to leave town until he gets back tomorrow. It's disgraceful when a person isn't safe in her own home because the neighbors are murderers, and the police won't do their job!" She turned on Pastor Briskin. "You'll get your own judgment day when Anton gets back, mark my words!" With that, Sasha stalked lopsidedly down the driveway towards Borofsky Castle.

It's too bad, Sarah thought, that the Borofskys didn't have a moat around their palace. A moat that would keep them inside, and the world safe outside.

"We must pray that the poor woman finds peace," Pastor Briskin said as he watched her back receding down the driveway.

"That's not quite what I'd expected," Oliver murmured to Sarah.

"It was a lot more than I expected," Sarah replied. "I wonder what else Anton said to her on the phone, other than telling her to leave town."

"Whatever he said certainly got her worked up."

Sarah nodded, and leaned close to whisper in Oliver's ear. "Ziggy could be in danger if he's really figured out who the killer is, the same way we did."

"Assuming we're right."

"It is a big assumption, but Ziggy could very well spill the beans to the wrong person."

"I'll warn him, and make sure he stays close by," Oliver said.

"I'll make sure you two aren't interrupted, at least until Charlie gets here."

Oliver took Ziggy aside and spoke quietly in his ear. The Can Man looked unhappy.

Sarah gave the pair a worried look. Would their scheme work, or were things already spinning out of control? Who could she trust in this bunch? She knew what Kate would say, and Oliver too: One can't get anywhere without trusting someone.

The trick was to find the right someone.

Chapter 27

Friday night was cloudy and cool as Ziggy, Sarah, Oliver, and a reluctant Charlie Howes sat in the thick underbrush. Their hiding place on the edge of Brian Curtis' lot provided them with a good view of the spot where Mabel, the well-traveled elephant, had been penned. At least it would have provided a good view if it weren't for clouds hiding the moon.

"Just so we're clear: I'm not going to arrest anybody," Charlie whispered. "All we're doing is observing."

"Of course," Sarah replied.

"Observing, like a pack of frozen penguins," Ziggy added, shivering.

"Bring warmer clothes next time," Charlie replied with a notable lack of sympathy. He turned to Oliver. "For all we know, last night was just some kind of naturalist, collecting nocturnal lizards, or whatever naturalists collect at night."

"Nocturnal lizards?" Ziggy said.

Charlie's scowl was lost in the darkness. "I'm just saying that this is probably one of your treasure hunters, or some innocent person with insomnia, or something like that. Your land isn't posted, after all."

"I welcome all, except killers of people and elephants," Ziggy replied.

Charlie muttered under his breath. "Second night in a row, I'm over here when I could be sleeping in my nice, warm bed. The only reason I'm here at all is because Pearly says that you clowns aren't as crazy as you seem."

"Thank you," Oliver said formally. "That's generous of him."

Charlie turned to Sarah and Oliver, indistinct blobs in the darkness. "Just don't give me a hard time."

"They are friends in need," Ziggy replied in a solemn whisper. "Ditch Lady Sarah sniffs out evil from the ditches of life."

"Ditches? Evil?"

"Don't get him started," Sarah hissed. "Did you talk to Bert Farley about why he was here yesterday evening?"

"Yes, I did, and he said he'd forgotten one of his shovels and came back to get it. Apparently, Briskin's crew weren't very friendly, so he waited until they were gone before coming back."

"They think he's trying to steal the Huggard's treasure," Oliver said.

"There isn't any treasure," Ziggy said.

"Whoever killed Bernie might have thought otherwise," Charlie replied.

"Or maybe not," Sarah murmured.

"How did I let myself get talked into sitting around in the dark with a bunch of nut-cases?" Charlie grumbled. "I don't get paid enough for this stuff. Another half hour, and we're out of here."

They didn't have to wait that long. Somebody wearing a headlamp appeared from behind the excavator.

"There's our sleepwalker," Charlie muttered.

"Or maybe our treasure hunter," Sarah replied.

"Or our killer," Oliver whispered.

"The only killer around here is Breener's elephant," Charlie rasped. "And I don't want to hear any more of that crazy elephant whisperer stuff. I got enough of that baloney already."

"Is it Myra and money, or Mabel and murder? That is the question," Ziggy murmured.

"I'm betting on the second choice," Sarah said softly.

"We'll see soon enough," Oliver whispered.

"Put a sock in it," Charlie muttered.

The stranger's headlight bobbed to and fro as he made his way across the rough, uneven ground. As he got closer, they could see a metal detector in one hand, and digging tools in the other. He put the tools down, and began to walk methodically up and down Mabel's former enclosure, sweeping the metal detector back and forth.

"Must be your treasure hunter, all right," Charlie whispered.

"There is no treasure," Ziggy replied. "Myra had no money."

"So you say, but I've heard talk over the years about buried gold."

"Haven't we all," Sarah said.

"There is no treasure," Ziggy repeated.

"Anyway, it's not necessarily illegal to look for buried treasure on someone else's land.

"There is no treasure."

"Well, he's looking for it, even so," Charlie replied, "and stop trying to get my goat."

They watched for almost half an hour while the stranger slowly walked back and forth, sweeping the metal detector from side to side, and occasionally stopping to reexamine a particular spot. The land inside Mabel's former enclosure was filled with dips, hollows, and tree stumps, all of which made for slow going.

"Didn't the Huggards have a trash pile somewhere?" Charlie whispered.

"It was closer to the house," Ziggy replied. "This was all thick woods back then."

"Whatever he's looking for must be pretty small, considering how slowly he's going," Oliver whispered.

Sarah was getting colder and colder.

Charlie must have been, too, because he shifted slightly, as though to get up. Oliver put a restraining hand on his shoulder and whispered in his ear, "Let's wait a bit longer. He hasn't got much more ground to cover."

Sure enough, the treasure hunter stopped suddenly at a small hollow and carefully swept his metal detector over the patch of ground. Apparently satisfied, he put the metal detector down on the spot, retrieved his pick and shovel, and began digging.

Chapter 28

"Geez, Harvey," Charlie said, as he emerged from the brush and aimed his flashlight at the mystery man, "if you wanted to do some treasure hunting, why didn't you just ask Ziggy instead of sneaking around in the dark like this?"

Startled, Harvey dropped the shovel as his headlight swept over the unexpected arrivals. "I didn't think he'd say yes," Harvey said. The light jiggled as he shrugged. "I'd have shared anything I found."

"Let's see what you did find," Sarah said brightly.

"I didn't find anything." Harvey sounded sullen.

"It sure looked like you did, Harv," Charlie said.

"I'll dig," Oliver offered, picking up the shovel. "It's probably not too far down, considering the soil here is hard-packed blue clay."

"Almost as hard as concrete," Sarah commented. She turned to Harvey. "You haven't had any luck looking around here, have you? Not with Mabel living in the middle of your search area."

"Especially when Mabel took such a dislike for you after Bernie died," Oliver added.

Harvey frowned at them. "That elephant is a killer. Look what she did to poor Bernie when he came in here at night."

"It was a lucky break for you when somebody took a shot at Mabel, and she and Asim left," Oliver said.

"The trouble was that even without Mabel and Asim there, Sasha saw you from her window last night and called the police," Sarah added.

"All I wanted to do was look for the Huggard's stash."

"I thought you didn't believe in the treasure," Sarah said.

"Maybe I changed my mind after all the talk."

"Maybe you changed your mind after Betty Boop turned up," Sarah suggested.

"Hold on a minute," Charlie interrupted as Harvey opened his mouth to speak. "You can't give Harvey a hard time just because he caught the treasure bug and decided to do a little harmless nighttime digging. Leave the poor man alone."

Oliver moved the metal detector from the spot where Harvey had carefully placed it, and sunk the shovel into the ground.

"Is that Bernie's metal detector?" Sarah said. Did you forget to give it back to his widow?"

"She let me borrow it."

It was heavy work to cut through the mat of dead leaves and roots, and Charlie took a turn with the shovel after a while.

"There could be anything buried there," Harvey grumbled as he watched the slow progress. "Who knows what you might find?"

"We know Bernie was doing some treasure hunting of his own," Oliver said. "Was he competing with you?"

"I didn't pay any attention to what Bernie was doing," Harvey said. "He did his thing and I did mine."

Charlie hacked at a root with the shovel. "That's a good policy, Harv. No point in picking a fight with an old friend, no matter how big the treasure might be."

Ziggy shook his head. "Two ghouls prowling around Myra's land. No wonder she's angry."

"Three ghouls, if you count Bert," Sarah said. "It's a good thing for Bert that he quit over Anton's phoney spearhead, since he was talking about bringing his metal detector into Mabel's enclosure after she left."

"Bert could have been a big problem if he'd stayed," Oliver said.

They had cut away the sod and packed roots from the area by now and were down to bare earth. Charlie put down the shovel and Oliver picked up the metal detector to sweep the area again. "There's metal right here," he said "It's small, and pretty close to the surface."

Charlie turned to Harvey. "Give Oliver your headlight, Harv, so he can see what he's doing."

Ziggy kneeled beside the hole and watched as Oliver carefully dug away the soil. The head light's battery was rapidly fading to a glimmer, so Charlie stood beside Harvey and helped illuminate the scene with his flashlight.

They found a heavily corroded clasp knife. Oliver wiped off the thick clay. It had the initials "EH" scratched into the plastic handle. Oliver handed it to Charlie, and glanced at Sarah, who looked back, her face white. He returned to the hole, where Ziggy was using a stick to scratch at the dirt.

"Those knives are common as dirt," Charlie said, oblivious to the irony. "Evan probably lost it here."

"And I wasted a whole evening, just to find Evan's old knife," Harvey said. "That's not much of a treasure. I don't know about you guys, but I'm freezing out here."

"Me too," Charlie agreed. He paused and rubbed his chin thoughtfully. "Of course, if somebody wanted to frame Evan, they could have scratched those initials on the handle pretty easily."

"Frame Evan? For what?" Harvey said.

Ziggy wasn't freezing from the cold anymore. His probing fingers had found a bone. And a fragment of cloth. "It looks like a human tibia and some clothing," he said, looking up at Charlie and pointing at his find. "This isn't about Myra and money; it's about Mabel and murder."

"Okay," the deputy sheriff said with a sigh, "I have no idea what you just said, but this doesn't look much like a treasure hunt anymore. We need to back away from here and call the state police."

"You don't think I have anything to do with Betsy Knowles, do you?" Harvey said.

"Why do you think that's Betsy Knowles?" Sarah said.

"Don't answer her, Harv," Charlie said. "I've had problems with this bunch before, and they love going around, stirring up trouble. That's probably just an old animal bone."

"I don't know what you're hinting at," Harvey said to Sarah, "but why would I dig her up if I'd buried her in the first place?"

"Because this is going to be a town park," Sarah said. "They'll have to dig out all the stumps, bulldoze it, and plant grass. With the body only a foot or two down, there's a good chance someone would find her, realize who it was and start to wonder what really happened. I'm surprised some animal didn't dig her up years ago."

"On top of that," Oliver said, "Mabel has been rooting around here, digging up brush, and she might have uncovered the grave site in the process. That's why you took a shot at her to encourage Asim to move her somewhere else, so you could get rid of Betsy's body."

"And I suspect that you're the person who left the threatening note on Bert's windshield," Sarah added.

"You'd better watch what you say," Harvey growled.

"You're right," Charlie said. "We don't even know for sure if this is a grave site. Like I said, it could just be an animal bone and some old cloth."

Sarah was beginning to wonder what was more important to the deputy sheriff: justice, or childhood friendship.

"That's true, it could be," Sarah said, "but I have a theory. I think Betsy told one of her boyfriends—"

"She was seeing both you and Dudley at various times, wasn't she, Harv?" Charlie said.

Harvey frowned.

"Anyway," Sarah went on, "she probably told one of her boyfriends that she'd left a note for her parents, telling them she was running away from home. My guess is that he didn't like the idea of Betsy walking out on him, so he fought with her."

Harvey opened his mouth to protest, but Charlie cut him off. "A perfectly natural reaction in that kind of situation. Her boyfriend must have thought about Betsy taking off to God knows where, and maybe ending up living on the street in Boston or New York. We hear horror stories about that kind of thing all the time. Naturally he'd try and save her from that, and there she is, saying no to him. Easiest thing in the world to lash out in the heat of the moment, trying to knock some sense into her, and accidently hitting the girl a little to hard, not meaning to, of course."

"She could have fallen and hit her head," Oliver suggested.

"That's right," Charlie agreed. "An accident, pure and simple. But there she is, lying dead. What's a guy to do?"

Sarah nodded. "The logical solution would be to frame somebody for it, and the note Betsy left for her parents was a good starting place. Betsy probably planned to use her bike to get to the bus station, so the killer would need to steal Betty Boop to make it look like she did just that."

"It was the perfect thing to plant on whoever the killer wanted to frame," Charlie added. "And who's more deserving than Evan Huggard, who had a certain reputation with young women?" Charlie was on a roll now. "I'm guessing the killer scratched Evan's initials on the knife—it would've only taken a minute or two—stabbed the body with it, and buried her and the knife right here in back of the Huggard's woodlot.

"Sam Merlew had a lot of you kids over every spring to help open up the camp next door, so you'd have known the lay of the land here, where to hide the bike and dig a grave in the woods—probably did it all that night."

"The beauty of it is that it wouldn't matter if the body or the bicycle were found," Sarah said. "If they were found, then Evan takes the blame, otherwise everyone assumes Betsy is off in the city somewhere, free of her abusive father."

Harvey snorted derisively.

"It was the perfect frame," Oliver went on, "except the killer didn't know that Evan had an alibi, thanks to Bernie. As it happened, the killer didn't learn about the alibi until Bernie got out his metal detector, discovered Betty Boop, recognized his sister's old bike, and realized something didn't add up."

Charlie looked at Harvey thoughtfully. "My guess is that Bernie decided to call one of his good friends and talk about what he'd found, maybe get some help figuring out the answers to his questions, like how did Evan end up with Betty Boop? Did he steal it, or what?" Charlie shook his head sadly. "The trouble is that he called the wrong friend and picked the killer—just plain bad luck. I expect his killer friend offered to come right over that night and talk it over."

"Talking probably turned into arguing pretty quickly," Sarah said.

"And arguing turned into murder," Oliver added.

Charlie shook his head sadly. "If Bernie had been a little smarter, he might have thought things out better, but he probably couldn't imagine that one of his best friends would kill his sister." Charlie sighed. "Hell, I'd have trouble thinking one of my best friends was a killer.

"Anyhow, I imagine the killer hit Bernie a little too hard, like he'd hit poor Betsy. And there he was with another body, a helluva nuisance. Lucky thing there was a killer elephant right there to frame."

Charlie turned to Sarah. "Tell him that crazy elephant theory you and Ziggy came up with. You'll get a laugh out of this, Harv."

"It's simple, really," Sarah said modestly. "Like Ziggy said earlier, Mabel knows who the killer is. If somebody killed Bernie and tried to frame Mabel by catching her unawares and smearing her tusk with Bernie's blood, then Mabel must know who that person is. Think about it. Mabel has been moody ever since Bernie died, friendly one minute and moping in the back of her enclosure the next."

"It must be a traumatic experience to have your tusk smeared with blood," Ziggy commented.

"Let me try to reconstruct last week," Sarah said. "Mabel was cowering in the back of her pen when Oliver and I got here the morning after Bernie died. I remember saying that she looked upset. The wind was out of the north that day—I remember because it kept blowing my hair around—so she would have gotten a good whiff of anybody who was here."

"Dudley, Harvey, Bert, and Pastor Briskin were here," Ziggy said. "That's the morning Dudley found the metal detector while he was cleaning Bernie's stuff out of the excavator."

"Then what?" Oliver prompted.

"Harvey went off with the metal detector, supposedly to take it back to Bernie's widow, and Pastor Briskin went off to arrange his 'save Mabel demonstration,'" Sarah said. "That left Dudley and Bert here when you turned up a little later."

Oliver nodded. "Mabel was looking quite friendly when I arrived; we commented on it. That lets Dudley and Bert off the hook."

"Mabel was in a funk again the next day, Tuesday morning, when I was here talking to Harvey and Dudley. Bert was there, too, but Pastor Briskin was away," Sarah said. "But she was fine later when everybody went away for lunch."

"She was looking forlorn after everyone came back after lunch, however," Ziggy said.

"She was fine when I was there Wednesday," Harvey said.

"That's right," Ziggy said. "Mabel was in a good mood. She even waved at Anton when he came over with his generous offer to buy me out, but the wind was southerly in the morning—you could smell elephant—so she couldn't have smelled any of us."

"Mabel was happy when the wind shifted to the north around lunch time," Oliver said, "but that was after Harvey left to rent a wood chipper."

"Of course it could be that she just doesn't like your aftershave, Harv," Charlie suggested. "Anyway, I don't think Mabel's trunk will stand up in a court of law. I just thought you'd get a kick out these guys and their crazy ideas. Can you imagine trying to get an arrest warrant on the basis of a harebrained theory like that?"

"That isn't funny at all," Harvey complained. "It sounds like you're trying to railroad me."

"No way I'd do that," Charlie assured him. "Of course, I can see the killer trying to shoot, or at least wound, Mabel to get her and Asim out of the way. And with Sasha out of town tonight, the coast is finally clear to get rid of Betsy's body once and for all."

"That's a nice new pickaxe, Harvey," Sarah said. "What happened to your old one?"

Oliver stared at Sarah, the uncertain light carving deep shadows of horror on his face. "My God, that's what happened."

Charlie shuddered. "I expect the police will be interested in your pickaxe theory," he said to Sarah. "It's a pretty gruesome thing to think about, but, hey, a guy's gotta do what a guy's gotta do, and that pickaxe is curved kind of like an elephant tusk. Anyhow, Bernie wasn't all that heavy, so the killer could have carried his body into Mabel's enclosure pretty easily, used the pickaxe on him, and smeared a little blood on the elephant's tusk for good measure. That must have given Mabel a start, where she was probably expecting a carrot or a handful of brush and got a handful of blood wiped on her tusk instead." Charlie shrugged. "Of course that theory won't stand up, where the pickaxe is gone."

"You're just kidding, right?" Harvey said to Charlie. "You don't believe any of this, do you?"

"Of course we're kidding, Harv. We're playing with your head, is all. You just happened to come across this grave—if it is a grave—while you were doing a little treasure hunting, like you said."

"In that case," Harvey said lightly, "I'll go home and get warmed up."

"Actually, I think we all need to stay right here 'til the cops talk to everyone," Charlie said. "We might have stumbled on Betsy's body, after all."

"Come on, Charlie; you know right where I'll be."

"Of course I do, Harv." Charlie put a hand on his friend's shoulder. "The thing is, we were watching, and you came right over and started sweeping the ground like you were going over a barroom floor looking for quarters. It sure looked like you had something particular on your mind. Don't take any of this personally; it's not about you. This is all just procedure. The police have got to do their thing, is all."

"None of this foolishness would stand up in court, even if it was true," Harvey said.

"I'm sure the police will clear the whole thing up in no time, and you'll be fine," Charlie said reassuringly. "On the other hand, as I remember, you were always a little possessive about your girlfriends.

Kind of a short fuse. Weren't there a few fistfights in high school? I imagine they'll ask around about that."

"Bernie did mention that you were short tempered," Sarah commented.

Harvey glared at Sarah. "Where the hell do you get off, talking like that?" he demanded.

"You're right," Charlie agreed, "They're just flat-landers, and like I say, nobody's accusing you of anything. We're just trying to make sense of it all, and the police are bound to ask questions."

"You can't keep me here against my will," Harvey grumbled.

"Well, I think maybe I can, at least 'til the state police get here and look things over."

"I was just looking for treasure," Harvey insisted.

"And I believe you, every bit," Charlie soothed. "I expect that particular spot just drew you in, like one of Ziggy's auras. Stranger things have happened, especially around this place." Charlie ignored Ziggy's scowl. "Let's go back to the vehicles and get warmed up while we wait for the cops," he suggested. "I don't know where you left your pickup, Harv, but we parked down a ways in that old tote road where the kids go to park. Anyway, there's plenty of room in my car for us to sit and get warm."

Charlie led the group towards Ziggy's driveway. He put his hand on Harvey's shoulder in an amiable yet possessive way.

"I don't have to put up with this," Harvey growled.

"I'm not saying you did anything," Charlie said, "but let's face it, the police will home in on the boyfriend in a situation like this. The fact is, Oliver is in as much trouble as you are."

"Me?" Oliver said.

"Sure," Charlie replied. "Just for the sake of argument, suppose Harvey did kill Bernie—which I'm sure he didn't. That's one thing. But if he *didn't* kill Bernie, then you're in trouble for hiding a killer elephant. That makes you an accessory after the fact."

"That's ridiculous," Sarah protested.

"They all say that. Hell, I can't wait to turn this business over to the state police."

"I am not hiding Mabel," Oliver retorted. "She's just staying safe until we can prove she didn't kill Bernie. I can hand her over to you any time you want."

"You can?" Sarah said.

"'Never underestimate animal wisdom,'" Oliver murmured.

"Ah," Sarah said, nodding.

They made their way slowly over the rough ground with the help of Charlie's flashlight. Sarah looked suspiciously at every hollow. Were other graves scattered around here?

"So tell me, Harv," Charlie said in a half-joking way, "if the state police go over to your place with one of those blood-sniffing hounds, are they going to find your old pickaxe lying around?"

Harvey stepped into a low spot and lurched against Charlie.

"Careful there, Harv. You could break an ankle on this rough ground. You want me to take your arm?"

"Leave me the hell alone," Harvey growled.

"Anyway," the deputy sheriff went on, "I'm only asking about the pickaxe because I know you're tighter than grease under a mechanic's fingernails, and you won't throw away a toothpick if you can help it."

Harvey swung around in one fluid movement, drove his fist into Charlie's midriff, and snatched the flashlight from his fingers.

Oliver fumbled with the anemic headlight and started to give chase.

Charlie, doubled over and gasping for breath, managed to grab Oliver's sleeve and throw him off balance.

"Let him go," Charlie wheezed in a strangled voice. "You'll break a leg chasing him over this ground without a decent flashlight."

Chapter 29

"What do you mean, let him go?" Sarah demanded, glaring at Charlie.

"Let me catch my breath," Charlie gasped, draping his arm over Ziggy's shoulder for support. "I didn't expect him to hit me so hard."

"We have to stop him before he gets to that pickaxe. It's the only evidence we have, and now he'll have a chance to get rid if it."

"You let him get away on purpose," Oliver said angrily.

"Why?" Sarah demanded.

"What's your rush? You don't even know for sure if that pickaxe business is for real."

"Why would he be running away if it's not for real?" Sarah said.

Harvey, with the advantage of Charlie's flashlight, was making good time, and was nearing the driveway.

Suddenly, they saw a hint of movement in the darkness just to Harvey's right.

Something was closing in on him.

A wild, animal howl split the darkness, and Harvey tumbled to the ground, the flashlight spinning through the air. His scream of terror was abruptly cut off as the apparition leaped on his back, pounding him into the ground.

"What in God's name was that?" Sarah said in a hushed voice.

"Myra's revenge," Ziggy murmured.

"I wish I'd brought my gun," Charlie muttered as they advanced cautiously towards the place where Harvey lay on the ground, prostrate and still.

The apparition, a shadowy figure, stood up as they came near.

"You're not supposed to be here," Charlie said disapprovingly as he retrieved his flashlight.

"I caught your killer for you, since you were letting him get away, as usual," Sasha replied, breathing heavily, an empty vodka bottle in her hand.

"I wish you hadn't done that," Charlie grumbled.

Harvey groaned.

"Did you want him to escape and get rid of the pickaxe?" Sarah growled.

Charlie rubbed his stomach gingerly. "I was hoping he'd help us *find* the pickaxe, if there is one."

Harvey groaned again and started to rise.

Sasha raised the vodka bottle, as though to hit him again.

"Stay right there, Harvey, you darn fool," Charlie said before turning to Sasha and relieving her of the bottle. "What the hell are you doing here? You're supposed to be hiding someplace safe. Look what you did to poor Harvey. Now, he's going miss Pastor Briskin's all-night prayer vigil."

"What prayer vigil?" Sarah asked.

"The one I arranged to have in Harvey's backyard, just in case," Charlie replied in a long-suffering voice. "It'll probably just be Pastor Briskin and Dudley over there, but that's okay. I expect that

Briskin can pray up a storm all by himself. Like I said before, can you imagine me trying to get an arrest warrant on the basis of an elephant's testimony? Not to mention trying to get a search warrant for Harvey's pickaxe, assuming he still has it. Having Pastor Briskin make sure Harvey didn't get away was plan B."

Ziggy gave Charlie a worried look. "Pastor Briskin was plan B? I hope you had a plan C."

"Plan C was to have Briskin keep an eye on Dudley in case you and Mabel were wrong about Harvey."

Harvey gave a muttered protest, and tried to sit up again.

Charlie pushed him back to the ground with his foot. "Shut up and lie down before you hurt yourself, Harv. You got pretty well clocked just now, and I'd hate to see you pop a fuse in your head."

"You were trying to goad Harvey into doing something stupid, weren't you?" Oliver said. "All that talk about 'I know you didn't do it, Harv,' and 'on the other hand,' was just leading him on."

Sarah looked at Charlie with newfound respect. "You were a regular Colombo back there."

The deputy gave her a sour look. "Colombo? Do you think this is some kind of joke? I grew up with Harvey, known him all my life. Do you think I'm having fun with this? Do you think I like the idea that one of my friends probably killed two people? I came here thinking the guy I went to school with couldn't be a killer—a little dumb, maybe, but not a killer."

Harvey started to say something, but Charlie cut him off. "Don't argue with me on being dumb, Harvey; you just proved it. Hitting an officer of the law is grounds for arrest, so your not going home tonight. Damn, I wish you hadn't hit me so hard, though."

"You're going to arrest him for assault?" Sasha said incredulously. "Is that all?"

"It'll be enough to hold him while the state police take a closer look at that junk heap he calls a backyard," Charlie replied. "I just hope Sarah's pickaxe theory is right, and they manage to find it. Otherwise, all we've got is the fact that he was digging up Betsy Knowles' grave—if it is her grave."

"Circumstantial evidence," Sarah said.

Charlie nodded. "There's a good reason why the state police haven't closed the book on Bernie's death, and that's because an elephant's tusk doesn't exactly match the wound, even if you try to make the wound look that way. Cops can be fussy about that kind of detail."

Sarah shuddered.

"Forensics," Charlie added. "This isn't like those cop shows on TV. Proper analysis takes time: days, not hours." Charlie glared down at Harvey. "Of course, finding the pickaxe would help."

"But he's a murderer. I know it. I recognized his voice when I heard it tonight," Sasha said, in a cold, even voice.

"Shut your mouth," Harvey snarled.

"What do you mean, you recognized his voice?" Charlie said ominously.

Sasha leaned over Harvey's prostrate form, her face purple with rage. "I heard him the night he killed that man."

There was a pregnant silence.

Charlie broke the spell, his face a mask of rage as he confronted Sasha. "Why the hell didn't you say anything earlier, for God's sake?"

"Say anything? You don't pay any attention when I do call."

Charlie glared at her. "Are you talking about all those times you called because somebody drove by with a loud muffler? Or when a drunk tossed an empty beer can onto your cobblestone driveway? Or when a couple of kids parked in the lot across the road? A man was killed that night, for crying out loud, and you didn't tell anybody who it was out there? Didn't it occur to you that there's a difference between a noisy muffler and a dead body?"

"I didn't tell you or the state police that this man was out there that night because I didn't know! All I heard were voices. I don't know any of the people who are working over here. How do you expect me to recognize their voices?"

"This is way, way too long past my bedtime," Charlie grumbled.

Sasha glared down at Harvey, and kicked his foot petulantly. "It wasn't until I heard all of you talking to each other tonight that I recognized the voice and came out here to make sure. It's a good thing I did or you would have gotten away." She gave Harvey's foot another kick, harder this time.

"I guess it's time to read you your rights, Harvey Cassell," Charlie said.

* * *

It was the wee small hours of the morning before the minions of the law left with Harvey in tow, leaving a sleepy-eyed officer to guard Betsy's presumed grave until the crime scene van arrived. Having brought Ziggy over, Charlie took him back to his rental cabin, leaving Sarah, Oliver, and Sasha standing in the driveway.

"You two look frozen," Sasha said, with unprecedented solicitousness. "Why don't you come over for a few minutes and get warmed up?"

"Thank you, but we don't want to bother you at this hour," Sarah said.

Sasha was silent for a moment. "I'd like you to come in," she said shyly. "Please. I owe you both an explanation." She stopped, her face seeming to reflect a range of conflicting emotions. "And an apology," she added quietly.

It was almost exactly a year ago, Sarah remembered, that she'd been in the Borofsky's gargantuan three-storey entry hall, fighting for her life with a psychopathic killer. The space soared up to the huge crystal chandelier, which was adjusted to give a dim, shadowy light.

At least it was warm inside.

Sasha led them to the study, and seated Sarah and Oliver on the fireside sofa. Sasha no sooner seated herself in the nearby wing chair when a mousy, grey-haired woman in a black maid's uniform scuttled in with a silver tea set.

"Thank you, Nika," Sasha said. "That will be all for tonight."

Nika stared blankly at Sasha, her head tilted to one side and her bright eyes focused on her mistress like an elderly and inquisitive crow. A flash of irritation flitted across Sasha's face, and she said something in Russian. Nika nodded and scurried away.

"We've been trying to teach Nika a few words of English for years, but she just doesn't seem able to learn. I'd have replaced her long ago, but Anton has a soft spot for the woman, and she is very efficient." She paused for a second before asking, "Was my tantrum this afternoon convincing?"

"You certainly had me going," Oliver said.

Sarah nodded agreement. "You were very impressive."

They sipped their tea in silence for a while, and Sarah could see their hostess becoming more and more uneasy, as though steeling herself to say something difficult. Finally, Sasha turned to Oliver and spoke.

"I wasn't kidding when I said that Anton would have you killed if he caught us having an affair. He doesn't do that with most of them, but you're different. He would see you as a bigger threat."

Naturally, Sarah knew the rumors about Sasha's reputation with men, and she couldn't help wondering how many of "them" there had been.

"I like to think that I'm attractive to men," Sasha went on haltingly. "But since the bicycle accident...seeing all the bruises...the scars on my leg, and..." She stopped and drank more tea before going on tentatively. "Do you think he saved my life?"

Oliver looked at Sasha, startled. "Yes, I think Ziggy Breener saved your life. Everybody thinks so, even the doctors."

Sasha's face crumpled for a second before she rallied. "He didn't have to stop, after all the things we've said about him...All the things we've done..."

"Yes, he did have to stop," Sarah said, "because that's who he is."

Sasha leaned forward to bury her face in her hands. Sarah and Oliver traded glances. Sasha's halting talk could be from the vodka, as the empty bottle suggested, or something more.

"I know that I'm not getting any younger," Sasha went on, "and I have a birthday coming up next month. The little lines and wrinkles...You do think I'm still good looking, don't you, Oliver?"

"I certainly do."

"Beautiful, even?"

"Absolutely."

Sarah was beginning to feel like a fifth wheel in this weird conversation. She took a generous swallow of tea.

"Maybe seductive, even?"

"That too," Oliver assured her.

Sarah thought about going back out to the entrance hall to admire the chandelier, whose predecessor had fallen, with her help, from on high and crushed Marlee Sue Ruggles to a gory pulp. Ah, the good old days. She hoped the new chandelier was more securely mounted than the old one.

"But you barely gave me a second look all those times you came over—" Sasha said, interrupting Sarah's musings.

"I wouldn't quite say that."

"Well, it felt that way," Sasha said. "You can't imagine how frustrating it was. Nobody did that to me before."

Lucky you, Sarah thought.

"I was very angry with you at first," Sasha confided.

"It wasn't about your looks—" Oliver began, looking trapped.

"Yes, yes, I've heard all that stuff—"

Sarah had heard enough. She clattered her teacup onto its saucer. "What happened on the night Bernie died?"

Sasha, her train of thought derailed, looked at Sarah blankly for a moment. "People may have been saying things about me and Oliver, but he didn't cheat on you at all, much as I tried. As I said, it was aggravating and frustrating. I just wanted you both to know."

"Thank you," Oliver replied uncertainly.

"Bernie?" Sarah prompted loudly.

Sasha pouted for a second. "Fine. It was warm that night, so the window was open and I heard two men talking. I went and looked out, but I couldn't see them because they were too far over towards the shore, but I could see Mabel. She was standing at the far side of her pen, looking worried. At least I thought she looked worried, though I'm not an expert on elephants, but I got the feeling—"

Sarah cleared her throat.

Sasha frowned. "Of course I didn't know who the men were, and I couldn't hear much of what they were saying, just a few words like, 'Evan did it,' 'Dudley did it,' from Harvey, and 'police' from the man who died–"

"Bernie," Sarah said.

"Yes, him. Then there was a thud, and that was all anybody said."

"What happened after that?" Oliver said.

"I don't know. It got quiet, so I stopped looking and went to bed. It was late and I was tired."

"That's too bad—" Oliver began.

"Too bad that I was tired?"

"Yes," he said tactfully, thinking that Sasha must have just missed the bloodying of Mabel's tusk.

"And you didn't call the police?" Sarah said, thinking the same thing.

"About what? Two people talking next door? I already told you and that clown-sheriff why I didn't call," Sasha snapped. She paused before asking, "What about the elephant? Is she coming back? I was sorry to see her go."

"I'll get her in the morning," Oliver said, "and she may be back here again, at least for a little while."

"I do enjoy watching them over there," Sasha said, as though embarrassed by the fact. "They'll need money to stay there, though, won't they?"

"Ziggy and Pastor Briskin? Yes, they will," Oliver said.

"And Anton cut off their funding," Sasha said.

"Yes, he did."

"That's not fair," Sasha said, iron in her voice. "I'll talk to him."

"And Mabel?" Sarah said to Oliver. "I assume the 'animal wisdom' you're talking about is Wes?"

"Wes has a good nose, like any bird dog, and I saw the way he was sniffing the air around Mabel's enclosure the day she disappeared."

"You think Asim has her hidden away in the woods out back?" Sarah said.

"It's must be nearby, so Asim can carry food to her, and there's a brook in there for water. I expect they hid Asim's pickup and camper before Phoebe went off to lead the gumshoe and the police on a wild goose chase. I doubt if she's gone far, and Asim will know how to reach her. In fact, he's probably camping next to Mabel."

Chapter 30

A week later

There's a special pleasure in the process of building a boat—turning the spiderweb of lines, arcs, and curves into a shapely, solid thing with your own hands. And with Sarah's hands too, of course. And finally to see her, *Daisy Mae,* that is, in her element, and feel her come alive at the touch of her helm.

Of course, there was that moment of suspense—even terror—as the boat slipped into her native element for the first time. Will she float to her lines, graceful and true? Will the carefully faired hull dance on the water, a thing of beauty?

Most important, will she sail well and bring joy to those aboard her?

All those thoughts, and more, roiled Oliver's brain as Abner's wife, Helen, broke a symbolic jug of moonshine over *Daisy Mae's* prow and the boat slid into the water.

By midday, they were well out into Penobscot Bay. For more than an hour, Sarah and Oliver took their turns at the helm, with Oliver and Abner talking happily about the boat's behavior.

A little later, with Helen and Abner absorbed in their new boat, Oliver went forward and sat, leaning against the mast as he gazed out over the bow. Sarah joined him a few minutes later and sat leaning against him.

"They're so wrapped up in *Daisy Mae,* I'm not sure they even know we're up here," Sarah said.

"Satisfied customers are the best kind." Oliver put his arm around her waist and she wriggled closer.

"The shop looks awfully empty without *Daisy Mae* there," Sarah commented.

"Yes."

After a moment of silence, Sarah glanced at his face, but his eyes were fixed on the endless procession of waves rolling up the bay towards them.

"I remember when *Daisy Mae* was just a skeleton with a few planks," Sarah said. "I never really dreamed that I'd be sitting here like this. It just seemed so far away."

"And yet here we are."

"Here we are," Sarah said. "*Daisy Mae* is in her element at last."

"As she should be," Oliver replied softly.

"As we all should be." Sarah thought about where her element lay. "It looks lonely in there, in the shop, I mean. And dead, somehow. It needs another boat. A future."

Oliver turned and smiled at her. "It certainly needs another boat if I want to pay the bills."

They were quiet for a while, lost in the moment, the eternal interplay of wind and water. Looking tiny in the distance, a schooner, probably one of the windjammer fleet, was making its way across the bay. There no other sailboats to be seen.

"A lonely woman, Sasha," Sarah said abruptly, thinking about the Borofsky's boat, "and insecure, too."

"I suppose it's a cliché, but money and looks really aren't

everything."

"Speaking of money, I hear that Pastor Briskin got his funding back," Sarah said.

Oliver nodded. "Anton apparently had a change of heart and pulled some strings again."

"I sense Sasha's hand in that."

"She's one tough cookie," Oliver said.

"It's too bad, in a way."

"Do you mean it's too bad that Pastor Briskin got his funding back? Why's that?"

"I kind of liked the idea of having a drive-in theater nearby. It brings back fond memories." Sarah lay her head on Oliver's shoulder. "It was thoughtful of Sasha to reassure me of your faithfulness and purity, by the way. Unnecessary, but thoughtful."

"Prudishness was the term she belabored me with at the time," Oliver commented.

Sarah watched *Daisy Mae's* bow wave roll off the hull as she cut through the seas. "It's surprising what a little bicycle accident did for her outlook on life. Bad as the accident was, perhaps something good did come out of it for Sasha. And Anton, too, with any luck. Maybe even Ziggy as well."

"My guess is that she's never had an injury that left scars like that before."

"Perhaps it made her realize that youth isn't timeless."

"Unlike the sea," Oliver said, still gazing at the waves as they rolled up the bay from over the horizon.

"It must have been something of a shock after being used to all the flawless skin. But you saw more of her skin than I did."

"I didn't make a detailed study of her skin, difficult as that was to avoid."

"It must be hard for her to have Anton going off all the time, leaving her to rattle around in that house with nobody but Nika to keep her company."

"And the occasional boy-toy, of course."

"I don't think of you as a toy," she said, toying with Oliver's ear. "Maybe I could take Sasha out on *Owl* and teach her how to sail. She could use a friend. A friend of the same gender, that is."

"Does that mean you're staying here this summer?"

"Most of the time, anyway. I sold the house in Sudbury. At least the buyers accepted my counter offer. We're aiming for a closing next month."

Oliver craned his neck, trying to see her face. "I'm thinking that might be a good thing," he said tentatively.

"It's one more decision crossed off the list, anyway," she replied, "and I know it's the right decision."

The wind was cool off the water, and Sarah snuggled closer while she lost herself to the *Daisy Mae's* motion over the waves, and the rise and fall of Oliver's breathing.

"Ziggy and Pastor Briskin seem to be getting along better now that Mabel is in the clear," she said after a while. "I was afraid they were going to have a major blow-up a couple of times, and the whole camp project would fall apart. The pair of them are so incompatible where their outlooks on life are so different."

Oliver watched as the distant windjammer slipped out of sight behind an island. "The last few weeks have been a struggle for both of them; they've had to rethink some of their basic assumptions."

"It's certainly been hard for Pastor Briskin to accept the idea that one of is flock is a serial killer," Sarah said. "It must be a blow to his self confidence. But what about Ziggy's basic assumptions? What does he have to rethink?"

"His relationship with Myra? You mentioned a while ago that you thought she'd given *Owl* to you in order to lure you back to Maine. I suspect she did the same kind of thing to Ziggy by leaving her property to him."

"You mean making him the keeper of her estate, her legacy?"

"Yes," he replied. "I don't think she really cared about turning her place into a camp, so much as having Ziggy preserve her way of life, somehow."

"Preserve her way of life? How? It's not possible."

"Exactly, and it was Mabel who made him realize it. At first, Ziggy hated having her in his back yard. What would Myra think about an elephant on top of everything else that was going on? Then you came along and suggested a connection between Myra and Mabel—that they were both thorns in his side."

Sarah nodded. "Myra because she resisted change and Mabel because she represented it—two sides of the same coin. No wonder he was miserable."

"Being, Ziggy, he chose the middle way, which is why he's decided to rebuild his shack on Meadow road. He figures that it's a better area, with higher class neighbors than the Borofskys."

"Myra's ghost being one of the neighbors he'll escape, I suppose. A better aura. Besides, I think he has a soft spot for Cindy Rice next door, even if she is younger," Sarah mused.

"You're quite the matchmaker."

"A man living alone like that needs a woman's companionship to keep him on track." Sarah gave Oliver an enigmatic smile. "It's good to see Mabel and Asim in your backyard again," she added.

Oliver wondered if Sarah would be living in his backyard again. He didn't push the issue. Watching the waves roll by reminded him that patience was a virtue, and understanding would come in its own time. Like the sea, the future was too vast to be rushed. "How could I say no when Mabel hadn't really left? It only took Wes five minutes to track her down. Phoebe and Asim had roped off a nice big enclosure for her a little way back in the woods."

"I gather Phoebe will be back in a few days to take Mabel back to Ziggy's place, all safe and sound now that Mabel is off the hook with the law," Sarah said "It sounds like the lawsuit against the zoo fizzled out when we proved that Mabel was framed."

"Is 'fizzled out' a legal term?"

"It is if only two people died in her pen, and one of them shouldn't have been there."

"It's lucky that you decided to wander around the remains of Evan's old shack and saw the bike before Harvey spirited it away, or we never would have figured out who killed Bernie."

"My finding Betty Boop was probably pure luck. Or maybe Myra Huggard."

An errant wavelet splashed icy water in their faces.

"You're not going to go Ziggy on me, are you?"

"Heaven forbid. Still..." She paused. "What about Betsy? Were those her bones?"

"Yes. The dental records match."

"What about Harvey and the pickaxe?"

"According to Charlie, they did find the pickaxe, squirreled away in Harvey's collection of cultch. The man is a hoarder, and his place really does look like a junk yard. According to Pastor Briskin, Harvey also had Betty Boop hidden there. He said the police spent all morning rooting through the stuff."

"Being a packrat isn't always a good thing. I assume they checked the pickaxe for blood?"

Oliver nodded. "Charlie wouldn't talk about an 'ongoing investigation,' but Harvey has been charged with Bernie's murder, which says they've got some evidence to go on."

Sarah sighed. "It's too bad there's no justice for Betsy. Her killer has been caught, but only after he murdered her brother. Harvey ended up wiping out the whole generation."

"They may do a plea bargain, where he pleads guilty to both murders in return for a reduced sentence."

"Two murders for the price of one?" Sarah's voice was bitter.

"Life is about compromise, making the best of a situation."

"Compromise," she mused. "I've been thinking. I've been living out of a pair of suitcases all year, either at the Merlews, my rental cabin, or your house. It's like I'm just squatting in somebody else's place all the time, never in my own home. I like being at your place, but it's your place, with some of my clothes stashed away in a spare drawer." She paused. "Well, a spare bureau, anyway. Most of my furniture will go with the house, though I did hold back a few pieces. And I've got ninety days to figure out what to do with the stuff."

"You could put it in my house."

"Or your barn."

"Or I could put some of my stuff in the barn, and some of your stuff in the house. And the rest of both our stuff in the barn."

The wind wafted a few strands of Sarah's hair across Oliver's face, and he glanced over to see a tear coursing down her cheek. He kissed the tear.

"I'm dreading the idea of going down there to clear out the house," she said in a small voice. "Would you come and help me close up the place?"

"And live out of a suitcase in your house? Talk about poetic justice. Can Wes come along?"

Sarah laughed. "I'll let you bring two suitcases. And a suitcase for Wes, too. Fair is fair, after all."

"Hey, are you two love birds hungry?" Helen called to them. "We're going to make sandwiches for lunch, if you want some."

The two hungry love birds headed back to the cockpit with smiles on their faces.

www.ingramcontent.com/pod-product-compliance
Lightning Source LLC
Chambersburg PA
CBHW031314170626
46807CB00001B/429